Her Lips Were Inches from His...

Patrick might not be able to read Jac, but he sure as hell desired her. He had never wanted to kiss a woman so badly in his life. It was like his lips were magnetized and she was solid metal.

"Are you married?" he asked.

"Not yet. I'm still working on it." Before he could figure out what that meant, she stood up. "So if you're not going to fix the tire, just what am I supposed to do?"

In heels, or at least in one heel, she was only a few inches shorter than he was. This woman looked like she could handle a man who liked things a little rough. And since she wasn't married, was in no way connected to his aunt's schemes, and was here...

Patrick smiled. "You're going to spend the night with me."

"What?" she squeaked. "I can't spend the entire night with a..."

"Patrick." He held out his hand. "And you are?"

Jac swallowed hard before answering. "In big trouble."

Acclaim for the Hunk
for the Holidays Series

RING IN THE HOLIDAYS

"A return visit to the headstrong McPherson family for another year of holiday high jinks...Lane's trademark brand of humor will keep the pages turning."
—RT Book Reviews

"Fans will enjoy this sexy and humorous story."
—Publishers Weekly

"*Ring in the Holidays* is all at once extremely sexy, intense, and a compelling story."
—FreshFiction.com

HUNK FOR THE HOLIDAYS

"4½ stars! Sharp, witty dialogue, a solid sense of humor, and a dab hand at sizzling sex is going to push Lane far, if this is an example."
—RT Book Reviews

"Lane's contemporary series launch sizzles from the moment Cassie McPherson's hired escort appears to accompany her to the company Christmas party...The romance is inevitable, but Lane makes the couple work for it, writing with warmth and humor. [Readers will] adore James, Cassie, and the affectionately jocular McPhersons."

—Publishers Weekly

"I was interested from the first page to the last...There was enough chemistry between Cassie and James to set the place on fire."

—Romancing-the-Book.com

"Katie Lane is an author who has the ability to create romantic magic with her words. Ms. Lane brings characters to life that readers love to bring into their lives."

—The Reading Reviewer
(MaryGramlich.blogspot.com)

Praise for the Deep in the Heart of Texas Series

A MATCH MADE IN TEXAS

"4½ stars! Lane's outlandish sense of humor and unerring knack for creating delightful characters and vibrant settings are on full display...She does a marvelous job blending searing heat and surprising heart."

—RT Book Reviews

"Fun-filled and heartwarming...a wildly sexy romance with a beautiful love story [that] old and new fans definitely do not want to miss."

—BookReviewsandMorebyKathy.com

FLIRTING WITH TEXAS

"4½ stars! [A] complete success, blending humor, innovative characters, and a wonderfully quirky town with an unlikely and touching love story."

—*RT Book Reviews*

"Every turn of the page is an unexpected journey full of humor as well as emotion."

—**FreshFiction.com**

TROUBLE IN TEXAS

"Sizzles with raunchy fun...[Elizabeth and Brant's] dynamic provides the drama to complete this fast-paced novel's neatly assembled package of sex, humor, and mystery."

—*Publishers Weekly*

"Lots of fun and games, enticing intrigues with tidbits of wisdom here and there make *Trouble in Texas* a tantalizing tale...Katie Lane's writing style keeps the reader turning pages."

—**LongandShortReviews.com**

CATCH ME A COWBOY

"Lane gives readers a rip-roaring good time while making what could feel like a farce insightful and real, just like the characters themselves."

—*Booklist*

"Nosy townsfolk, Texas twangs, and an electric romantic attraction will leave readers smiling."

—*BookPage*

"Katie Lane is quickly becoming a must-buy author if one is looking for humorous, country romance! This story is an absolute hoot to read! The characters are real and endearing...the situations are believable (especially if one has ever lived in a small town) and sometimes hilarious, and the romance is hot as a June bug in July!

—*Affaire de Coeur*

MAKE MINE A BAD BOY

"Funny, entertaining, and a sit-back-and-enjoy-yourself kind of tale."

—**RomRevToday.com**

"I absolutely loved Colt! I mean, who doesn't like a bad boy? Katie Lane is truly a breath of fresh air. Her stories are unique and wonderfully written...Lane, you have me hooked."

—**LushBookReviewss.blogspot.com**

GOING COWBOY CRAZY

"Katie Lane has a winner on her hands; she is now my new favorite author!"

—TheRomanceReadersConnection.com

"Romance, steamy love scenes, humor, witty conversation with a twang, all help the pages keep turning. I'm looking forward to reading other books written by Katie Lane."

—BookLoons.com

"I enjoyed this book quite a bit. It really reminded me of an early Rachel Gibson…or early Susan Elizabeth Phillips. Faith became a sassy, intriguing heroine…The chemistry between these two ratchets up to white-hot in no time."

—TheSeasonforRomance.com

Unwrapped

ALSO BY KATIE LANE

Unwrapped

Katie Lane

FOREVER

NEW YORK   BOSTON

Forever
Hachette Book Group
1290 Avenue of the Americas
New York, NY 10104

HachetteBookGroup.com

Printed in the United States of America

First Edition: September 2015
10 9 8 7 6 5 4 3 2 1

OPM

Forever is an imprint of Grand Central Publishing.
The Forever name and logo are trademarks of Hachette Book Group, Inc.

The Hachette Speakers Bureau provides a wide range of authors for speaking events. To find out more, go to www.hachettespeakersbureau.com or call (866) 376-6591.

The publisher is not responsible for websites (or their content) that are not owned by the publisher.

To my mother-in-law, Billie Kay, for all the fun shopping sprees, movie matinees, birthday parties, and football games... but especially for giving birth to the love of my life.

Unwrapped

Chapter One

"Let me guess...the Bride of Frankenstein?"

Jacqueline Danielle Maguire wasn't surprised by the assumption. With her wind-whipped hair and smudged makeup, she probably did look like she'd just stepped out of an old horror movie. But if she was the Bride, then the man who stood behind the gas station counter was the Creature. He certainly had the huge body and square head for it...not to mention the thick unibrow. If Jac was smart, she'd turn right around and get the heck out of there. Two things kept her from it: her need for a telephone, and the rack of candy bars.

Brightening her smile, she turned on the Southern charm. "Happy Halloween. Or should I say 'trick or treat'?" She selected a Snickers from the rack. "I just loved *Bride of Frankenstein*, didn't you? But my all-time favorite horror movie is *Young Frankenstein*. Do you remember the part where Madeline Kahn came out of that bathroom after she'd married the monster?" She touched her finger to the tip of her tongue, then thrust out a hip and placed her finger on the full skirt of her wedding gown. "S-s-s-t-t." She laughed, but it faded when the store clerk didn't join in. Obviously the man wasn't into small talk.

She placed the candy bar on the counter before pulling a twenty out of her Gucci bag. "I was wondering if you might have a phone I could use. My cell phone doesn't seem to work here in the Rockies."

"Sorry, can't help ya." He took the twenty. "The storm knocked down some branches and screwed up the lines." He tipped his head at the window behind him. Outside, a wood chipper sat amid a pile of pine branches. "Phone's been out since midday. If it weren't for the generator, we wouldn't have no power either." His unibrow lifted. "You lost?"

Jac might've conceded if he hadn't opened the cash register and her gaze hadn't landed on the wicked-looking knife next to the stack of one-dollar bills. Just that quickly, an entire *CSI* episode played out in her mind, ending with the murderer being apprehended and the runaway bride's remains being discovered in the wood chipper.

The gas station attendant followed her wide-eyed stare. "Fishin' knife."

Her gaze remained riveted on the jagged edge that could easily have cut a humpback whale in half, to say nothing of a twenty-six-year-old carb-counter. "Y-you fish with a knife?"

He grinned, and a squirt of brown spittle flew through the air, missing the bodice of her Vera Wang by inches. "I don't kill 'em with this." He lifted the huge weapon, the overhead florescent lights reflecting off the shiny steel blade. "I just gut 'em."

The words *gut 'em* set Jac in motion. Grabbing her candy bar, she raced for the door. A strong wind pushed against one side of the glass as she pushed against the other. She might've lost the battle if the man hadn't stepped around the counter. The big, big man with the big, big knife.

Please, Lord, if you don't let me be gutted like a fish, I promise I'll never eat sushi again. With that prayer she used every underdeveloped muscle she had to shove open the door, and plowed out into the freezing night air.

"Hey!" the attendant yelled.

Lifting the hem of her gown, Jac made a mad dash for her sister's MINI Cooper, popping up the locks in mid-flight. It felt like it took a full thirty minutes to get the car door open and stuff herself, and a good twenty yards of organza, inside. But by the time she had the doors locked and the engine revved, the mad fish gutter had just made it out the door. With the knife clutched in one hand and her change in the other, he watched as she squealed away from the gas pumps.

Two miles later Jac finally caught her breath and stopped looking in the rearview mirror. Two more miles and she realized that she had probably overreacted. But it was hard not to be a little spooked on a dark and stormy Halloween night while lost in the horror-movie setting of the Rocky Mountains.

To help calm her nerves, she turned up the radio and scanned through the stations until she landed on classical. She thought the soft violin music would soothe her. Instead it reminded her of the string quartet that had been hired for her wedding. The four musicians in black had just been arriving when Jac had been leaving—or racing across the lawn with her purse slung over her shoulder and her sister's stolen car keys. The quartet had probably gone home by now, along with a hundred guests, the florist, the chef and pastry chef, the valets, the cute little flower girl and ring bearer, the six ushers and six bridesmaids, and the wedding planner.

Correction: Gerald, the wedding planner and her best friend, would still be there. Probably frantically dialing Jac's number. This was his first wedding, and he had been determined it would be a success. Now, thanks to her, his fourth business in four years might fail.

Taking her phone out of the side pocket of her purse, she speed-dialed his number. She hit speaker and placed the phone in the cup holder while she unwrapped the Snickers bar and took a big bite. Chocolate, caramel, and nougat weren't part of her diet plan. Not that she had ever stuck to a diet. The only willpower genes in the family had gone to Aunt Frances and Jac's sister, Bailey. Jac had little will and no power. Just a wild imagination and compulsive tendencies.

"Jac! Where the hell are you?"

Bailey's booming voice came through the phone speaker and caused Jac to swerve toward the wall of dense forest. Dropping the candy bar, she used both hands to steer back toward the double yellow lines.

"Bailey," she breathed with relief. Her relief was short-lived.

"'Bailey'?" Her sister's voice hit a high note that didn't bode well. "You run off from your second wedding in less than a year and all you can say is 'Bailey'? I swear, Jac, when I get my hands on you—"

"I'm sorry, Bay, but I didn't really run off. I just needed to take a little drive and think things through."

"Three hours is not a little drive!"

Jac picked up the candy bar from her lap and finished it off as she tried to explain. "I know it looks bad, Bay, but I got lost. And my phone wouldn't work so I couldn't call or use the GPS. I even tried stopping at a gas station to get directions, but there was this really creepy attendant who I think killed the real gas station attendant with his big ugly fishing knife and then disposed of his body in the wood chip—"

"Oh, for the love of Pete." Bailey groaned. "I should've never let you watch so much television growing up. You live in some kind of fantasy world where gas station attendants are murderers and brides run off from their weddings without any repercussions. Wake up, Jac. That's not how the real world works."

Jac's shoulders slumped. "So I guess Bradford is upset. And Gerald's probably heartbroken that I screwed up his first job as a wedding planner."

"Actually, Bradford looked more relieved than upset. But I don't think you'll be getting any more party invitations from his mother. As for Gerald, he's already planning your next holiday wedding." Bailey paused. "But this is it for me, Sis. I refuse to attend another wedding where I'm the only Maguire present. The whole runaway bride thing has gotten old. It's time to give up on the crazy stipulation in Aunt Frances's will and get a job."

"Unlike you, Bay, I can't ignore that much money. And I don't want a job. I want to be like Aunt Frances and spend my summers in Italy and my winters in Cancún. Which means I only have two months left to choose a groom before all Auntie's money goes to the Mysterious Mr. Darby, who I think is trying to take me out so he'll inherit. I told you that I saw him lurking around my and Gerald's apartment."

"According to Gerald, he wasn't lurking. He rang the buzzer like any normal person, and you refused to answer it."

"Because it's too suspicious. He never said more than two words to me all the times he visited Aunt Frances. Now suddenly he shows up and wants to 'talk' to a woman who's going to keep him from inheriting billions of dollars. Well, that's not going to happen. Not unless I have a big bodyguard with me."

Bailey sighed in exasperation. "He's not trying to kill you. Why would he have to kill you when you keep running away from your weddings? All he has to do is wait you out. Geez, Jac. How many weddings is it going to take before you realize that you're not attracted to men in Aunt Frances's social circle? Or at least to the loser men you keep choosing."

"I have to choose the losers who need money, Bay. No one else would agree to a one-year marriage. And that's how long I need to stay married in order to get my inheritance."

There was a long pause. "Do what you want, I'm not your keeper."

That was a lie, and they both knew it. Bailey had been Jac's keeper since birth. Which was a good thing, since their mother had been better at serving a bottle of Bud than a bottle of milk and more accomplished at changing lovers than changing diapers. Five years older, Bailey was the one who had fed and changed Jac. The one who helped Jac up when she fell and cuddled her close when she cried. Not that Maguire women cried all that often. They were more yellers than criers.

Suddenly feeling contrite for all she'd put her sister through, Jac whispered, "Thanks, Bay."

"For what?"

"For being such a good sister."

She snorted. "Don't thank me yet. When I get my hands on you, I might just strangle you and dispose of your body in the Gerhardts' wood chipper."

"They have a wood chipper?"

Bailey laughed. "While I'm looking for it, I want you to find out where you are so I can come get you. Do you see any mile markers?"

Jac looked around. "No. But I'm sure there has to be one up ahead."

"As soon as you find it, call me back."

"Love you, Bay."

"Love you too."

After hanging up, Jac felt much better. Things would work out. They always did. When a door closed, a window opened. Her life was a testament to this. Who would've thought that two orphaned Mississippi kids would end up living the good life? But it had happened.

One minute the police were standing in their small apartment telling them their mother and her newest boyfriend had been killed in a motorcycle accident, and the next minute Jacqueline and Bailey were living with their wealthy aunt Frances in a mansion in upstate New York.

Well, maybe not exactly the next minute. The next minute they were shipped off to Alabama to live with their uncle Bud, their aunt Sissy, and their six hillbilly cousins. Then, after Bailey set fire to Uncle Bud's tool shed, they were sent to child services. It was during their stay there that Jac had remembered their great-aunt Frances or, as Granny Lou had liked to refer to her, "the Rich Bitch."

It seemed Frances Rosenblum hadn't gotten the gene that made Maguire women get with losers. She'd had the foresight to completely distance herself from her Southern relatives by getting educated and marrying money. So much money that she could easily take in two orphaned nieces.

It had been like the musical *Annie* all over again. Except they didn't have a Daddy Warbucks who sang and took them on cool helicopter rides. They had the Rich Bitch, who sent them off to boarding school the first chance she got. Still, boarding school was better than living with Uncle Bud.

Just like being lost in the Colorado Rockies was better than being married to Bradford. As much as she wanted her aunt's money, she would've been miserable with Bradford—and he would've been miserable with her. He hated her constant chatter, and she hated his overbearing mother.

Tired of the depressing classical music, Jac dialed through the radio until she found a seventies station. The Donna Summer song reminded her of Granny Lou. Her mother's mama had loved anything to do with disco—polyester, platform shoes, mirror balls, and John Travolta. Since she and Bailey had stayed with Granny every summer until she died, Jac knew all the words to "Last Dance." As she sang along, a mile marker came into view. She reached for her phone, but before she could call Bailey, Bigfoot leaped out in front of the MINI Cooper.

Jac hit the brakes, but they barely slowed the car down. Making the split-second decision that hitting a huge beast with a tuna can was a bad idea, Jac swerved and ran right into a signpost. The airbag opened, forcing her head back and whooshing all the air out of her lungs, before quickly deflating. She slumped against the seat and took a few quivery breaths as Donna continued to sing about her last chance for love.

Besides a sore shoulder from the seat belt, Jac didn't appear to be hurt. The car wasn't as fortunate. The front of the MINI sat a good three feet off the ground, its yellow hood curved around the bent signpost like a bee that had crashed into a really hard flower. The sign said *Deer Crossing*, a warning she could've used earlier.

Reaching for her phone, she tried dialing 911, and then both Bailey's and Gerald's cells. Unfortunately, this time she had no service. A gust of wind blew against the car, causing the bumper to creak back and forth on the metal post. As she sat there in the dark, she thought about all the television shows she'd seen about people who got stuck on dark, deserted roads. An image of the creepy gas station attendant with his knife flashed through her mind. What if she'd gone in a circle and the guy was right around the corner? Or what if the animal that had jumped in front of her really wasn't a deer? What if it *was* Bigfoot? Or a mountain lion? Or a grizzly bear?

The engine sputtered and died, taking with it the soothing Donna Summer song and the warm air from the heater. Within seconds the car started to get cold. Jac figured that she had two choices: She could stay there and freeze to death, or she could get out and see if she could get phone service farther down the road. Neither was appealing, but since freezing to death seemed more likely than becoming Bigfoot's dinner, she grabbed her phone and Gucci bag and released her seat belt.

Once she pushed open the door, the car tipped precariously, making her descent anything but graceful. She tumbled out surrounded by a pile of petticoats and ivory organza. As soon as she got to her feet, the cold wind sliced through her, pulling at her hair and freezing her bare shoulders. Fighting against the wind, she grabbed the billowing full skirt of her dress and pulled it up around her shoulders and head. It wasn't a ski jacket, but it worked. Although her nose soon felt like a block of ice and her toes had lost all feeling—which was probably a good thing, considering her Christian Dior heels were too tight. Stopping at a bend in the road, she leaned against a mailbox and tried her phone again. She was still out of service—

A mailbox?

Jac lowered her phone and stared in awe at the gray metal box on the rustic wooden post. Her gaze traveled up the narrow, rutted road that wound through the trees.

She was saved! And not a moment too soon. Icy flecks of snow swirled down from the dark skies, hitting her face and bare hands like stinging insect bites. Using her phone for light, she started up the dirt road.

It was much darker and scarier than the highway. The dense forest seemed to close around her like a thick, cold blanket. An owl hooted, and Jac stumbled, catching her heel in a deep rut. The heel snapped, and she fell to her knees, ripping her dress and landing in mud.

At any other time, Jacqueline would've been horrified. She'd spent the last sixteen years of her life trying not to get dirty—trying to be the clean, pristine niece her aunt expected her to be. But tonight she was too cold, too tired, and too scared to care about a little dirt. She struggled to her feet and continued up the hill. Her efforts were rewarded a few moments later when she spotted a light through the trees.

Civilization.

Sort of.

The small, dilapidated cabin was nothing like the Gerhardts' large mountain home. In fact the cabin would have easily fit in their living room. But to a cold, mud-covered woman, it looked like heaven with its warm, beckoning lights and curl of smoke coming from the chimney.

A pickup truck was parked in front. As Jac stumbled past, she held up her phone and read the words printed on the side door. *M&M Construction*. It sounded like a reputable business and made her feel much less scared.

The wind wasn't as bad on the porch. So she took a moment to release the skirt of her dress and fluff it out before knocking on the door. It took ten polite taps followed by a bout of hysterical pounding before the door was jerked open.

Jac's hand froze in midair.

A man wearing nothing but a kilt stood in the doorway—or more like filled it—his half-naked body outlined by the flickering fire behind him. Having only been to bed with older men, Jac had never been this close to so much...hardness. This man had chest muscles you could crack an egg on and a stomach that looked like her Granny Lou's antique metal washboard.

Jac's gaze swept up to his face. A face that was just as hard as his body. His angular jaw was tight, his lips pressed into a firm line, and his eyes intense and unforgiving. For a second she wondered if she wouldn't have been better off with the gas station attendant. Although she'd never seen a *CSI* episode about a murdering Scotsman. In fact the only murdering Scotsman she could think of was in *Braveheart*. And William Wallace hadn't killed irrationally. He'd just wanted revenge for his dead wife. Which Jac thought was so romantic. Unfortunately, her romantic theory was shot to hell when the man opened his mouth to speak. His lips parted to reveal a set of pearly white teeth with two very long—very sharp—fangs.

"Trick or treat," he growled.

Chapter Two

Patrick McPherson watched the woman in the long white dress hurry down the steps and out into the flying snow, holding her lit cell phone in front of her like a groupie at a rock concert. Most men would have been surprised, or at least a little curious, at finding a lone woman in a wedding gown at an isolated cabin in the middle of a blizzard. But most men didn't have a matchmaking great-aunt. A great-aunt who was too stubborn for her own good. No matter how many blind dates Patrick refused to go on, or how many times he ignored the women his aunt dragged to family gatherings, Aunt Wheezie wouldn't give up. In fact his refusal to go along with her match-making schemes had only resulted in out-and-out war. In the last month, Wheezie had started to meddle in areas of his life that she had no business meddling in. Every day he would arrive at an M&M Construction jobsite to find a newly hired female assistant, contractor, or even metal-worker who looked at him like his dogs and cats did when he brought home Boston Market. And not more than a week ago, Wheezie had rented out one of the family condos to a prospective bride who kept stopping by for a cup of sugar.

Patrick didn't have any sugar. He drank his coffee black and ate his cereal with nothing but a splash of 2 percent milk. But even if he had been a sugary kind of guy, he wasn't about to be bulldozed by a ninety-two-year-old woman. No matter how much he loved his aunt. Or how many marriage-crazed women she threw at him.

The frigid wind and snow whistled under the eaves of the porch, causing bumps to rise up on his arms and reminding him that he still wore the costume he'd pulled together for his friend's Halloween party. Between the party and the drive to the cabin, it had been a long night. All he wanted was to go back inside by the fire and get some sleep. It didn't look as if that was going to happen. The bride took a mean tumble and didn't get up. And while Patrick could ignore crazy behavior, he couldn't ignore someone hurt. With a heavy sigh, he headed down the rickety porch steps.

When she saw him, she lifted her dress to run, but Patrick easily caught up with her and flipped her none too gently over his shoulder. She was tall for a woman, as tall as, if not taller than, his sister, Cassie. But she wasn't as strong as his sister. Her attempt to get out of his arms was pathetic at best.

He strode up the steps and into the cabin, kicking the door closed before tossing her onto the sofa. She landed in a pile of muddy material and wild blond hair. He didn't care for blondes. Blondes usually had bad attitudes—which might explain his own golden locks. He plucked a pebble from his foot as she fought her way up from the couch, showing off a set of dirty but extremely long legs.

"Don't you touch me," she said in a voice that held a slight Southern twang. Clutching a bright-pink handbag to her chest, she pointed her phone at him. "I-I'm warning you. I know Pilates and...I ate a lot of garlic for dinner." She edged around the couch until she had it safely between them.

Patrick studied her. She wasn't a pretty sight. With her long tangled curls, she looked like she'd spent the last four hours on the back of his Harley. She had makeup under her eyes and mud smudged across one cheek and shoulder. Her lips might've been nice if they hadn't been pressed together in a tight line. As far as he could tell, the only good thing about the wild apparition before him was the set of creamy breasts that swelled above the edge of her dress.

"Let me guess, the Corpse Bride?" he asked.

"Let me go," she stated in a voice that quavered with either fear or cold. Since her chin was hiked at a stubborn angle, he figured it was cold.

"Look"—he pointed a finger, and then grew more annoyed when he saw it was covered in mud—"there's nothing I'd like better than to let you go. Except we have a slight problem." He raised his eyebrows. "Would you like to take a guess on what that is?"

She didn't answer. Her gaze seemed to be pinned on his mouth. Surprisingly, a twinge of desire sizzled through his veins. Or not so surprisingly, considering the fact that he hadn't had sex for months. Aunt Wheezie's matchmaking attempts had really screwed over his sex life.

Frustrated with the entire situation, he answered for her. "It seems you have no transportation. With the nearest town a good twelve miles away, the only place I can let you go to is a cold, dark forest with large, hungry mountain lions. So I suggest you call whoever dropped you off and have them come get you. And if it was my Aunt Wheezie's chauffeur, he and I are going to have problems."

She hesitated for only a second before lowering her gaze from his mouth and tapping the screen of her phone. He didn't need to hear her frustrated groan to know her attempt had failed. That was one of the things he loved about the cabin—you rarely got good cell phone service. Which meant no calls from his overbearing father, his protective mother, his teasing siblings, or his matchmaking great-aunt Wheezie. Of course right now he would've given his left nut for a phone that worked.

Patrick released a long, tired sigh. How had his plan for a fun, relaxing weekend run so amuck? Instead of spending the weekend in Denver attending his nieces' and nephews' Halloween parties, where little devils raced around on sugar highs, cute princesses had major screaming meltdowns, and poopy-diapered pumpkins smeared cupcake frosting everywhere, he'd planned to spend the weekend the adult way. First at a Halloween party with Jell-O shots and women in nasty costumes and then at his cabin...alone.

The Halloween party hadn't disappointed. Besides the usual nasty nurses, police officers, and French maids, there had been nasty witches, nasty storybook characters, and his favorite—nasty team sports. He hadn't complained a bit when the brunette wearing a Broncos jersey and stilettos had pulled him into a bedroom and asked to see what was under his kilt. It was only after her cute tight end had him primed and ready that he noticed her wedding band and sent her back to the locker room.

Women. Was there a man on the face of the earth who understood them? He sure didn't. He didn't understand their preoccupation with gossip, their ability to fire off a good twenty texts between each paltry bite of grilled chicken salad with low-fat dressing, or their strong desire to meet the "right one."

Patrick wasn't the right one. He loved his single life too much to give it up for the rules and regulations of married life. He was willing to give up a weekend for great sex, but that was where he drew the line. Let his three brothers and sister carry on the McPherson name; he was more than happy to be the bachelor uncle of the family.

"Look," he said, "I don't know what plans you and my aunt cooked up—or why you've suddenly changed your mind. And frankly, I don't give a damn." He walked over to the sink in the small kitchenette. "You made your bed, Goldilocks, and now you'll have to sleep in it. Because I'm not driving you back to Denver tonight."

He turned on the faucet, but barely had time to slip his hands beneath the cold water before he heard the door open. He might've let her go if not for the blast of snow and frigid air that accompanied her departure. With a grumbled oath, he went after her, grabbing her arm before she even made it past his truck. A truck that now leaned to one side with a flat tire.

"What the hell!" he yelled as his grip tightened on her arm. "Did you do that?"

Instead of answering she swung at him with her huge purse. Her aggression coupled with the flat tire and escalating snowstorm took the last of his patience. Dragging her back inside, he kicked the door closed before jerking the purse from her hand. Which resulted in her pummeling him with her fists.

"Enough!" He dropped the purse and grabbed her wrists, pulling her hands behind her back and bringing her body flush against his. The contact caused her to still and Patrick's anger to take a backseat to sexual awareness.

The woman was soft. Not fat soft, but feminine soft. The kind of soft that females were born with, but few kept. Not with their crazy diets and hours spent in Zumba classes. But this woman didn't have hard muscles or sharp bones. Just round curves and warm valleys.

Patrick glanced down. It was a mistake. Her creamy breasts spilled over the edge of the satiny neckline like two soft, sweet dollops of heaven. Snuggled between his hard pectoral muscles, they looked—and felt—sexy as hell.

His cock came to full attention. And since he was a true Scotsman and never wore anything under his kilt, there was nothing to hold him back. Thank God her dress was made of yards and yards of material. But then she gasped, and he figured even yards and yards weren't enough to hide his desire. What did he expect? After four long months without sex, he was surprised his cock hadn't burned straight through her dress.

She stopped struggling, and her gaze lifted. Not to his eyes, but to his mouth. Her conflicting actions confused him. Did she want to leave, slash his tires, or kiss him?

Maybe she was one of those women who liked to play rough. The type who liked to heighten the sexual tension by playing hard to get. Well, it was working. His sexual tension was at an all-time high. And since she was the one who had knocked on his door, he decided to release some of it.

Tugging her closer, he kissed her. Unlike most women, she didn't try to take control. Nor did she try to stop him. She just stood there with her eyes wide and her breath held as he deepened the kiss. She tasted like chocolate and caramel, making him realize that he had a sweet tooth after all. Her lips were soft and heavenly, her mouth hot and habit-forming.

Worried about losing control too quickly, he pulled away and nibbled his way to the pulse beneath her ear. She smelled like Aunt Wheezie's homemade bread baking in the oven. Wondering if her skin tasted as good as it smelled, he sucked the sweet flesh into his mouth before taking a nip.

The woman in his arms released a sexy little moan before going completely limp. Not an I'm-so-turned-on-I-can't-stand kind of limp, but a completely-passed-out kind of limp—as in fainting dead away. Luckily, Patrick caught her before she slipped to the floor. Scooping her up, he carried her to the couch and checked her pulse. Her beat was rapid, but then again, so was his. He picked up his cell phone from the end table and checked for service. When he found none, he tossed down the phone and headed for the kitchen. He had always remained calm in emergency situations. Not that this was an emergency situation.

Yet.

It didn't take him long to light the kerosene lamp and wet a dish towel with water. He set the lamp on the coffee table before sitting down on the edge of the couch and running the cold, wet towel over her forehead.

"Hey, Goldilocks, wake up." He gently washed away the streak of mud on one cheek before moving to the streak on her shoulder. Beneath the drying mud, he found a nasty-looking red welt. A welt in the exact shape of a seat belt.

Holy shit. He sat back. She wasn't some woman his aunt had sent. She was a victim of a car accident, and from the look of the welt, a pretty good one. He released a snort of disgust. His sister was right. At times he was an inconsiderate jerk. While this woman was probably concussive, he had been trying to figure out how to get her in bed. He went to press his fingers to the pulse at her throat, but stopped when he noticed the two red indentions. Indentions he'd put there.

"Dammit!" He reached up and pulled out the fake fangs. They weren't the cheap plastic kind kids used. These were porcelain and made exclusively for him by a female dentist he'd once dated. The dentist had sent the fangs after he'd ended their relationship, along with a note about how well they went with his cold heart. Patrick hadn't been insulted as much as impressed. The fangs fit to perfection and looked real as hell. Real enough to scare his nieces and nephews every Halloween. And real enough to intrigue some nasty women. Unfortunately, after spending the night drinking beers and scoping out women, he'd completely forgotten about them.

No wonder the brunette Bronco had kept offering her neck. Except he hadn't wanted to bite the brunette's bronzed neck—just the pale neck of an accident victim. He ran a finger over the welts. Never in his life had he hurt a woman. At least not physically. He'd broken a few hearts, but never skin. A moan came from Goldilocks's slightly parted lips, and her eyes fluttered open. He watched as a myriad of emotions passed through their sky-blue depths. Confusion. Fear. And finally resignation.

"Am I a vampire?"

He chuckled at the joke and smoothed the damp hair off her forehead. "No. I don't change my victims...I just snack on them." She didn't crack a smile, but her shoulders relaxed, bringing his attention back to the welt. "How badly are you hurt?"

Her hand went to the marks on her neck. "Surprisingly, it didn't hurt as much as I thought it would."

Patrick felt his face heat with embarrassment. "I'm sorry. I forgot about the fangs."

Her gaze flickered to his mouth, and damned if he didn't get hard again. "Well, I guess since you didn't... umm...overindulge, it's not a big deal."

Overindulge? Oh, he wanted to overindulge. Especially with those phenomenal breasts just a reach away. But he wasn't that big of a jerk. "So can you tell me what happened? Are there any other victims?"

"No. No one else was in the car with me when Bigfoot—I mean, a deer jumped out in front of the car. I would've been okay if my brakes had worked properly. It was almost like someone had tampered with—" She paused, and her eyes widened. "Mr. Darby." She glanced at the door. "And he's probably the one who flattened your tire."

Patrick started to wonder if she wasn't suffering from

a concussion. She seemed to be talking irrationally. Of course most women talked irrationally. "I thought you said no one was in the car with you. Who is Mr. Darby?"

"No one was in the car with me. Mr. Darby is the guy who's trying to k—" She stopped and cleared her throat. "Never mind. It's not important. So you were saying?"

His brow knotted. Why couldn't women be as easy to read as a blueprint? He released his breath in a sigh. "I was wondering how badly you were injured."

"I'm fine now. I was just a little light-headed before." She sat up to prove it, bringing her full pouting lips inches from his. He might not be able to read her, but he sure as hell desired her. He had never wanted to kiss a woman so badly in his life. It was like her lips were magnetized and he was solid metal. But before he could kiss her, she got to her feet and started picking up the items that had spilled out of her purse. Since there was a lot of crap, he knelt down to help her.

"So what are you doing up here?" he asked as he lifted her wallet and handed it to her. "I'm assuming by the costume that you were coming back from a party."

There was a slight hesitation before she nodded. "And I got lost." She leaned over to reach the tube of lipstick that had slid under the coffee table, and her breasts swelled forth in twin mounds of bodacious beauty. "So if you can't take me back to Denver, do you think you could get me to a working phone?"

It took her grabbing the lipstick and straightening before he could talk. "I could if I didn't have a flat tire." Now that his temper had cooled, he realized that she wouldn't have had time to flatten his tire. He'd probably run over a nail at one of the jobsites, so it had been slowly leaking air all day.

"Don't you know how to fix it?" she asked.

"Yes, but I'm not going to do it in a blizzard." He picked up her phone and tried it. There was still no reception so he tapped the screen closed. A screen saver picture of two people popped up. Patrick didn't know why he was more interested in the skinny guy than the pretty dark-haired woman. Or maybe he knew why, but just wasn't willing to admit it.

"Are you married?" he asked.

"Not yet. I'm still working on it." Before he could figure out what that meant, she got up and took the phone and her purse from him. "So if you're not going to fix the tire, just what am I supposed to do?"

In heels, or at least in one heel, she was only a few inches shorter than he was and sturdily built. He realized that he liked that about her. He was tired of petite women he had to worry about breaking. This woman looked like she could handle a man who liked things a little rough. And since she wasn't married, was in no way connected to his aunt's schemes, and was here...

Patrick smiled. "You're going to spend the night with me."

"What?" she squeaked. "I can't spend the entire night with a..."

"Patrick." He held out his hand. "And you are?"

She swallowed hard before answering. "In big trouble."

Chapter Three

Jac stretched out in the deliciously hot water and propped her feet on the rim of the tub. It was funny how a nice soothing bath could make a girl accept the fact that she was stuck spending the night with a bloodsucking vampire. A bloodsucking vampire with hungry green eyes and hard, sculptured muscles that made Jac understand why all those women in horror movies offered up their necks. There was something extremely erotic about having your blood sucked by a really hot guy. Especially if he didn't suck you dry.

She touched the spot behind her ear. The indentations were still there, but no puncture marks. And she had to wonder if she'd let her overactive imagination get the best of her. It wasn't like it hadn't happened before. When she was eleven, she'd discovered spaceship-landing marks near the horse stables. At twelve she'd been convinced that a ghost lived in the attic. And when she was fourteen she and Gerald had spent the entire summer trying to catch the mass-murdering groundskeeper who buried his victims' body parts in the garden. She had been extremely disappointed when they turned out to be tulip bulbs.

But Jac had been young and impressionable when those things happened. Now she was an adult. An adult who knew the difference between normal incisors and sharp fangs. The man might not have fangs now, but he'd had them before. And he'd bitten her with them. Not hard. Just enough to scare the crap out of her and cause her to faint. Of course her tight bustier might've added to her lack of oxygen, along with the bolt of lust that had speared through her at just the touch of his firm lips.

The lust had surprised her. Jac had always thought that sex was overrated. It was nice, but not as nice as spending a day in the kitchen whipping up some of Granny Lou's recipes, or a night watching movies with Bailey and Gerald. And it wasn't even close to being as earth-shattering as her friends made it out to be.

Of course Jac had learned early on that wealthy, spoiled women had a tendency to exaggerate about everything, from how much money their fathers made to the authenticity of their breasts. Which was why Jac fit right in. She could stretch the truth about almost anything—including her sex life. Her friends all thought that Jac's boyfriends had been excellent lovers, men who had sent her over the moon and back again. But the truth was that she'd had sex, but she'd never really liked it. Yet all it had taken was the soft brush of vampire lips to make the spot in her panties light up like Times Square at night. Even now she felt all warm and breathless at just the thought of his kiss.

"Are you okay, Jacqueline?" Her vampire's deep voice came through the door, causing her to sit up and slosh water onto the floor.

"I-I'm fine, Patrick," she called back. *Patrick.* She had always liked the name. Patrick Swayze. Patrick Dempsey. Saint Patrick. Count Patrick.

There was a long pause before he spoke. "Well, I'm glad you're fine, but do you think you could hurry it up so I could take a bath?"

"Oh!" She jumped up and unplugged the drain before reaching for the towel on the rack. "Of course, I'll just be a second."

She didn't waste any time toweling off and getting dressed in the clothes Patrick had given her. The gray sweatshirt had a Denver Broncos logo on the front and the pants an orange-and-blue swish. Since she couldn't stand the thought of wearing her bustier and Spanx, she went commando, enjoying the feel of the cozy, soft cotton against her skin. After pulling on the warm wool socks, she studied her reflection in the mirror. Her hair was a mess, and even in the dim light from the kerosene lamp, she could see the brown freckles that sprinkled her nose and cheeks. Her aunt had hated her freckles and forced Jac to cover them ever since she'd been old enough to wear makeup. But her aunt was dead, and Jac had no business trying to impress a vampire.

After putting her underwear in her purse, she picked up her wedding gown. The gown was pretty much ruined, but it didn't matter. Her next wedding would be small. Maybe just close family and a knee-length Versace. And not somewhere cold. Possibly Mexico or the Bahamas on Thanksgiving or Christmas. She would've liked a New

Year's Eve wedding, but that was the deadline in Aunt Frances's will, and Jac refused to cut it that close.

She pulled open the door to find Patrick waiting just outside. He held a candle, the light flickering in the green of his eyes and on the bronze of his naked chest. As his gaze swept her from head to toe, she blushed with embarrassment and tugged on the ribbing of the sweatshirt.

"I didn't have a brush...and these clothes are a little big."

A smile played on his firm lips. "You look cute."

Cute? Jac didn't know why the statement annoyed her. She should be happy he thought she looked cute. Vampires probably wouldn't want to snack on cute women. Which might explain why Jac felt so annoyed. Deep down she really wanted to be his Hostess snack cake.

"Are you still cold?" he asked.

With his naked chest so close, she wasn't cold. She was burning up. "Actually I'm a little warm."

"Really?" His gaze lowered.

She glanced down and realized that her nipples had pitched a little tent on either side of the Broncos logo. She quickly crossed her arms. "Well, I better let you use the bathroom—I mean, I should get out of your way so you can do...whatever you need to do." She tried to scoot past him, but he didn't seem to be in any hurry to move.

"There is something I need to do." He lifted a hand and smoothed her hair behind her ear, his hot fingers causing her to release a sound that she'd never released before— a cross between a high-pitched sigh and a breathy moan. The sound turned his eyes a shade darker as he dipped his head and gave her a thorough kiss that curled her toes in the wool socks. Then, without another word, he walked into the bathroom and closed the door.

Jac didn't know how long she stood there staring at
the scarred wood of the door and fighting down the desire
to follow him into the bathroom and ask for another toe-
curling kiss. Her brain might know Patrick the Vampire
was bad business, but her body hadn't gotten the memo.
It took the sound of water filling the tub to bring her back
to her senses.

*No, Jacqueline. No. No. No. You CANNOT become a
vampire's snack pack.* Not when she had to concentrate
on finding another husband and marrying him before the
first of the year. Even a sexy, good-kissing vampire wasn't
worth losing billions. She turned and walked into the living
room. Patrick had taken the time to make up her bed. The
sofa mattress had been pulled out, the pillows plumped, and
a fluffy comforter invitingly folded back.

Dropping her dress and purse on the floor, she sat
down on the mattress. Of course she couldn't go to sleep.
Man or vampire, she wasn't that stupid. She would just
sit there until morning. Morning couldn't be more than
five hours away. Five hours that suddenly began oozing
by like molasses out of a measuring cup.

The wind howled outside the window. The logs shifted
in the fireplace. And a splash came from the bathroom.
Since the sitting position was uncomfortable, Jac eased
back against a pillow and stared at the dancing flames
and glowing orange embers of the fire. She felt bad about
leaving Bradford. Even if he was only marrying her because his mother wanted Aunt Frances's money, she
should've talked with him before just running off. She
also felt bad about wrecking Bailey's car and screwing
up Gerald's hope for a career in catering. But there was
nothing she could do about it now. When she got Aunt

Frances's money, she would make it up to them. Her eyes slid closed.

Yes, Aunt Frances's money would fix everything.

Jac didn't dream about money. She dreamed about Granny Lou. Granny hovered over the sofa couch in her polyester pantsuit and platform shoes and warned Jac about vampires and adding too much salt to cream gravy. After the warnings, her grandmother sang Donna Summer's "Last Dance." Of course Jac had never been able to ignore good music, so she jumped up on the mattress and danced while her grandmother sang. Jac had just completed an arm roll and finger point when someone grabbed her from behind and pulled her down to the mattress. As she was enfolded in hard muscles and warm skin, Granny Lou faded away, her singing drowned out by the loud thump of a heart and the sharp bite of a vampire.

Jac's eyes fluttered open, but the dream continued.

She was in Patrick's arms, and he was nibbling on the spot right behind her ear. Or not nibbling as much as tasting, his mouth open and his tongue swirling. His hand slipped beneath her sweatshirt, encasing her breast in strong fingers and rough calluses. It wasn't a gentle cradling, but rather a possessive, undulating squeeze that made her breathing as loud as her thumping heart. The weird sigh-moan escaped her lips again, then got muffled in folds of cotton as her sweatshirt was jerked over her head.

When Jac was free, she looked up to find Patrick leaning over her, the dying embers of the fire casting his shoulder-length hair in flaming gold and orange. He studied her with hot, intense eyes for only a moment before he lowered his head and kissed her nipple. He brushed his rough tongue over it once before sucking it into the heat of his mouth. It was like being plugged into a power socket. A burst of tingling energy shot through her body straight to the spot between her legs, where it settled into a sweet ache that begged for attention. As if they had a will of their own, her legs wrapped around Patrick's hard thigh as her hips did a bump and grind.

It briefly crossed her mind that she must look like her aunt's shih tzu, Walter, going to town on one of Bailey's UGG slippers. Patrick didn't seem to mind. With a deep moan that vibrated against her nipple, he slid his hand down her pants and gave her the exact friction she needed. His fingers expertly located her clitoris, and then found a rhythm that ignited her. The flame caught and sizzled through her body, causing her hips to lift, her muscles to tighten, and her eyes to roll back in her head as all the energy inside her expanded in an orgasmic shower of crackling light. As the sparks began to settle to the ground, Patrick's rhythmic strokes and nipple sucking slowed along with them. A contented shiver ran through her, and he gave her nipple a gentle kiss before rolling to his side. She heard the slide of a drawer, followed by a curse and the jostle of mattress springs.

Jac opened her eyes to find Patrick gone. He returned only a few seconds later, his perfectly honed body outlined by the fire. He stopped at the foot of the bed, and she watched as he tore open the condom and placed it on his erect penis. Her eyes widened, but before she could get over his size, he was back on the bed and giving her a hard, deep, possessive kiss.

His mouth tasted of beer and lust, an intoxicating combination that caused desire to swell once again. He pulled back from the kiss and jerked down her sweats, his gaze sweeping her from head to wool socks. She had never been proud of her body. Her hips and thighs hung on to every calorie she ate. And being appraised by such a perfect human specimen, it was hard not to feel a little embarrassed. She reached for the sheet, but he stopped her.

"I want to see you," he said before he spread her legs and knelt between them. Her gaze settled on the condom-covered penis that jutted out in front of him. It had grown. Suddenly she didn't feel fat. She just felt hot. Especially when he released a low, hungry growl.

Jac instinctively placed a hand over her neck. But it turned out that he didn't crave her blood as much as her body. Hooking his hands behind her knees, he bent her legs and lifted her hips off the mattress. She barely had time to adjust to the position before she was impaled. This time the fuse was set from the inside out. The deep thrust set off a chain reaction of sensations that completely took Jac's breath and sanity. And before she could get them back, Patrick tightened his grip on her legs and thrust again. And again. And again. Until the sofa bed squeaked and rattled and Jac moaned and trembled. The orgasm that broadsided her was even more intense than the first one. It burst in a huge sunburst of colors and glimmering sparks that filled her entire body. When she finally floated to earth, she wasn't surprised that the words to Donna Summer's song popped into her head and seemed to fit perfectly.

Jac was bad. So, so bad.

And it felt so, so good.

* * *

Loud banging woke Jac from a sound sleep. She rolled to her side and tried to muffle the noise with her pillow. The banging continued. Giving up on sleep, she opened her eyes and blinked at the sunlight that streamed in through the small window. A small window she didn't recognize. She glanced around the room until her gaze landed on a plaid kilt slung over a scarred end table.

In an instant Jac sat straight up and grabbed her neck. The two tiny indentions were still there, but they weren't worse. Obviously her vampire was into sex more than blood. The banging stopped and was soon followed by a soft tap. Jac glanced at the window to find a woman peeking in, her gloved hand cupped against the frosty glass. The woman smiled and pointed to the door.

Jac nodded, and then as soon as she disappeared, scrambled for the ugly sweatshirt on the floor and slipped it over her head. After finding her sweatpants and pulling them on, she quickly checked the bedroom and bathroom. It was a waste of time. Her toothy lover was gone. When she finally got the door pulled open, the woman had moved off the porch and stood next to the sheriff's deputy's car. A car that sat in the exact same spot the white truck with the flat tire had been sitting in the night before. Obviously vampires could love you and leave you as easily as mortal men.

The deputy pulled the radio away from her mouth. "Jacqueline Maguire?" she yelled up at her. When Jac nodded, she went back to talking to whoever was on the other end of the radio while Jac huddled in the doorway and stared out at the winter wonderland.

The blizzard had left a good twelve inches. Patrick had been right. She would've never made the cross-country trek to town. The fact that he had quite possibly saved her life made her feel even more disappointed, and she couldn't help staring longingly down the road as the deputy clipped the radio to her belt and walked back to the porch.

"I'm Deputy Stanopoly from the County Sheriff's." She climbed the steps and stretched out a gloved hand. "I've been looking for you. Are you okay?"

Jac tried not to cringe from the firm handshake. "I had an accident up the road from here."

"I know. We found your car an hour ago. Would've found it sooner if the snow hadn't covered it." The woman studied her. "So around what time did you have the accident?"

"I'm not sure. I guess around midnight. I tried calling for help, but there was no service."

Deputy Stanopoly nodded. "We figured as much. You should be thankful that you found a place to spend the night." She leaned to the side and looked in the cabin. "This has been vacant for years, but last I heard it had been sold. Did someone let you in?"

The question caused the events of the night to parade through Jac's mind like a bad porn flick. In the light of day, they seemed outrageously fictional. Who would believe that a Scottish vampire owned the cabin and had saved her from freezing to death, bitten her neck, and given her two amazing orgasms? She had a wild imagination, but even she had trouble believing the story. And her logical sister Bailey would never believe it.

"Actually"—Jac smiled brightly—"I don't know who

lives here. The door was open, and I just came in." She
held a hand to her chest. "Thank God there was firewood
and blankets."

"And three little bears?" the woman asked as she
glanced at Jac's neck.

Jac laughed and covered the marks with her hand.
"N-no. No bears. Just Goldilocks." And a really hot
vampire who hadn't minded sharing his bed.

"Sounds like you lucked out," Deputy Stanopoly said.
"You wouldn't have survived out in the cold all night."
When Jac didn't reply, she nodded at her car. "I'll just let
you get your things while I radio my boss. You have a lot
of people worried about you."

"I guess you've spoken to my sister?"

The woman laughed. "Not me. But my boss got his
butt chewed out by a woman in your family. Along with
the sheriff's department in every county within a two-
hundred-mile radius. Even the feds got an earful."

Jac could only imagine the tirade her sister had gone
on. "I'm sorry," she said.

The deputy thumped her none too gently on the arm.
"I have five brothers and sisters, so I understand. When
family gets worried, all hell can break loose." She trotted
down the steps.

Once back inside the cabin, Jac shut the door and leaned
against it. She hated to lie, but she couldn't tell the truth either. Not when she didn't know what the truth was. In the
forgiving glow of a fire, the cabin had been cozy, warm, and
seductive. In the bright light of day, it was bare, cold, and
shabby. There were no pictures of vampires, with or without fangs, no coffins or bats hanging from the high ceilings,
and no black capes or bright red sashes.

Just a kilt.

Walking over, she picked up the soft plaid material. She had a vivid imagination, but last night hadn't been a dream. There had been a man. A handsome man with sharp teeth and a really hot body. And he'd had sex with her. Amazing sex. She might not ever share her secret lover, but she would never forget him.

Not as long as she lived.

Chapter Four

Patrick had always been an early riser. It didn't matter how late he'd stayed up the night before. When the sun peeked its head over the horizon, sleep was no longer an option. But sex was. Sex was always an option. Especially when you woke up to a full-figured woman who ignited your passion like no woman before her. Unfortunately, Jacqueline had been out cold and no amount of kisses and caresses had roused her. So he'd gotten dressed, fixed the tire on his truck, chopped more firewood, and, when she still wasn't up, he'd headed into town for groceries.

And condoms.

The condom situation had him a little nervous. He'd never had a condom break before. Of course he'd never used a condom that he hadn't purchased himself either. If he'd been thinking with his brain, he might've checked the expiration date before using a condom he'd found in the kitchen drawer of the cabin. But he hadn't been thinking with his brain. He'd been thinking with his hard dick. When he realized that he'd wasted the only condom in his wallet on the brunette Bronco, he didn't think twice about using the other condom. Not that he needed to worry. Nowadays most women were on birth control. But he still needed to have a long talk with Jacqueline when he got back to the cabin.

Jacqueline. Her name surprised him. It brought up images of a snooty little rich girl. Having grown up with his fair share of snooty little rich girls, he pretty much couldn't stand them. But a woman who was willing to dress up like the Corpse Bride for Halloween, said, "Sweet Lord have mercy" when she reached orgasm, and drove a MINI Cooper couldn't be some snooty rich bitch.

Patrick had discovered her car—if that's what you could call the pint-size vehicle—perched on a road sign as he pulled out onto the highway. Even with the snow covering it, he could tell that the car was totaled. Which made him realize that the accident had been much worse than Jacqueline had let on. As he drove past, he couldn't help feeling a little guilty for being so rough with Jacqueline the night before. But damned if the woman didn't make him lose control. He got hard just thinking about her pouting lips and sweet curves. Which made him drive a little faster.

When he got to town, he stopped by the sheriff's office to tell him about the accident and let him know where they could find the car and Jacqueline. Unfortunately, it was Sunday, and the sheriff's office was closed up tight. So he called the number stenciled on the door and left a message. After that he got gas and groceries and headed back to the cabin. On the way he called his brother.

Matthew didn't answer until the fifth ring.

"What?" His little brother sounded pissed and winded. Since it was Sunday and Matthew hated to exercise, Patrick could pretty well guess why he was out of breath.

"So? What's goin' on, baby brother?" Patrick tried to keep the teasing humor out of his voice. "You running on the treadmill?"

"Not funny, Patrick," Mattie growled. "Call me later."

"Sorry, I can't. I'm up at the cabin. Remember?"

"Shit." There was the muffled sound of the phone being shifted, followed by distinct complaints from his sister-in-law Ellie.

"This better be good," Mattie said only seconds later.

Teasing aside, Patrick cut to the chase. "I'm not coming into work tomorrow."

"Are you sick? Hurt?" The concern in his brother's voice made Patrick smile.

"Nope. I just want to take a day off."

"Are you kidding me?" The concern was replaced with anger. "You bothered me on a Sunday morning to tell me that you finally decided to take a day off?"

"Of course, little brother. Who else would I bother? Jacob, Rory, and Cassie have so many rug rats screaming in the background, it's hard to be heard. You're the only one that's kid-free—at least at the moment. Which brings up a good point. Do you think it's wise to be heating up the sheets with a woman who's so pregnant?"

"The obstetrician said it was—wait a minute! It's none of your damned business what I do with my wife."

Patrick grinned. Nothing felt better than ribbing one of his siblings. "Just a thought, Mattie. Just a thought." Unsure of how long he could keep the connection, he moved on to business. "Here's what I need you to do. Let Rory know I won't be there for the lunch meeting with Sanchez and tell him that the specs are on my desk. Then call my pet sitter and ask if she can stay another night. I'll text you her number. And in the morning, I need you to stop by the Welbourne site. I chewed Harper's ass out on Friday for being too lax about ear protection. I want to make sure he got the message."

"And you think a visit from me will make a difference?"

"You're a big scary corporate lawyer, aren't you?"

Mattie snorted. "Not as scary as the big mean project manager. But I'll do my best. Anything else I can do for you?" he asked snidely.

"Yeah." He paused just long enough to piss his brother off.

"What, Paddy?"

"Give Ellie a kiss for me." He was still grinning when he hung up. As much as he liked to tease his family, he loved them. Even his father, Big Al, whom he constantly locked horns with. His mother said it was because they were two peas in a pod. Patrick didn't see it. He might have his father's stocky build and green eyes, but he wasn't even close to being as arrogant or demanding. Although he did have a tendency to put work before pleasure. But only because work was his pleasure.

He loved construction and never minded staying late or going in on weekends to make sure the job got done. Some people might have called him a perfectionist. He wasn't. He just liked things done right and on time. But after talking with Matthew, Patrick realized that a few days off here and there wouldn't make a difference.

Maybe he should start coming to the cabin more often. Like every other weekend. Or even every weekend. Not only would it get him away from his aunt's matchmaking, but it would give him more time to work on remodeling the cabin. And if he should run into a certain sexy blonde, all the better.

Suddenly feeling extremely happy, Patrick started to whistle. He had learned to whistle from his dad—just like he had learned to swing a hammer and wield a power saw. The skills had come easily to him. While his siblings had needed years of practice, Patrick had built his first birdhouse at the age of five, all while whistling the theme song to the movie *The Bridge on the River Kwai*. It was the same song he whistled now. But he'd only gotten halfway through it when his phone rang. He glanced at the number and rolled his eyes. So much for thinking that being surrounded by mountains would keep him away from Aunt Wheezie's matchmaking.

He pulled his cell phone from the front pocket of his flannel shirt. "Hey, Wheeze."

"Hey yourself," she replied in a sassy voice. "So when are you getting home today? I thought I'd stop by with some cookies."

He shook his head. "And, no doubt, another one of your friends' granddaughters or great-nieces who are looking to get married and start a family? Wasn't moving Donna in right next door to me enough?"

"Deirdre. Her name is Deirdre. And if you had given her a chance, you would know that." She paused for only a second before continuing. "It's time for you to start a family, Patrick."

"I have a family. I have a mom and dad, and enough

brothers, sisters, nephews, nieces, cousins, uncles, and aunts to fill Mile High football stadium."

"Then let me rephrase that. You need your other half."

He rolled his eyes. "Please, Wheezie, just give it up. I'm quite happy with my life. I have a good job. A comfortable home. And plenty of company when I want it. The key words being *when I want it.*"

Wheezie snorted. "That's your problem, Paddy. You're too much of a loner. If you're not careful, you'll end up like your great-uncle Wesley. Since he died before you were born, all I can tell you is that the man was the unhappiest crotchety old hermit you'd ever want to meet. And I won't have my nephew living that kind of lonely life. You need a mate. Someone to soften your rough edges and teach you the enjoyment to be found in female company."

An image of Jacqueline stretched out naked on his sleeper sofa popped into his head. "I enjoy female company."

"I'm not talking about sex, Patrick. I'm talking about finding a woman that you're not just physically attracted to, but mentally attracted to. A woman you want to share everything with. Your thoughts. Your fears. Your deepest desires."

His deepest desires. Right now his deepest desire was to get back to his cabin and Jacqueline's warm body.

"A partner," Aunt Wheezie continued. "That's what I want for you, Patrick, and why I've been such a pain in the keister the last few months. You're not getting any younger…and neither am I."

His aunt was always using her impending death to get her way, and since she was over ninety, her death was impending. Which was one of the reasons he hadn't completely disowned her after all her matchmaking schemes. Knowing that she only had a few more years on this earth kept his anger in check. But it wasn't easy.

"Okay, Wheeze, I get that you want me to be happy. But not everyone is cut out to be a husband and father. I work long hours, and I like to work long hours. After I get off work, I like to have a beer with the guys without worrying about pissing off some woman because I didn't meet her and her friends for sushi. And when I get up in the mornings, I like to drink my power smoothie and go for a run without worrying about hurt feelings because I didn't eat the strawberry waffle that the same woman slaved over a hot skillet to make me."

Wheezie snorted. "That's why you need a woman, Paddy. You make waffles in a waffle iron, not on a skillet."

"Whatever. My point is that I like my routine, and I don't need a woman messing it up." There was a weird clicking noise, and he figured he only had a few more minutes before he lost her. "Look, Wheeze, can we call a truce? You stop throwing women at me, and I'll make an effort to do more dating. Or at least keep my eye open for…my other half. In fact I'm kind of on a date as we speak."

"A woman is with you?"

"She's staying with me at my cabin."

"A living, breathing woman? Not that silly life-size doll that Matthew bought you as a joke."

"Yes, a living, breathing woman. I left Miss Featherbee at home." There was silence, and he could only imagine his aunt rubbing her hands together with glee.

"Truce," she said with a smile in her voice. "But only if

you bring your young lady over to visit so I can see if she's a good fit. I don't trust you to make the right choice."

He laughed. "Thanks for the vote of confidence. I'll call you when I get back in town."

"Enjoy the rest of your weekend." She hung up.

Patrick might've felt relief about the truce if he hadn't made it with his aunt. Aunt Wheezie never cried uncle. She might take a little break from her matchmaking, but she wouldn't be content until he was standing at the altar. The poor old gal was in for some major disappointment.

After slipping his phone back in his pocket, Patrick continued his whistling. He whistled as he drove the rest of the way to the turnoff. Whistled as he headed up the dirt road that led to his cabin. Whistled as he carried the grocery bags through the door.

He stopped whistling when he got inside and saw the empty sofa bed. Placing the bags on the kitchen counter, he took the time to slip a few condoms out of the box and into his back pocket before heading to the bathroom. Visions of silky white flesh surrounded by slippery, sudsy water crowded his mind and lengthened his cock against the fly of his jeans.

It wasn't until Patrick stood in the doorway of the bathroom, with the note he'd left still attached to the mirror, that his mind finally comprehended what his libido couldn't.

Jacqueline was gone.

Chapter Five

I love this scene," Gerald sighed. "Rock Hudson is so cute when he's angry. God, what I wouldn't give to have him fling me over his shoulder and take me back to his tawdry apartment. Oh, the things I'd do to him behind those locked doors."

Jac giggled and took the last handful of popcorn from the bowl that sat on the mattress between her and Gerald. She should've left it for Gerald or Bailey, especially after the extra pounds she'd gained. But it was Thanksgiving weekend, and everyone fudged on diets during the holidays.

Everyone but her sister, who never fudged on anything.

Bailey glanced up from the laptop she'd been working on. "You do realize that Rock Hudson is dead."

Gerald rolled his eyes. "Way to ruin a fantasy, Bay. You don't hear me reminding Jac that Mel Gibson is old with at least a hundred children and grandchildren every time she fantasizes about him. I'm not such a party pooper." He stuck out his tongue at Bailey, who had gone back to tapping away on her keyboard. He reached for more popcorn and then sent Jac an exasperated look when he came up empty-handed. "What is your pre-occupation with *Braveheart* these days anyway, Jac? I swear I'll throw up if I have to see his filthy, stringy hair one more time."

"I only chose *Braveheart* twice," she said, fluffing a pillow behind her back.

"Twice in the last month," her sister grumbled. "Along with every vampire movie ever made." The computer keys clicked as she spoke. "And I'm not wasting another Saturday night watching some guy suck the blood out of women. I get plenty of that in the courtroom."

Gerald snorted. "I'd love to meet the man who dares to try and suck your blood, Bailey." He winked at Jac. "You need to choose a movie with dark-haired female vampires next time. Because if there's any bloodsucking going on, Bailey's doing the sucking."

Jac ducked as a throw pillow sailed past her and hit Gerald in the side of the head, mussing his perfectly styled and highlighted hair. And no one mussed Gerald's hair and got away with it. He grabbed the pillow, knock-ing over the popcorn bowl as he jumped up on the bed. Bailey barely had time to close her laptop before the pil-low pounding began.

Laughing, Jac got to her feet and wielded a pillow of her own. As far as she was concerned, Saturday night was the best night of the week and had been ever since they'd moved in with her aunt. Movie nights had started the summer after she and Bailey had returned from their first year at boarding school. That was when they'd met

Gerald, the skinny, pale boy who was the only child of their closest neighbors.

Gerald was closer to Bailey in age, but had more in common with Jac. They both liked to play dress-up, style Barbie hair, and watch old movies. And coming from different backgrounds, they had a lot to teach each other. She taught him how to cuss, cook, and explode a mailbox using an M-80 firecracker. He taught her how to dress appropriately, how to decorate, and proper etiquette. There were a few blunders. Like the time he accidentally dyed her hair a bright magenta and plucked her eyebrows so thin she constantly looked surprised. Or the time she set the roof of the gardener's cottage on fire with the exploding whizzer firework. That incident had been the final straw for Aunt Frances, and Jac would've been sent away for good if Gerald hadn't taken the blame.

Which explained why Jac took his side in the pillow fight against Bailey. Not that having her on your team was an advantage. During a misaimed swing, she stumbled and fell into Gerald, knocking him down and cracking the back of his head on her cherrywood footboard.

"Oh my God." Jac bounced down next to him. "Are you all right?"

Bailey reached out a hand and pulled Gerald up to a sitting position. "Geez, Jac. First you almost ruin his event planning business and then you try to kill him."

"You know I would never intentionally hurt Gerald," Jac defended herself. "And he's already forgiven me for the wedding fiasco."

Looking slightly dazed, Gerald nodded. "I don't blame her for walking out on the wedding. The canary-yellow roses clashed horribly with the daffodil-yellow bridesmaids' gowns. I never should've chosen Robert as the florist...even if he is great in bed." He pressed a hand to the back of his head. "Although the date was all Jac's fault. Why you chose Halloween for a wedding is beyond me."

"What better date to have a fake wedding than on a holiday where everything is fake?" Bailey answered for her.

Gerald shrugged. "It would've been completely unique if your fiancé hadn't refused my Vegas costume idea. A costume wedding in Vegas on Halloween would've been the talk of the town. But without Vegas and costumes, the date was just boring and crass."

"The entire idea of marrying for money is crass," Bailey said. "But I can't seem to get that through Jac's screwed-up head."

"Everyone marries for money these days, Bay." Gerald got up and walked over to the mirror on the closet. "I've been looking for a wealthy lover ever since Mother disinherited me for being gay." He lifted the top of his hot cowboy pajamas and pinched his waist. "And if I keep eating Jac's butter-injected country cooking, I'm not going to find one."

"You wouldn't need to find one if you hadn't gotten involved with your jealous personal trainer. Then your homosexuality would never have gotten back to your mother." Bailey opened her laptop.

Gerald sighed. "Ahh, Ramon. You were almost worth losing millions for."

"Ahh, millions." Jac flopped back down on the bed. "Just thinking about all that money makes me weak."

Gerald glanced over. "So who's your next victim?"

Jac rolled to the side and rested her head in her hand. "I'm not sure. My friend Renie has a really cute divorced father who has six car dealerships that are going bankrupt. I figure he'll be willing to cut a deal for a year. He's sixty-seven and likes younger women."

"Good God," Bailey muttered. "Can't you find someone your own age? Charles and Bradford were over fifty."

"It's the absent-father thing," Gerald said. "She's looking for the father she never had."

"Maybe," Jac conceded. "Or maybe I'm just looking for a man who won't be upset with the no-sex clause in my prenup." Of course after her night in Colorado, sex didn't seem so overrated. In fact it had consumed her thoughts for the last month. Or maybe what had consumed her thoughts wasn't sex as much as sex with a certain Scottish vampire. Thankfully, after the sheriff's deputy had driven her back to the Gerhardts', Bailey had been too relieved to interrogate her thoroughly. So Jac's secret was safe. Now if she could just get her libido in check, things would go back to normal.

"It's too bad that your aunt excluded me from possible grooms," Gerald said. "I wouldn't mind at all if we didn't have sex." He touched the spot on the back of his head and winced. "If you ladies will excuse me, I'm going to get some ice."

When he was gone, Bailey stopped typing and looked at Jac. "I'm not coming to another wedding."

Not believing her sister for a second, Jac hugged her legs to her chest and rested her chin on her knees. "I think I'll have the next one in Mexico."

"I really won't attend one in Mexico. I'm not driving all the way there. Colorado was bad enough."

"If you weren't such a chicken about flying, you wouldn't have to drive." She leaned over the side of the bed and picked up the popcorn bowl and the un-popped kernels that had spilled on the carpet.

"And my MINI wouldn't be totaled and my insurance rate increased," Bailey muttered.

"I'm really sorry about that, Bay. But you can't blame that on me. Not when Mr. Darby tampered with the brake lines."

"Geez Louise!" Bailey threw up her hands. "For the umpteenth time, no one tampered with the brakes. I told you that I needed new brake pads and an icy highway probably didn't help."

"That doesn't explain the flat tire."

"The tire on my MINI went flat before you hit the sign?"

Jac realized her blunder and quickly changed the subject. "It doesn't matter. All that matters is that I need to get married quickly before some other freakish accident happens." She tossed the last of the kernels back in the bowl. They landed in the congealed butter at the bottom. The sight of the yellow, foamy grease caused her stomach to flip. She took a deep breath to try to settle it, but instead a waft of butter and popcorn filled her lungs, making her even more nauseous. The fried chicken and mashed potatoes and gravy she'd made for dinner swished around in her stomach before rising to the back of her throat. Dropping the bowl, she placed a hand over her mouth and jumped from the bed.

She made it to the toilet just in time. After she'd emptied her stomach of dinner and what looked like the Chinese she'd had for lunch, she flushed the toilet and sat back, resting her head on the wall.

"How come you didn't tell me you're sick?" Bailey stood in the doorway, her hazel eyes filled with concern.

"Because I'm not." She got up and moved to the sink. "It's probably just something I ate."

Bailey placed a hand on her forehead. "You don't feel like you have a fever."

"Because I'm not sick." Jac pulled away from her sister and picked up the glass from the granite countertop. "Lately I've just felt a little queasy after I eat."

"Lately? How lately?"

Jac shrugged. "For about a week, I guess." She filled the glass and rinsed out her mouth while Bailey stood behind her, her narrow gaze reflected in the mirror.

"You've had your period, right?"

Choking, Jac spewed water out of her mouth and spattered the mirror. Her stomach churned as she stared at her sister through the dripping droplets.

"Tell me you've had your period, Jac." Bailey's voice shook with anger and something that sounded a lot like the emotion that coursed through Jac's body. Fear. Unmitigated fear.

"I…I…" She swallowed. "I-I'm just a week late. Or maybe two." She tried to breathe, but a huge lump had filled her airway.

"Shit! I thought you were on birth control." Bailey pointed a finger at the mirror. "You told me you were on birth control."

"I was!" Jac yelled back, now feeling as hysterical as Bailey. "I got off it because it was making me retain water. Besides, I didn't need it when Bradford and I weren't having sex."

Bailey grabbed Jac and turned her around. "So you haven't had sex with Bradford?"

"No."

"Or anyone?"

"No." She kept direct eye contact, but she couldn't keep her right eye from twitching.

It was enough to clue Bailey in on the lie. "For God's sake, Jac." She released her and turned away. "What the hell were you thinking?"

"But he wore a condom, Bay. I swear."

"Who wore a condom?" Gerald stood in the doorway holding a box of frozen waffles to his head.

"Jac's lover," Bailey said before she pushed past him.

After she was gone, Gerald looked at Jac, and his eyebrows waggled. "Shame on you, Jac, for not sharing that tasty little morsel with me." But his teasing brown eyes grew concerned when Jac didn't laugh. "He-e-ey." He walked over and placed a hand on her shoulder. "It's okay to have a lover, honey. Especially one who knows how to wear a condom."

"Except he still got her pregnant!" Bailey yelled from the other room.

"I'm not pregnant!" Jac yelled back before she lowered her voice. "Contrary to what happened in the Twilight series, vampires can't have babies—not even with humans. I looked it up on the Internet."

"Have you lost your mind?" Her sister raced back in with her trench coat flapping and her briefcase clutched in one hand. "Vampires? What do vampires have to do with you being pregnant?"

"A lot." Suddenly tired of being bullied, Jac glared back at her and told the truth. "I had sex with a vampire on Halloween night."

Bailey's briefcase thumped down to the floor as her mouth dropped open. Always the peacemaker, Gerald grabbed a towel off the rack and gently wiped the water off Jac's chin. "Well, that does explain all the vampire movies."

Bailey finally found her voice. "Don't give in to her, Gerald. That's exactly what got us into this predicament. We've gone along with her craziness for so long that she's lost touch with reality."

"I'm not crazy. The man had fangs, and I had a bite mark to prove it." Jac turned to Gerald. "Tell her, Geri. Tell her that vampires can't make babies." There was a desperate edge to her voice. Probably because she didn't believe the crazy story any more than Bailey did.

Gerald lowered the towel and looked like a deer caught in headlights. But after only a few seconds, he nodded at Bailey. "It's true. I think it has something to do with not having a soul. They have no souls, therefore there's no divine conception."

Bailey stared at him in disbelief. "You've got to be kidding me."

"No." He shook his head. "Although they can bite babies and turn them into little vampires. We need to be thankful we're not talking about the Devil. He has no problem impregnating women. Just look at *Rosemary's Baby* and Damien."

Bailey dropped down next to her briefcase and put her head in her hands. "I don't know what I ever did to deserve this."

Crouching, Gerald patted her back. "Don't worry, Bay. If Jac said the man"—he winked at Jac—"wore a condom, I believe her. Still, it might be a good idea to get one of those pregnancy tests. Just to be on the safe side. If it's positive, then we'll worry about baby vamps."

Positive? Jac slumped down on the floor with her sister.

It couldn't be positive. Jac couldn't think of one positive thing about being pregnant. Kids had never been part of her plan. She didn't want a life with kids and a family. She wanted a life with no worries and lots of money. Children didn't fit into the scenario. Especially when her motherly example had been a bartender who got knocked up by losers and got her two illegitimate daughters' names from Jack Daniel's and Bailey's Irish Cream whiskeys.

No, Jac wasn't pregnant.

She couldn't be.

Chapter Six

The holiday season was more of an annoyance than an enjoyment for Patrick. It slowed down the delivery of building materials and equipment. Gave employees an excuse for taking days off. And made his family even crazier than they were to begin with.

"Lose something?" Patrick looked down at his father, who was crouched behind Patrick's desk.

Even on all fours, the man was intimidating. His thick hair curled over his scowling forehead in a mixture of faded red and gray, and his face was weathered from years of working in the sun. But while his face looked every bit of sixty-five, his body looked closer to forty. His chest was wide, his biceps defined, and his hands as big as dinner plates.

He used those hands to push up from the floor and brush off his jeans before sitting down in Patrick's chair like it was his office instead of his son's. "I thought you were working at the Welbourne site today. We're already a week behind on that project. Which means you need to move your tail." Patrick had a hard time keeping his temper in check. Of course he always had a hard time keeping his temper in check with Big Al. Which might've explained his terse reply.

"More like two weeks."

"Two weeks!" Big Al's voice boomed before he glanced at the closed door and lowered it a few levels. "What do you mean we're behind two weeks? I gave Sam Welbourne my word that we'd have it done by the end of January. What in the hell is the problem?"

Trying not to show his irritation, Patrick leaned against the desk and crossed his arms. "The problem, Dad, is you. You had no business promising Sam anything. Especially when you're supposed to be retired."

His father's eyes darkened. "You had better watch the way you talk to me, Paddy. This is still my company, and I can still hire—and fire—anyone who gets too big for their britches."

"Go right ahead and fire me." Patrick came away from the desk, now as angry as his father. "But then who will do the actual building, Dad? Cassie's husband, James, is busy securing all the bids and contracts. Jacob and Matthew take care of all the legal issues. Cassie and Rory design the buildings. Which leaves one person in charge of making sure things get built." He tapped his chest. "Me. And I'm getting pretty damned sick and tired of getting all the shit when things don't go the way you think they should." He glanced at the plans rolled open on his desk. "And what are you doing in my office when you have one three times as big down the hall?"

His father's face turned almost as red as his hair and

beard. It took Patrick only a second to figure it all out. As quickly as his temper had flared, it cooled. Finding a chink in his dad's armor was much more fun than fighting.

Patrick grinned. "Mom doesn't know you're working, does she?" The hard gleam in his father's eyes told Patrick that he'd hit the mark. He looked back at the plans. "So how long have you been sneaking in here to avoid being caught?"

His father studied him for a moment, then surprised Patrick by not denying it. "The last couple months." He slumped back in the chair and ran a hand over his close-cropped beard. "I've tried to forget about business and be the attentive husband your mother wants. But damned if I can do it and still keep my sanity. Doesn't the woman understand that I'll go crazy if I don't get to build things?"

As much as Patrick didn't like agreeing with his father, he understood where he was coming from. Once construction was in your blood, it was hard to get out. Even as a child, Patrick's favorite toys had been Legos and Lincoln Logs. He'd spent hours in his room erecting multicolored plastic cities and entire log cabin communities. Unlike his sister, Cassie, and brother Rory, he wasn't interested in the design aspect as much as the actual hands-on building. There was nothing like taking an architectural concept and turning it into reality. A sleek modern hotel. A sprawling shopping mall. Or even a tiny office building. So he couldn't blame his father for not wanting to give that up.

"Don't get me wrong," Big Al continued. "I enjoyed going to Hawaii with your mother and looking at the fall leaves in New England. Hell, I didn't even mind the golf lessons she signed us up for in the summer." He leaned forward and thumped his fist on the desk. "But damned if I'm going to put on some sissy shoes and learn how to tango, or hop on a river cruise ship so I can come home with pictures of some old crumbling castles, or get another pedicure, or—"

Patrick laughed. "Mom talked you into a pedicure?"

His father shot him a warning look. "Your mother can talk me into just about anything. Something you'll figure out once you're married." He lifted his bushy eyebrows. "How's it going with that little brunette you brought to Thanksgiving? Your mother is convinced that she's the right one for you."

"Heather's not the one," Patrick said irritably. At least he thought her name was Heather. He wasn't good at remembering women's names. Although there was one name he'd had trouble forgetting. Even now just the thought of her name brought up an image of full, pouting lips and sweet, supple breasts. Which in turn caused a swift kick of depression. It was this depressed feeling that had caused him to invite Heather to Thanksgiving dinner with his family. He'd thought it would clear his head of Halloween night. All it had done was make his parents jump on the marriage bandwagon.

Walking over to the drawing hanger that held the blueprints, he searched for the building specs he'd stopped by the office to get. "So why don't you just tell Mom that you miss work and want to come out of retirement?" The thought of having his father breathing down his neck day in and day out had him rephrasing. "Not full time, but a couple hours a day."

"Because it would break her heart. In the last few

months, your mother has grown extremely attached to me. Hell, she can't go to the grocery store without dragging me along."

That didn't sound like Patrick's mother. Mary Katherine McPherson had always been a strong and independent woman who had her own interests, including working at a domestic violence shelter. She wasn't the clingy type. Something Patrick had always admired. But now that his father mentioned it, his mother hadn't been herself lately. Of course, being that she was a woman, it could just be a mood swing.

"So if she doesn't like you out of her sight," he said, "how did you get away today?"

"She's at the doctor with your Aunt Louise."

Patrick glanced over. "Is Wheezie okay?"

"She's fine. Your mother is just hoping the doctor can talk her into using a walker." His father shook his head. "Damned ornery woman. After her fall last spring, you'd think she wouldn't want to go anywhere without one."

Wheezie was stubborn. And a bit of a know-it-all. While Patrick's entire family had liked Heather, Wheezie had taken Patrick aside during dessert and informed him that he had the wrong girl and they needed to keep looking. Patrick wasn't looking for anything but a few minutes of peace and quiet.

Finding the specs, he pulled them from the hanger and rolled them up. "I'm heading back to the Welbourne job."

His father got to his feet and followed him to the door. "If we offer the crew overtime, do you think we can get it done by January?"

"Maybe. But you have to remember that people don't like to work overtime around the holidays."

"Try a bonus and see if that doesn't work," his father said. When they reached the door, he grabbed Patrick's arm. For a guy in his mid-sixties, he had one hell of a firm grip. "I'm assuming my secret is safe with you."

"Unless Mom asks me." Patrick shrugged. "Then you're on your own."

His father's scowl deepened before he poked his head into the hallway. The coast must've been clear because he hurried out and headed for the stairs. Since the M&M offices were on the eighth floor, taking the stairs instead of the elevator proved how much his father didn't want to get caught.

"Was that Grandpa?"

Patrick turned to find his niece Gabby standing behind him. Since starting high school, she'd worked at the office in the afternoons as the receptionist. Today she wore a business suit and a pair of trendy black-framed glasses. As cute as she looked, Patrick couldn't help missing the tomboy who'd loved riding dirt bikes and following him around the jobsite with the tool belt he'd given her cinched around her waist.

"Hey, Gabs," he said. "Since when do you wear glasses?"

She pulled her gaze from Big Al's retreating back and blushed. "They aren't real glasses. They're just for fashion."

He really didn't understand why anyone would want to wear glasses for fashion. Unfortunately, the expectant look on Gabby's face said that he needed to come up with a reply.

"Well…they look fashionable."

"You don't think that they're stupid?"

His eyes narrowed. "Did someone tell you that they looked stupid?"

"No-o-o." She drew out the word. "Geez, Uncle Patrick, you don't have to be so protective. You embarrassed the heck out of me the last time you showed up at my high school."

Just the thought of the incident had Patrick scowling. "Male teachers have no business keeping sixteen-year-old girls after school. I don't care how much they're messing around in class. If he had a problem with your behavior, he should've called your parents. Although I think the problem was his more than yours."

She giggled. "That's because you think I can do no wrong, Uncle Paddy."

He smiled. "There might be a little of that." He went to ruffle her hair, but she stepped out of his reach before he could and held out a message slip. "Some man from the city called this afternoon and wanted to talk with you. It sounded like it was important."

Patrick took the note and glanced at the name. He didn't recognize it, but that didn't mean anything. The city was always hiring a new pain-in-the-butt inspector who made Patrick's life hell. Deciding to return the call later, he pocketed the note as he followed Gabby to the receptionist's desk.

"So what do you want for Christmas this year, Gabs? There's a new four-stroke motocross bike out that I thought we could talk your dad into."

She took her seat behind the desk. "Actually, I'm not into motocross as much as I used to be." Some of Patrick's disappointment must've shown because she quickly added, "But if you want to go riding this weekend, I'm up for it."

He grinned. "That's my girl. I'll pick you up around eight on Saturday."

*   *   *

Patrick spent the rest of the afternoon trying to play catch-up at the Welbourne site. By six thirty he was beat and decided to call it a day. Normally he picked up take-out on the way home, but tonight he was too tired to make the effort. Which proved to be a mistake when he got to his condo and looked in the refrigerator. His dinner choices consisted of green-tinted bologna, two slices of moldy pepperoni pizza, and a bag of shriveled mini carrots.

A whine had him looking down at his overweight bas-set hound, Gilmore, who sat next to Gomer, a large pit bull mix.

"I know how you feel, buddy." Patrick took out the bag of carrots and tossed Gilmore and Gomer each one before taking one for himself. They actually weren't too bad, so he finished off the bag as he got out the dry food for the dogs and his three cats—Jinx, Tom, and Hellcat. It had never been his intention to have such a large menagerie of animals, but for some reason, strays kept showing up in his life.

After the animals were fed, he got a bottle of Scottish ale from the fridge, then grabbed some stale crackers and a jar of peanut butter from the cupboard and sat down on the barstool next to Miss Featherbee. The blow-up doll had been a college-graduation prank from Matthew, a gift that most men would've trashed long ago. But Patrick had never trashed a gift from his family, and over the years, he'd grown attached to Miss Featherbee. She didn't text, never complained about his coming home late, and was a great listener.

"How ya doin', dollface?" Patrick said as he dipped a cracker into the peanut butter jar. "Anything exciting happen today?" He popped the cracker in his mouth and washed it down with a gulp of ale. "Yeah, me neither. Just another day of dealing with unions, inspectors—shit!" He wiped his hands on a paper towel before pulling the message memo that Gabby had given him from his pants pocket and reaching for his phone. It wasn't until after he'd dialed that he glanced at his watch and realized that there was no way in hell a city inspector would still be at work. It turned out he was wrong.

"It's about damned time."

Surprised by the way the inspector answered the phone, it took a moment for Patrick to reply. "This is Patrick McPherson from M&M Construction. I got a message that you called."

"Oh yes...Mr. McPherson. I'm afraid that we're going to have to shut down your building on Eighth Avenue. It seems that you have numerous code violations."

Patrick bristled. "Wait a minute. We already had the inspection and everything passed. Now you're telling me that we're in violation?"

"That's exactly what I'm telling you."

It took a real effort not to lose his cool. "I'd like to talk to your department head. I believe his name is Ross Williams. Is he there?"

"Yes, but he's bopping his secretary right now so he'll have to call you back."

Patrick blinked. "He's what?" A booming laugh came through the receiver. A laugh Patrick remembered all too well. "Jonesy?"

"Got ya!" Jonesy said. "I swear I could almost see the

veins popping out of your neck, Paddy. Although you've learned to control your temper much better than you did in college. In college you would've already been here and had me in a choke hold. Remember the time that we were in the rugby scrum and the guy on the other team said something about your mother? It took five of us to pull you off him."

Patrick relaxed and smiled. "I've mellowed a little since then. When did you get in town, Jonesy?" He looked at the number Gabby had given him, with the Denver area code. "And whose number is this?"

"Mike Morrison's guesthouse. You remember Mike? The geeky guy who hung out in the computer lab?"

"Yeah. I ran into him a couple years ago. He's made some major money with an Internet company."

"*Major* is an understatement. He's rolling in it."

"And I heard you weren't doing so bad yourself. Sounds like your sports bar idea took off. How many do you have in California?"

"Just three, but I've got big plans for a lot more. Which is exactly why I'm here in Denver. I just talked Mike into investing in my company. With his financial backing, I plan to build a Sports Fanatic in every major city in the United States. But I'll need a builder I can trust. Someone who won't let me down. You think you can handle it, Paddy?"

Patrick was a little taken back. Usually you did a bid for big projects like this. He was amazed that Jonesy was giving him the job without getting a price first. "That's great, Jonesy. And I certainly appreciate you giving M&M the business. How many locations and what kind of time frame are we talking about?"

"We're starting with ten—the first right here in Denver. And we want them completed in the next two years."

Patrick's excitement died a quick death. "Ten in two years?" His mind scrolled through the other jobs they had to finish. There was no way they could get it done— especially with the crews they had. They could hire more crews, but whom would they get to spearhead the jobs? Before he could come up with one name, Jonesy spoke.

"And of course, you're the only one I'd want as the project executive."

Patrick released his breath. "I don't know if that will work. I have projects I need to finish here."

There was a long pause. "Then quit and start your own business," Jonesy said. "You can work exclusively for us—or get other jobs. It doesn't make any difference to me as long as you spearhead my sports bars. You're still single, right? No kids?"

Still in a bit of a daze, he shook his head before realizing Jonesy couldn't see him. "No. I'm not married. And I don't have any kids."

"Good. Since I'll expect you to be on site in each city, it's best if you don't have a family. Not to mention how much fun it will be when I come to check on the progress. It will be like college all over again." Jonesy laughed. "Except with more girls and money."

Patrick's brain finally kicked in. "I don't know, Jonesy. I can't just leave M&M."

"Why not? I'm sure your family won't care if one brother leaves the nest. Not that you have to leave Denver. Your company can be headquartered anywhere you like as long as you're willing to travel." He pulled away from the phone. "Hold on, Mike, I'll be right there! Listen,

Paddy, I've got to go. I'm taking Mike to a strip club tonight. I mean, the guy is loaded and I don't think he's ever had sex. Hey, you want to come?"

Patrick grabbed the first excuse he could think of. "Thanks, but I can't. I promised my Aunt Wheezie I'd stop by."

"That old bird still alive? Wow, you McPhersons are some tough Scots. Which is exactly why I want you on my team. Think about it, buddy, and I'll call you next week."

After he hung up, Patrick felt a little like he had after getting tackled by a brute of a linebacker while playing high school football. Quit M&M? As much as he fought with his father and disagreed with his brothers, he had never even considered the possibility. Ever since he could remember, M&M had been part of his life. But maybe Jonesy was right. Maybe it was time to leave the nest. To experience the excitement of building a company from the ground up without having his father breathing down his neck.

Suddenly Patrick realized the amazing opportunity Jonesy had just handed him. An opportunity that only a fool would pass up. And Patrick had never been a fool.

Lifting his bottle of ale, he toasted the blow-up doll sitting next to him.

"Why not, Miss Featherbee? There's not a damned thing holding us back."

Chapter Seven

"Do you think you could be any more conspicuous, Geri?"

Gerald looked down at his skinny jeans and navy pea-coat. "What's the problem with what I've got on?"

Jac shook her head. "Nothing if you're hanging out at a designer coffeehouse."

He looked around the diner. "We are in a coffeehouse."

"No." Jac slid her sunglasses down on her nose and glared at him over the top. "We're in a greasy-spoon diner filled with very heterosexual, blue-collar men."

His eyes followed a muscular construction worker on his way past the table. "Mmm, and don't I know it. All this testosterone is making me light-headed."

"Well, get a grip." She pushed the glasses back up. "I'm light-headed enough for both of us. At least take off the pink scarf."

Gerald retied the hot-pink scarf around his neck in some elaborate knot that Jac couldn't have duplicated if her life depended on it. "No, my outfit would be boring without it. And contrary to what you think, I did dress down for this little reconnoitering escapade. I could've worn my plaid fur-lined hoodie, which would still be a lot less conspicuous than your Liza Minnelli wig and Paris Hilton sunglasses."

Since he had a valid point, Jac only stuck her tongue out at him and adjusted the wig she'd bought at Party City before leaving for Denver, Colorado. "It's Cleopatra, not Liza."

"What it is is a waste of time. Especially when you went back to your natural hair color." Gerald took a sip of coffee, and then shivered with disgust. "But even if you were still blond, he probably couldn't pick you out of a lineup. Not unless you were naked and offering up your neck."

"Very funny." Her gaze wandered out the window to the large building that was going up across the street. "You won't be laughing when he sinks his fangs into you."

"If he wants to sink his fangs into me, then you wouldn't be in the condition you're in." He took another packet of artificial sweetener out of the ceramic holder and shook it. "Besides, I thought we concluded that your sperm donor isn't a vampire?"

"You and Bailey concluded that," she said. "I haven't concluded anything yet. Not until I see him out in the sunlight with my very own eyes."

"Which is exactly why I let you drag me across the country. You need to see the truth for yourself so you'll stop having all those nightmares about vampires. It's not good for the baby."

It wasn't so good for Jac either. Probably because most

of her vampire dreams weren't as scary as they were erotic. Contrary to what Gerald believed, she didn't wake up moaning in fear. She woke up moaning in frustration that the only man available was gay.

The waitress came to take their order, and before Jac could order the pecan caramel cinnamon roll, Gerald cut in.

"She'll have oatmeal, wheat toast, and a bowl of fresh fruit. And I'll just have coffee."

Jac might've said something if Gerald hadn't just been following Bailey's list of dos and don'ts. A list her sister had put together after Jac decided to keep the baby. The dos included prenatal vitamins, plenty of fruits and vegetables, and exercise. The don'ts included hair dyeing, because of the harsh chemical fumes, and eating too many sweets. And since Bailey had made up the list, regardless of the fact that she wasn't happy with Jac's decision, Jac kept her mouth shut and handed the waitress back the menu.

Jac didn't know what had made her decide to keep the baby. It might've been the movie *Baby Boom*, which had come on Turner Classic Movies the night the pregnancy test came back positive. Or it could've been Gerald's infectious excitement about adding a baby to their odd family. Or maybe it had nothing to do with movies or Gerald. Maybe it just had to do with Jac wanting to prove to herself that she wasn't her mother. That rather than ignoring a mistake, she could love her little girl and nurture her.

Not that she knew the gender of the baby. Jac just wanted it to be a girl. A girl whom she would name Lulu Bay after her granny and Bailey. Jac would dress Lulu in designer outfits with cute little shoes and hats and take her for walks in Central Park in one of those jogging strollers that fashionable mothers used. She would show her off to all her friends and—

"Ooo, Jac," Gerald whispered breathlessly, cutting into her baby fantasy. "There's your lover now. And he looks like my kind of a guy."

She pulled herself from her daydream and looked out the window in time to see an old hearse drive past. It had been painted hot pink, and flowered curtains swung in the back windows. "Real cute, Geri. You should be a stand-up comedian."

"Not in this lifetime. I couldn't take the hecklers. But I'm thinking about starting a new reality show. *Gay Spy on Your Straight Guy*." His brown eyes twinkled as he poured the sweetener into his coffee. "Especially now that my event planning business has breathed its last breath."

"I'm sorry," Jac said. "I shouldn't have talked you into letting me do the catering for your last event."

He shrugged. "They were a bunch of snobs if they didn't like your Granny Lou's pigs in a blanket and macaroni cups. So how did you find out where Patrick was working?"

Jac took a bite of the bland oatmeal the waitress had delivered and coveted the pecan caramel cinnamon roll even more. "I didn't exactly. When I called M&M Construction, I told the receptionist that my boss was looking for a contractor to build a new shopping mall and wanted a list of jobs M&M was working on. There were only four in the city. I thought we'd start with the biggest and work our way down."

Gerald pressed his hands together and looked up at the ceiling, which was hung with tinsel and shiny red Christmas ornaments. "Please God, let there be a Starbucks close to the next one."

It turned out that they didn't need to go to another construction site. Not more than fifteen minutes later, a truck pulled up across the street. At first glance it was no different from all the other trucks parked around the building site—white, big, and muddy. Then she noticed the *M&M Construction* stenciled in bold red letters across the driver's side door. Her stomach tightened as the door opened and a scuffed work boot appeared. A muscular body in faded jeans, a flannel shirt, and down vest followed.

"Well, hello, sweet thang," Gerald cooed. "Now that's my kind of a construction worker. Thor in work boots."

Gerald was right. With his broad shoulders and the morning sun gleaming off his long golden hair, the man did resemble a Norse god. A Norse god who had rocked Jac's world on Halloween night.

"That's him," she whispered.

"You've got to be kiddin' me." Gerald leaned so close to the window that his nose almost touched the glass. "That's him? Jac, that's no vampire. That's one hundred percent hot-blooded man."

Jac watched as Patrick leaned over the bed of his truck. His jeans had a rip in one pocket, and his shirt molded itself to the muscles of his arms as he pulled a hard hat and small cooler from the bed. He walked around the front of the truck, and a breeze caught his hair, brushing the blond strands back from the hard angles of his face. His head turned in her direction, and she ducked behind the snow scene that was painted on the window. When she peeked back around, Patrick had put on his hard hat and was disappearing through the small opening in the fences that surrounded the skeleton frame of the building.

"All right then." Gerald buttoned up his jacket. "Let's go back to the hotel, order room service, and take a nap. Then this afternoon we'll go to the art museum and do some Christmas shopping at the 16th Street Mall. What are you getting Bailey? I was thinking about getting her a new cell phone. The antiquated one she uses doesn't even have text messaging. I swear the woman is a worse miser than my mother."

"I want to talk with him."

Gerald glanced up from rearranging his scarf. "What?"

"I want to talk with him," Jac repeated. "I want to make sure."

He leaned over the table and took her hands. "Jac, I played along with your little story about vampires because it was amusing—and because it pissed off Bailey so much. But it isn't funny anymore. That man is not a vampire." He waved his hand through the air. "Because vampires do not exist. Whatever you saw was an illusion brought on by the accident and the fact that it was Halloween night."

When Jac didn't say anything, he held up his hands in surrender. "Fine, let's go talk to him. I think you need to tell him about the baby anyway. A man should know he fathered a child, even if he wants nothing to do with it." He scooted out of the booth.

She followed him. "I'm not going to tell him who I am."

"So what are you going to tell him?" He smiled at

the cashier as he handed her his credit card. "'Hi, I'm a weird pregnant woman who likes to dress up in bad wigs and go around to construction sites and check out men's teeth'?"

"You can tell a lot about a man from his teeth." The cashier nodded her head at Jac. "I dated a guy once who had the whitest teeth you've ever seen. I should've known he was hiding a lot of dirty secrets behind those pearly whites."

Jac nodded in agreement. "Mine had big sharp fangs—"

"Thank you." Gerald quickly signed the receipt and pulled Jac out the door. "Geez, Jac. Would you please monitor what comes out of your mouth? I'd rather not end up in the psychiatric ward."

"He had sharp fangs, Gerald. Not the kid kind, but real ones." She hooked her arm through his as they walked toward the rental car. "What about if we tell him that we're a married couple looking for someone to build our house?"

Gerald rolled his eyes. "And we saw his truck out in front and thought—we need a house built and here's a construction company. What a co-winkie-dink. Try again, Jac. Thor didn't look like the type to fall for stupid lies."

"It's not a stupid lie." Jac buttoned her coat and wished she had Gerald's pink scarf. For being so sunny, it was extremely cold. "Besides, it's not the lie, but the execution. And I'm world class at executing."

"You think you're world class." He stopped at the rental car that was parked next to the curb and pulled the key from his pocket.

"It worked on Bailey. She thinks we're catering a

Christmas party in Rochester." She walked past the car and headed for the corner, thankful when Gerald caught up with her.

"I mean it, Jac. I have a bad feeling about this."

"It will only take a second"—she pulled him down the street—"and then we'll go sightseeing and Christmas shopping."

They stopped at the corner, right next to a group of street people who huddled against a building. A bent coffee can had been placed on the concrete in front of them with a sign that simply read, *Hungry*. Having gone hungry a time or two in her life, Jac couldn't help digging through her purse for money. She had barely finished dropping a ten-dollar bill into the can when a man separated himself from the group. A man in a tattered red coat and a bright green stocking cap. Long white hair spilled from the ribbing of the hat and fell well past his shoulders, perfectly matching the snowy beard that obscured most of his face.

"Santa." The word popped out of her mouth, bringing a blush to her cheeks and a twinkle to the man's eyes.

"Merry Christmas," he said, his voice kind and calming. He nodded at the coffee can. "And thank you. You have a kind heart, Jacqueline."

For a brief second, she was surprised that he knew her name. Then she realized that he must've overheard Gerald. Her eyes narrowed. Although Gerald always called her Jac. Before she could figure it out, the light changed, and Gerald pulled her across the street. She didn't realize that Santa followed until she smelled the distinct scent of peppermint and glanced around to see where it was coming from.

Santa stepped up on the curb. "I forgot to ask you. What do you want for Christmas this year?"

"How about some sanity?" Gerald butted in.

Jac swatted at his arm. "Don't listen to him, Santa. He's more or less a Scrooge. I would like..." She started to say "money," but then quickly changed it to something that sounded less greedy. Something she wanted more than just money. "A happily ever after." Not just for her, but for Bailey, Gerald, and Lulu.

The little old man's whiskers lifted in a smile. "I think I can arrange that." He winked before he walked off down the street.

"You shouldn't throw your money away on old winos, Jac," Gerald said as they headed in the opposite direction. "Especially now that you won't be inheriting your aunt's fortune."

"Who says I'm not inheriting my aunt's fortune? Renie's dad has his lawyers looking over the contract as we speak. Since Bailey refuses to fly, I decided to have the wedding in New York City. Maybe in Central Park with one of those horse-drawn carriages. Those have always reminded me of fairy tales."

"In the winter in Central Park, your fairy-tale wedding would be Disney's *Frozen*. And does Renie's father know about the baby?"

"No, and he doesn't need to know." She searched for the small opening between the chain link fences that she'd seen Patrick go through. "It's a business deal. Nothing else. And didn't you hear Santa—I'm getting my happily ever after."

Gerald only grunted.

It wasn't as windy inside the steel structure as it was

outside. But it was louder and colder. There were whining drills, screeching saws, and ringing metal. Jac clung to Gerald's arm as they wove their way through the equipment and men. She knew she was being crazy, but she couldn't seem to stop herself. Man or mythical creature, she had come to Denver to exorcise Patrick from her mind once and for all. And she wasn't leaving until she'd done it.

She was tired of spending her days dreaming about Scotsmen and bloodsuckers. And even more tired of spending her nights dreaming about skilled fingers and hot lips. If talking to Patrick made her realize that he was only an ordinary man, not some mythical vampire or dream lover, then so be it. Hopefully, seeing him in the light of day would allow her to move on with her plan to get her aunt's money. This time she wouldn't run off from the wedding. She rested a hand on her stomach. The stakes were much too high.

"Hey!" A man yelled at them. "You can't walk through here."

Gerald started to stop, but Jac tugged him along. Once her eyes adjusted to the shadowy building, she immediately spotted Patrick.

He stood at a makeshift worktable, one hand resting on his hip while the other held a cell phone to his ear. His attention was pinned on the plans rolled out on the table. The closer they got to him, the louder his voice got.

"I don't give a damn what excuses the guy has, I want that crane here now."

The sound of his deep voice sent a shiver through Jac's body. Or maybe it wasn't his voice as much as the image that popped into her head. An image of Patrick standing in front of her, his muscled body highlighted by the fire that flickered behind him. That breathy sigh/moan escaped her lips. Gerald glanced down at her and lifted an eyebrow.

"It's not too late to change your mind," he said. She ignored him and continued to pull him toward Patrick.

"Hey, did you hear me?" The man grabbed Gerald's arm and stopped them. "You can't be in here."

Patrick looked up, his green eyes zeroing in and taking all the air from Jacqueline's lungs. "What the hell, Jimmy? Get those people a hard hat."

"I'm trying, boss." He looked back at Gerald and Jacqueline. "You can't be in here. Not without—"

There was a loud clang from overhead, then an even louder shout to "Look out below!"

Jac glanced up just in time to see an object bounce off a steel beam. It spun end over end just like Thor's hammer, heading straight for her. There was a burst of pain.

Then there was nothing but darkness.

Chapter Eight

Patrick couldn't quite believe his eyes. Not only because two civilians had slipped through the barricades but also because of the precision with which the thermos bounced off the steel girder and headed straight for the woman with the really ugly hair. It ricocheted off her forehead with a dull thud, and she dropped like a stone. Luckily, the guy with the pink scarf caught her before she hit the cement foundation. Unluckily, the woman looked like she was out cold.

Shit. Here's a lawsuit.

"Gotta go, Charlie. I'll expect to see that crane here by this afternoon." He hung up without waiting for a reply and dialed 911 on his way over to the limp woman. As he knelt, he noticed her black hair was now askew. The wig sat on her head at an angle, and her large sunglasses had slipped off her nose to cover her mouth.

"I'm sorry, Patrick." Jimmy, the college kid he'd just

hired, stood over them with panic in his eyes. "They wouldn't stop when I yelled at them."

"We'll discuss it later," Patrick said. "For now, go get me some ice out of a cooler." He pushed the wig up on the woman's forehead and examined the large bump that was forming. The 911 operator finally answered. While he gave her the pertinent information, the victim's eyes fluttered open. They were a clear robin's-egg blue. And when they focused on him, they widened, and her hand covered her neck.

Patrick's heart thwacked against his ribs. "Jacqueline?"

The woman didn't answer. She just stared at him—mostly at his mouth. Even in a cold building, a shaft of heat speared through him. He pulled his gaze away and finished talking with the operator. When he ended the call, he turned to find Jacqueline being mauled by the guy in the pink scarf.

He was the same guy in the picture that had been on Jacqueline's phone. Patrick instantly disliked him. He didn't like his navy coat or his fancy designer jeans or his perfect haircut. He really didn't like the way he hugged Jacqueline to his chest.

"My God, Jac. Are you all right?" he asked in a frantic voice. "That missile thing just came out of nowhere. Then it hit you, and you went limp in my arms. For a brief moment, I thought you were...dead." He looked like he was about to burst into tears.

"I'm all right," she whispered as she pulled back. Even with the sunglasses covering her eyes, Patrick could feel her gaze riveted on him. The man continued to ramble. This time at Patrick.

"How fast will the ambulance get here? Would it be

faster if I took her? Or maybe we should get a helicopter."

Patrick didn't answer him. Instead he got to his feet and swept Jacqueline up in his arms. He didn't care that it might piss the guy off. Or even that it might piss Jacqueline off. She was lucky he didn't chew her ass out. Fool woman. What was she doing parading around his construction site without a hard hat? Standing right in the line of a wayward thermos? Hanging out with a jerk in a pink scarf?

And why the hell had she left his cabin when Patrick hadn't been finished with her?

But instead of asking her that question, he carried her through the building to the jobsite trailer at the back of the lot. Her arms hooked around his neck, her hands brushing the skin above his shirt collar. He couldn't explain the heat her cold fingers generated. Nor could he explain his strong desire to punch the guy she was with.

"Bailey's going to kill me," the man said as he hurried along next to them. "Kill me. I don't know why I let you talk me into this. Let's fly to Denver, she says. It'll be a fun little getaway, she says. Well, there was nothing fun about this. Not one thing. Not the long plane trip or the bad coffee or the crazy spy thing. And certainly not the flying object thing. Oh God, Bailey is going to kill me!"

Ignoring the man's nonsensical jabbering, Patrick climbed the steps of the trailer and shifted Jacqueline so he could open the door. As soon as they entered, his foreman Steve jumped up from the chair behind the desk.

"Patrick, what happened?"

"A thermos hit her in the head." He moved to the decrepit sofa and laid her down. She tried to sit up, but he warned her with one look. She shrugged and relaxed back against the cushions, causing the wig to shift. A strand of red hair fell from beneath. Not bright red or strawberry blond, but a deep auburn. He studied the curl for a brief second before he turned to Steve.

"Find out who dropped the thermos. I'll want to talk to them after the ambulance leaves. And get Matthew or Jacob on the phone." He nodded at the door. "Use your cell."

"I'm on it." Steve grabbed his phone off the desk and brushed past the man in the pink scarf. The man looked about ready to drop.

"What can I do?" he asked.

Patrick didn't hesitate to answer. "Wait outside."

"No!" Jacqueline sat up. The action must've made her dizzy because she closed her eyes and put a hand to her head. It was déjà vu all over again. The memories he'd been trying to wipe from his mind flooded back in vivid color—full breasts, smooth thighs, a sweet center all warm and waiting for his touch.

"Out," he tossed over his shoulder.

There was only a slight hesitation before he reached for the doorknob. "I'll be right outside, Jac."

She turned the huge lenses of her sunglasses toward him. "Don't call Bailey, Gerald. I'm okay...really."

Gerald didn't look convinced, but he nodded as he slipped out the door. When he was gone, Patrick asked the question that had been resounding in his head since he first recognized her.

"What are you doing here?"

She continued to look at the door, almost as if plotting her escape. And a part of Patrick really wished he could let her. Her return was bad timing. Right now he had more on his plate than he could handle. He'd decided to take

Jonesy up on his offer and had spent the last week crunching numbers and coming up with a business plan. Starting his own company was going to take time and money. The work didn't bother him and he had plenty of money in his bank account—that was, if he didn't have to pay his family back for money lost in a lawsuit.

"Do I need to repeat the question, Jacqueline?"

She pulled her gaze from the door and cocked her head, causing the wig to shift even more. "Am I supposed to know you?"

Pissed didn't even come close to describing how he felt. He wasn't sure what game she was playing, but he wasn't going to join in. "Let's see if this will jog your memory. Halloween. Two orgasms."

Behind the lenses, her eyes didn't even blink. "Hmm? I'm sorry, it doesn't ring a bell. You must have me confused with someone else. What did this woman who had two orgasms look like?"

"Long blond hair and blue eyes."

She held out a strand of the wig. "Short. Black."

Patrick's shoulders tightened. Women confused and annoyed him, but they rarely made him so angry that he wanted to strangle them. Jacqueline seemed to be the exception. But he wasn't about to let her know that.

He leaned on the edge of the desk and crossed his arms over his chest. "You do realize that your wig is on crooked, right?"

She straightened it with a jerk. "Look, I don't know you. I wasn't with you on Halloween. And I didn't have two orgasms. The only reason I'm here is to find a contractor to build a house for me and my husband."

"Your husband?"

"Yes." Her cheeks beneath the frames of the glasses turned a rosy red. "My husband and I were eating breakfast across the street when the idea came to us."

Patrick held back a snort of derision. She had to be the worst liar ever. But for now he'd play along. "Really? And just where are you planning on building this house?"

She fidgeted. "I don't have a clue. Gerald did all the land buying. We're from Cincinnati."

"How long have you been married? And what were you doing last Halloween night?"

"Three years. And we were attending a wedding."

"On Halloween?"

"Yes," she sniffed. "I think Halloween is a perfect date to have a wedding."

Tired of the game, he pushed away from the desk. "And I think you're lying. I've never met a woman yet who didn't know exactly what neighborhood her house would be built in. People who dress like you don't eat at greasy-spoon diners. As for Halloween night, you didn't attend a wedding. You were with me. You took a bath in my tub. You slept on my sofa bed. And you fu—" Jacqueline released an outraged squeal and tried to get up from the couch, but he blocked her way. "So answer the question. What the hell are you doing here getting hit in the head with thermoses and screwing up my workday?"

If he thought he could intimidate her, he was wrong. Releasing an exasperated breath, she sat back on the couch with her expensive coat buttoned up to her neck and her hands crossed over her stomach. The sunlight from one of the small windows reflected off the red strand of hair that rested on her shoulder. After seeing her naked by firelight, he knew she wasn't a true blonde. And now it all fit. The red hair. The freckles sprinkled across her nose and cheeks. The ivory skin.

"Irish," he breathed. "Which would explain all the blarney."

Her mouth dropped open, but before she could get a word out, Jimmy hustled in the door.

"The ambulance is here. They're pulling around back." He handed Patrick a towel filled with ice, then held up a candy cane–striped thermos. "This is the thermos that hit her."

Since it looked like something a kid would have in their lunchbox, Patrick was a little taken aback. "Whom does it belong to?"

"I don't know," Jimmy said. "When I asked around, no one on the crew would claim it."

"Leave it on my worktable and I'll deal with it later. For now, direct the paramedics in here." Once Jimmy was gone, Patrick knelt next to the couch and brushed the wig bangs off her forehead. The bump had gotten much bigger, causing his anger to lessen. "Does it hurt?"

"A little."

"It could've been a lot worse." He cradled her jaw in his hand and placed the towel of ice on the bump, surprised at the desire that tightened his gut at the feel of her soft skin. Okay, so maybe he wasn't too busy to pick up where they had left off. Because, regardless of the crazy lies she'd told, she was here for a reason. And her flushed skin and the way she closed her eyes and leaned closer said it had to do with the same desire that swirled around in him.

But before he could kiss her, the door opened and two paramedics came in, followed by the so-called husband. Gerald whispered something to one of the paramedics before shooting a guilty look at Jacqueline. The look turned to one of fear when Patrick relinquished care of Jacqueline to the paramedics and motioned for Gerald to follow him to the desk.

Once Patrick was seated behind it, he nodded for Gerald to take the chair in front. "So how's married life?"

Gerald sat down so quickly that he almost tipped backward in the wobbly chair. He used the edge of the desk to right himself before answering in a quavering voice. "G-g-good. Umm, we want to build a house and need a good construction...guy." The man was a worse liar than Jacqueline. He cleared his throat and fidgeted with his scarf, loosening it and then sliding it back and forth on his neck. "But I guess you don't build houses, do you?"

"No."

"Somehow I didn't think so." After an awkward pause, he focused his attention on retying the scarf. The way he meticulously retied it finally caused Patrick to see him in a different light. The realization made Patrick feel much better, and he actually smiled as he leaned over the desk.

"Let's cut to the chase, Gerald. You aren't married to Jacqueline, any more than I am. So what are you doing here?"

Gerald swallowed hard before glancing back over his shoulder at the paramedics, who were taking Jacqueline's blood pressure. One of the paramedics spoke to her. Patrick couldn't hear what the man said, but it caused her eyes to widen and then narrow on Gerald, who took the opportunity to turn back around. "Are you a violent man by nature?" he asked.

"Not normally. But if you don't start talking, that could change."

Gerald released his breath. "Jac has a wild imagination that sometimes gets the best of her. But underneath all the craziness, I think she really wants to do the right thing. But I want you to know that I won't allow you to harm or bully her. What happened is both your responsibility, and you need to work toward a solution in a calm, nonviolent—"

"Excuse me." One of the paramedics moved over to the door and opened it. "I'm going to need someone to hold this so we can get the gurney in."

Both Gerald and Patrick jumped to their feet. "The gurney?" Patrick said as he came around the desk. "You're taking her to the hospital?"

The paramedic nodded. "Normally we wouldn't be too concerned. Her vitals are good. Her pupils responsive. But I think she should have some tests run."

Patrick relaxed. "Of course. I want to make sure she's all right."

The paramedic nodded. "Especially since she's pregnant."

All the oxygen in the room seemed to evaporate in one fell swoop, leaving Patrick unable to take a deep breath. His knees gave out, and he sat down so hard in the chair Gerald had vacated that the damned thing flipped backward, taking him with it. Luckily, the back of the chair hit the floor before his head did. But at that point he didn't really care.

"Are you all right?" The paramedic crouched next to him.

Patrick blinked, trying to breathe and process the words at the same time. All right? No, he wasn't all right. His organized life had just spiraled out of control, and there wasn't a damned thing he could do about it.

Chapter Nine

"All I can say is that I'm happy I'm a married man," Matthew McPherson said as he watched the movers load his furniture into the back of the van. "I would hate to still be on the receiving end of your matchmaking, Aunt Wheezie."

Louise McPherson Douglas shook her head. No matter how many times she explained things to her family, they still didn't get it. She wasn't a matchmaker. Matchmakers were unintuitive people who liked meddling in other people's lives just for the fun of it. Wheezie had always been able to read people like the morning newspaper and only meddled in their lives when they were screwing things up on their own.

"Well, I, for one, am grateful for Aunt Wheezie's matchmaking." Matthew's wife, Ellie, came out of the garage carrying a large houseplant. "If she hadn't fixed things so I moved right next door to you, we might not have gotten together."

With a scowl marring his handsome face, Matthew hurried over and took the plant from Ellie. "Didn't I tell you not to lift anything bigger than a toothbrush?" He handed the plant off to one of the movers. "I should've moved us into our new house on the sly like Patrick and I did for James and Cassie."

"I'd tell you to stop fussing over me"—Ellie hooked her arms around Matthew and smiled up at him—"but I find it very cute... and sexy."

Matthew's face softened, and he flashed a smile. "Sexy?"

It did Wheezie's heart good to see her nephew so happily married. Especially when there had been a time she'd thought he wouldn't be happy with anything less than a harem of women. But Ellie had changed all that. And if love could change a playboy into a one-woman man, it could change a confirmed bachelor into a family man.

One more McPherson. That's all Wheezie had left. Once Patrick had someone to watch out for him, she could die happy knowing her family was taken care of. Unfortunately, Patrick was proving to be more stubborn than his father. The young man had thwarted every prospective bride she sent his way. But she wasn't ready to throw in the towel just yet. Which explained what she was doing at her nephew's condo complex.

"So can I count on you to rent out your condo to a woman of my choosing, Matthew?" she asked. "Like Ellie pointed out, it worked for you. So why wouldn't it work for your brother?"

Matthew stopped cuddling his wife and glanced over. "In case you haven't figured it out, Wheeze, Patrick and I are two different people. I loved women, while he merely tolerates them. It doesn't matter if they're living next door to him or not. And didn't you figure that out when you moved Deirdre into Ellie's condo?"

He did have a point. Patrick hadn't said more than two words to the waitress from Wheezie's favorite restaurant.

"I take full responsibility for that," she said. "I picked the woman for her sweet personality, not realizing that she was easily intimidated by assertive men—or that she was allergic to cats." She glanced at Patrick's condo, which was only two doors down from Matthew and Ellie's. In each window there was either a cat or a dog— or both. The man might be as stubborn as the day was long, but he had a heart of gold. All a woman had to do was get past the surly disposition.

"But I think I've found the right one this time," she continued. "Tabitha's a personal trainer at my gym. Not only can she keep up on your brother's runs, but she also loves animals. It seemed like a godsend when she told me she was looking for a place to rent."

Matthew glanced at Ellie. "What do you think?"

"I think that it couldn't hurt to try," Ellie said. "As much as Patrick acts like he's happy with his life, I have to wonder if he truly is. Usually when people surround themselves with numerous pets and spend hours at work, it's because they're trying to fill a void in their lives. I'm not saying the void is a woman, but it could be."

Wheezie smiled. It was such fun having a psychologist in the family. Especially when Ellie agreed with her.

"Okay," Matthew said. "Have this Tabitha give me a call." He pointed a finger. "But this is it, Wheezie. Patrick is a big boy who can choose his own—" His cell phone rang, and he pulled it out of his coat pocket and answered. "Hey, Steve...sorry, I must've been talking with the movers. So what's up?" His face registered surprise, quickly followed by concern. "How badly is she injured? The hospital? Who went with her?" His eyes widened. "Damn, Patrick isn't good with people. I'll call him and try to keep him from causing problems, then I'll meet you at the office." He hung up and turned to Ellie. "There's been an accident at one of the jobsites so I need to go. Are you going to be okay handling this?"

"I'm not an invalid, Matthew. I'm just pregnant. Now go to work and I'll call you once we get to the new house."

He gave her a stern look as he pulled the zipper higher on her coat and tugged the knit cap down around her ears. "No lifting, and don't stay out in the cold for too long." He kissed her before turning his attention to Wheezie. "You shouldn't be out here either, Wheeze. Especially without your walker." He glanced around. "Where did Barkley park? I'll get it for you."

Since her walker wasn't in the car, Wheezie ignored the question. "So who got hurt?"

"I guess some bystander. I'll have more information when I talk with Patrick."

"Well, don't let us stop you from doing your job." Wheezie flapped her hand in a shooing motion. "I'll stay here and keep Ellie company until the movers finish loading." Matthew gave her a quick kiss on the cheek and headed to his Range Rover.

Ten minutes later Wheezie was sitting in the window seat of Matthew and Ellie's empty condo, enjoying the heat of the gas fireplace and the relief of being off her feet. "So just in case Tabitha doesn't work out, what about your friend Sidney? Does she like animals and angry men?"

"I'm not sure that Sidney would be a good match for Patrick." Ellie handed her a Styrofoam cup of hot tea and sat down next to her, fidgeting on the cushion until she and her large stomach were comfortable. "Like Patrick, she's not really looking for a husband. Especially since she just started her new job."

"I thought she was your assistant."

"She was. But since I've put my second book on hold until after the baby, there's just not enough to keep her busy." Ellie blew on her tea. "So she decided to become a part-time travel agent. In fact, Matthew's father is her first client."

"Well, that doesn't surprise me. Big Al and Mary Katherine have done a lot of traveling this year. Where are they going this time?"

"On a European river cruise."

"I'm happy for them. Mary Katherine has always wanted to go to Europe."

Ellie studied her tea. "I hope the rest of the family feels the same way."

"What do you mean?" Wheezie asked. "Of course their children want to see them travel and have fun."

Ellie glanced up. "Even if it's during the Christmas holidays?"

Wheezie set her cup on the windowsill. "You mean Albert booked a trip over Christmas?"

Ellie nodded. "It was the only cruise available at such late notice, and I guess Albert wanted to surprise Mary with it for Christmas."

Mary was going to be surprised all right, and not in a good way. She loved everything about Christmas— the baking, shopping, decorating, and especially the big family get-togethers. But maybe Mary was tired of all the holiday excitement and would enjoy a nice quiet cruise with her husband. After the craziness of last Christmas, Wheezie couldn't very well blame her. Between Mary kicking Big Al out of the house, Cassie being convinced that James was having an affair, and Wheezie trying to get Matthew and Ellie together, it had almost done Wheezie in. She was ready for calmer holidays this year.

"Well, I'm sure the kids will get over their mother and father not being here," Wheezie said as she picked up her cup of tea. "Although if I was you, I'd let Big Al or Mary Katherine break the news. We McPhersons have been known to shoot the messenger."

Ellie laughed. "Good advice."

"Ma'am?" A mover stood at the top of the stairs. "We're ready to head out."

With her big stomach, it took a while for Ellie to get to her feet. Of course Wheezie wasn't much better. Getting old was hell. Once they were outside, Ellie hugged her close. Obviously a year with the McPhersons had changed her from a non-hugger to a hugger. Something that made Wheezie smile as she patted her back.

"Do you need me and Barkley to follow you over to the house and help you unpack?"

"No, thank you, Aunt Wheezie." She gave her an extra squeeze before pulling back. "The sisters-in-law—Melanie, Amy, and Cassie—are going to come over and help me. Although Cassie probably won't be much help. She hasn't been feeling well lately."

Wheezie didn't comment. Even though Cassie hadn't said anything to the family, Wheezie thought she knew

exactly what was behind her niece's sickness. If anyone
had told her six years ago that her tomboy niece would be
laying kids like eggs, she would've laughed her sides out.
But love had a way of changing people. And always for
the better.

Ellie hooked her arm through Wheezie's. "Let me
walk you to your car. Matthew is right—you should've
brought your walker."

"A walker is just one wheelchair away from a coffin.
I'm not ready for that yet." Wheezie patted Ellie's hand.
"Now you go on and make sure those movers get to the
right house. Barkley is parked just out front."

It was a bit of a lie. She had released her chauffeur
to do whatever he did on his time off until she called
him to come get her. She shuffled around the building
and parked her arthritic hips on a bus stop bench before
taking the phone out of her pocket and squinting at the
tiny screen. The damned thing looked more like a makeup
compact than a phone. Where was the keypad? The receiver? The curved case that fit nicely in your hand?

Releasing a frustrated sigh, she swiped the arrow on
the screen as Mary Katherine had repeatedly shown her.
A clutter of little squares popped up—little squares that
did all kinds of things but call someone. She shook her
head. Alexander Graham Bell was probably spinning in
his grave.

It took her a good five minutes to locate the square
with the phone. She very carefully tapped it and was relieved when a keypad popped up. Mary had programmed
Barkley's and the family's numbers in the phone, but it
was harder to pull those up than it was to dial a number.
Wheezie wasn't senile. She remembered people's num-

bers. She punched in her chauffeur's, then placed the phone to her ear and waited. And waited. And waited.

She glanced at the phone. The screen had turned black again.

"Good merciful Lord," she muttered.

"Having problems?"

She glanced up and was surprised to find an old bum sitting next to her. She had been so wrapped up in the silly phone that she hadn't noticed him sit down. Which in downtown Denver wasn't too smart. She scooted over a couple of inches and sent him a no-nonsense look.

"If you want a handout, I'm afraid you'll have to wait until my driver returns. I don't carry any money on me." That was a lie, but sometimes lies were necessary.

The eyes above the curling mustache and snow-white beard twinkled merrily as he nodded at the phone. "Crazy inventions. Seems like only yesterday that all you had to do is crank a handle and an operator would ask who you wanted to call."

Wheezie snorted as she started the phone sequence all over again. "Then you must be a lot older than I am. In my day you had a dial."

The man laughed. "I guess I am pretty old. Although when I get up in the morning and look in the mirror, I don't see an old man with a white beard and wrinkles. I just see me." He paused. "The body might be different, but the soul's still the same."

The truth of his words had Wheezie glancing up. His coat and running shoes might have been tattered, but they looked clean. And instead of body odor, she smelled peppermint. It was a calming scent that reminded her of childhood Christmases back in Chicago.

She and her brother, Big Al's father, had grown up poor, but their parents had always had enough money to fill their stockings with peppermint candies.

She smiled at the memory. "I know what you mean. Unfortunately, everyone else just sees a senile old woman who should be using a walker. And a walker is almost as bad as these silly phones."

The blue eyes that studied her were clear and direct. Almost too direct. It was like he looked right through her and understood her thoughts and fears much better than she did herself.

"Sometimes the greatest gift we can give ourselves is acceptance." Before she could ask him what he meant, he held out a hand. "Let me see if I can figure it out."

If she were smart, she'd refuse. She watched the news and knew thieves loved to steal cell phones. But the man didn't look like a thief. He looked like Santa Claus. Besides, if he took off with the danged phone it would be a blessing.

She handed it over. With only a few swipes and taps, he handed it back. She held it to her ear, surprised to hear it ringing. More than a little annoyed that the man had figured it out when she couldn't, she was a bit snappy when Barkley answered.

"I'm ready," she said. "You can pick me up in front of the condos. I'm sitting at the bus stop."

"By yourself?" Barkley didn't sound happy.

"Of course by myself. What? You don't think I can sit at a bus stop by myself? I'll have you know that when I was a teenager, I took the city bus every day to school."

"Stay put," Barley ordered. "I'll be right there." He hung up without saying good-bye. Wheezie pulled the phone from her ear and felt relieved when it appeared to hang up on its own. Suddenly feeling foolish for her bad behavior, she turned to thank the bum for his help.

The words died on her lips.

The man had disappeared.

Chapter Ten

Jac hated hospitals. They reminded her of the state home she and Bailey had lived in for a month—all sterile and squeaky-clean with hard, uncomfortable beds and bad wall art. The picture across from her bed was of huge white dandelions. Who wanted to look at weeds when they were sick? Of course she wasn't sick. Or even that badly injured. She had tried to explain this to the emergency room doctor, but he'd refused to listen and insisted she be admitted for more tests.

"I see they've got you all settled." Gerald swept into the room, his arms loaded with snacks and magazines. He'd arrived at the hospital earlier, but since she had been on her way to get the MRI, they hadn't had a chance to talk. Not that Jac was talking to him. She was still mad at him for exposing the truth of her pregnancy to the EMT who'd then exposed it to the one man she didn't want to know.

"I bought you some KitKats," Gerald said. "I would've gotten you M&M's, but I thought it might bring up bad memories." When she remained mute, he meticulously organized the snacks and magazines on the hospital tray in front of her. "Okay, so I'm sorry I spilled the baby beans to the paramedic, but I was only concerned for your health. And if you remember correctly, it wasn't my idea to walk into that deathtrap of a building."

Picking up a KitKat, Jac carefully unwrapped it and snapped off a bar. Then she took a big bite and slowly chewed as she stared at the ugly dandelion picture. With a shrug Gerald grabbed one of the magazines and sat down in the chair to wait her out. Since she'd never been good at the silent treatment, it didn't take long.

"Well, how was I supposed to know that a thermos would fall from the sky?" She took another bite of chocolate and wafer. "Which should make you and Bailey rethink the entire Mr. Darby situation. Freak accidents don't just happen."

"They do if you're dumb enough to walk into a construction site without a hard hat." Gerald flipped through the magazine. "But you're right, maybe it wasn't an accident. Maybe it was God's way of knocking all those wild fantasies out of your head."

It had done the trick. Jac now realized that Patrick wasn't a misunderstood vampire with good self-control. Or a tortured Scottish warrior with talented fingers. He was just a man. A man she knew all too well. Not from one night of phenomenal sex, but from years of watching all the men her mama had dated parade through their life like ducks in a carnival target shoot. Patrick wore the same faded blue jeans and work boots. Had the same overdeveloped biceps and pecs. And had the same arrogance and overbearing attitude.

But now she understood how her mama had fallen head over heels for alpha men. The way Patrick had swept her up in his arms had fed all of Jac's romantic fantasies. No man had ever swept her up in his arms before. Bradford had caught her once when she'd tripped in her six-inch Christian Louboutins, but he had just sort of pushed her upright. Patrick had effortlessly lifted her and carried her back to his trailer like she weighed no more than any other woman.

She had to admit that she liked the way his muscled arms had felt tucked around her back and legs. The way the hard angles of his face had been shaded beneath his hard hat. And the way his hair had gleamed gold in the sunlight. It was longer than she'd remembered, the ends brushing her hands that she'd looped around his neck. Beneath the side of her breast she had felt his heartbeat, a strong, steady thump that spoke of virile health. But the romantic fantasy had ended the moment he put her down on the couch and turned mean.

"Hel-lo? Earth to Jacqueline." Gerald pulled her away from her thoughts. "Did you hear me? When will we have the test results?"

"A couple hours." She snapped off another candy bar.

"Thank God. I'm ready to leave. And I'm not just talking about the hospital. I'm talking about Denver." Before she could take another bite, Gerald snagged it and joined her on the bed.

"You and me both. But somehow, I don't think it's going to be that easy." He took a bite and glanced at the door. "Patrick doesn't seem like the type who will just let you go."

"I don't know what you're talking about." She tore

open the bag of Cheetos. "If he didn't care enough to show up at the hospital, what makes you think he'll try to stop me? He's probably sitting at a local bar, downing beers with his friends and celebrating the fact that he doesn't have to pay child support."

Gerald stared at her as if she'd gone nuts. "I hate to burst your bubble, Jac, but Patrick's not at a bar. He's in the waiting room talking on his cell phone."

She choked on her Cheeto. It took Gerald whacking her on the back twice before she could get any words out. "In the waiting room? How long has he been there?"

"Since he spoke to the doctor and demanded more tests and a private room."

Her stomach did a giddy flip-flop before the feeling was stifled by anger. "He has no right to order tests for me. Especially when he doesn't even know if my child is his. For all he knows, it could be yours."

Gerald finished off the KitKat and brushed off his sweater. "I think we settled that on the ride to the hospital."

"You let him drive you to the hospital?"

"*Let* is not the word. I didn't have much choice. Not when I happen to like my face just the way it is." He held up a hand. "And before you start acting like a drama queen or come up with another screwball scheme, you need to know that the guy is not an idiot. After spending thirty minutes with him in morning traffic, I figured out he's smarter than most of the snobs you con into marrying you. He knows you're the woman he spent Halloween night with and he knows the baby is his."

She sat up on the bed and pressed a hand to her forehead. "So what did he get out of you?"

"Not much. He fired out questions, and I gave vague answers. Is she pregnant? Yes. Are you married to her? No. Is she married to anyone? No. Where do you live? New York City. What does she do for a living? Nothing."

She glanced up. "You said nothing?"

He squinted at her. "What was I supposed to say? You're an astrophysicist? A brain surgeon?"

"No. But you could've said I help cater your events."

He shot her a sardonic look. "And we both know that would be a lie since I've only had one event in the last two months—and the pigs in a blanket you made didn't exactly go over well. If it weren't for my grandmother's trust fund, we'd both be living with Bailey the Miser in her tiny studio apartment."

"So why do you think he's still here?"

Gerald shrugged as he picked up the bag of Cheetos. "I don't know, but I don't think we're going to get rid of him anytime soon."

Jac hesitated for only a second before she jumped up and headed for the tiny closet next to the window.

"What are you doing?" Gerald asked.

"We're leaving." She pulled her plastic bag of clothes off the top shelf. "Call the airport and see if you can get us an earlier flight. It shouldn't take long to grab a cab back to the hotel and get our things. You didn't tell him where we were staying, did you? Because so help me God, Geri, if you—"

"No." A deep voice had her hands freezing on the knot of the plastic bag, "Geri didn't tell me where you're staying." The thump of boots against tile had Jac peeking over her shoulder. Patrick stopped only a foot away, his green eyes direct and his blond hair mussed like he'd been run-

ning his fingers through it. "But I'm about to find out."
He glanced at Gerald.

Gerald held up his hands as he rose from the bed and
talked to Patrick like they were old friends. "I'll give you
two some privacy. But remember her condition, Patrick."
He sent her an apologetic look before slipping out the door.

When he was gone, Jac turned and faced Patrick. She
should have been intimidated by his close proximity and
dark look. She wasn't. After spending her childhood terrified of her mother's badass boyfriends, she'd grown a hard
shell. Or maybe she'd just gotten good at hiding her fear.

She crossed her arms over her chest and tipped her
chin up. "You really are a bully, aren't you? You bully
all the people at your work, and I heard that you bullied
all the people at the hospital, and now you think you can
come in here and bully me. Well, think again, Mr. Macho
Man. I've been bullied by the best, and you don't even
compare."

He took a step closer, and she had to fight the urge to
take a step back. Yet instead of bullying her, he lifted a
hand and gently brushed it over the bump on her forehead. "Is the baby mine?"

She wanted to lie, but for some reason—the gentleness
of his touch or the uncertainty in his eyes—she told the
truth. "Yes." His hand dropped, and there was a moment
where he seemed to stop breathing. Then his chest filled
with air, and he slowly released it. "I realize that it's hard
to believe," she continued, "especially when you used a
condom."

He turned and walked to the window, resting his arm
on the frame. "I believe you." A few seconds ticked by.
"So do you plan on keeping...it?"

She didn't know why the question made her so angry. It wasn't like she hadn't asked herself the same question when she read the results of the pregnancy test. Maybe she was just angry that he'd called the baby "it." Like Lulu was some kind of inanimate object.

"I'm not getting an abortion, if that's what you're getting at," she snapped.

He turned back around. "I wasn't getting at anything. I'm merely trying to get the facts."

"The facts? By all means, let's deal with the facts." She held up a finger. "Fact number one, I'm pregnant with your child. Number two, I want this child. Number three, you don't." He started to say something, but she held up her hand. "Don't lie. I know your type. My mother had a thing for men in tight Fruit of the Looms and scuffed boots. You might like to take charge, but deep down, you really don't want the responsibilities that come with being a father." She stared directly into his green eyes. "It was a foolish mistake to come here, Patrick. So let me go back to New York, and you can go back to pounding nails and guzzling beer."

Then, before she could do something really stupid like cry, she turned on a heel and headed for the bathroom. Unfortunately the door didn't have a lock, and she had no more than removed the hospital gown, when Patrick barged in.

"What are you doing?" She hugged herself. "Get out of here." She tried to shove him out, but he pulled her close and trapped her arms at her sides. Like Halloween night, her breasts snuggled against his chest like two kittens to their mama.

"Fact number one, I don't wear Fruit of the Loom," he

said. "I wear Jockey. Number two, I don't drink beer. I drink Scottish ale. And number three, I don't pound nails. I use a gun." He lifted her up to her toes so her eyes were level with his. "And fact number four, you're not going back to New York... at least not yet."

Before she could even collect her thoughts, his gaze lowered to her neck, and he lifted a hand to touch the spot right below her ear. "I see that the marks are gone."

The teeth marks were gone. They had disappeared a day later. Of course it appeared that he'd marked her in other ways. The mere brush of his fingers caused desire to pool hot and heavy inside her, and she released that crazy sigh/moan sound. His eyes registered surprise for only a second before they sizzled with heat, and he lowered his mouth to her neck.

This time he didn't bite her. Instead he softly kissed the spot, his lips scorching her skin like a brand. They rested there for a moment as he breathed her in, then they slowly sipped a path toward her mouth. He gave her plenty of time to turn away. She didn't. Instead her fingers scraped through his hair, and she welcomed his kiss, opening her mouth to his moist heat and teasing tongue. Then things turned a little wild. He walked her back against the wall and hungrily devoured her mouth while his hips pressed into hers, causing Jac to drown in a sea of lust. It was crazy, but she really didn't care if he took her right then and there. In fact she wanted him to.

Unfortunately, a forced cough broke through her desire and she pulled back. Jac expected to see Gerald standing in the bathroom doorway. Instead it was a stranger with a friendly smile.

"And here Matthew was worried about how you'd handle things, Paddy. But it looks to me like you're handling things just fine."

"Dammit, Rory." Patrick stepped in front of her, shielding her nakedness. "What are you doing here?"

"Sorry to interrupt, Bro. But there's been some new developments."

Bro? Jac peeked over Patrick's shoulder at the man in the suit. But it wasn't the suit that held her attention as much as his familiar green eyes. Obviously the word *bro* wasn't just street slang.

Without looking at her, Patrick issued an order. "Get dressed." Then he stepped out and closed the door behind him. As she put on her clothes, she couldn't help but eavesdrop on the conversation going on in the other room. Even though she could only catch bits and pieces through the thick door, she heard enough to figure out that Rory was the friendly brother and Patrick the mean one. This was confirmed when she stepped out of the bathroom and found Patrick scowling and Rory all smiles.

"Rory McPherson." He held out a hand. "I'm one of Patrick's older brothers."

One of? Jac tried not to roll her eyes. It figured that a man as arrogant as Patrick would have an entire football team of siblings. It also supported the entire theory that poor people had a tendency to breed like rabbits. She should know. If her mother and grandmother hadn't had endometriosis and been forced to have hysterectomies at an early age, she'd be one of a large family.

"I'm Jacqueline Maguire," she said. "It's nice to meet you."

"The pleasure's mine." He exchanged a measured look with Patrick. "I was just telling Patrick about the connection you have to our family. It seems that our father worked with your uncle a few years before he passed away."

"Really?" Jac plastered on a smile. "Well, that is a co-incidence. Now, if you'll excuse me, Mr. McPherson. I need to catch a plane."

"You're not leaving." Patrick stepped in front of her, and their eyes clashed before Rory spoke.

"What my gruff brother is trying to say, Ms. Maguire, is that our family would love to meet you. In fact my mother has dinner all planned."

"That's very thoughtful," she said, "but I really couldn't—"

"Jac?" Gerald peeked his head in the door. There was little doubt that he'd been listening to the entire exchange. "I was wondering if I might speak to you in private for a moment." Relieved to be out from between two such intimidating men, she nodded and met him in the hall, where he hooked an arm through hers and led her to a vacant waiting room.

"You're not using your head, Jac," he said. "Did you notice Patrick's brother's suit? It's Armani or I'm the pope. Which means that he has money."

"So?" She flopped down in a chair. She was exhausted and hungry and really sick of men yakking at her. Even Gerald. Although she became more alert when he continued.

"Enough money to hire a lawyer and sue for custody."

She stared at him. "Are you kidding me? Regardless of how nice his brother dresses, Patrick is a crude, overbearing construction worker. No judge in their right mind would give him custody. Not over a Rosenblum."

He rolled his eyes. "Not a Rosenblum, but an illegitimate Maguire who has no job or way of supporting herself." He counted off on his fingers. "Has a boatload of debt. Lives with a gay man. And ran out on two weddings."

Jac eased back in the chair and covered her stomach as fear like she'd never known welled inside her. Until this point the trip had just been a bad idea. Now it had suddenly turned into her worst nightmare.

"He can't have Lulu, Gerald," she whispered. "I can't let him take Lulu."

"Of course we won't let him take the baby." He sat down next to her and took her hand. "But you have to stop being so antagonistic. Don't you always say that you get more flies with honey than with kerosene—or something like that? So if Patrick wants you to go to dinner with his family, we go to dinner with his family. We sit at their table and feast on Kentucky Fried Chicken while we talk about hunting and fishing and manly things, and we do it with bright smiles on our faces. We do whatever it takes to convince him and his family that we're good people and that his child will be loved, taken care of, and have more advantages then he could ever offer her."

She shook her head. "But what if he wants joint custody?"

"He won't. Does he look like the kind of guy who would want to be saddled with a screaming baby? Nor does he look like the kind of guy who would travel across the country to see his baby. At least not very often."

The fear subsided, replaced with determination. "You're right, Geri." She squeezed his hand.

Gerald grinned. "Then it's a plan. Once we turn on the charm, his country bumpkin family won't know what hit them, and we'll be back in New York City before Bailey gets suspicious."

Chapter Eleven

The sunny morning had given way to an overcast afternoon. Dark clouds rolled over the Rocky Mountains, covering the city like a sheet of gray aluminum siding. It seemed fitting. Patrick's mind was as troubled as the skies, his thoughts a brewing storm with no ray of sunshine. A baby. It didn't seem possible. Not for a man who had always prided himself on self-control, moderation, and responsible sex.

Until Halloween night. That night he'd forgotten all about self-control, moderation, and responsible sex. And look where it had gotten him.

He glanced over at the woman who sat next to him in the truck. The ditzy blonde who had given him a night he couldn't forget had turned into a redhead who seemed to change as quickly as the Denver weather. After the accident she'd been belligerent and stubborn. Now she was all friendly and accepting. Almost too friendly and accepting.

She glanced over and caught him studying her. She smiled, but it didn't quite reach her eyes. "So how much further to your parents' house?"

"Not far," he said and returned his attention to the road. He wasn't exactly thrilled about the dinner with his family. In fact he was more than a little pissed off that his father had butted his nose in where it didn't belong. Of course Big Al was only trying to prevent a lawsuit. His father must've had his brothers do some major digging to come up with the information about Jacqueline's uncle. Rory hadn't had time to go into detail about how their father knew her uncle, but he was probably some union worker on one of their previous construction sites.

Probably a union worker who could use money.

Although Patrick was no longer worried about a lawsuit. He had much bigger problems. Like how to tell his family that he'd gotten the thermos victim pregnant. And there was a moment when he actually considered bypassing his parents' house and postponing the moment. Instead he pulled into the circular drive.

"Your parents live here?"

Jacqueline's high-pitched, almost frantic voice had him glancing over. Her face had lost most of its color. In fact she looked like she was about to pass out as she stared at the house.

For the first time in his life, he viewed his family home as something more than just the place where he'd grown up. His gaze took in the aged stone and multi-paned windows. The steep shingled roof and huge oak doors. The sculptured shrubs and neatly tended flowerbeds. It wasn't as large as some homes in the neighborhood, but its elegant grace and subtle richness could be intimidating.

"You don't have to worry," he said as he cut the engine. "They're not rich snobs." He got out and walked around to her side of the truck. After the kiss back at the hospital, he wasn't in any hurry to touch her again. But his truck was high, and all the manners his mother had drummed into his head not easily forgotten. Although he released her hand as soon as her feet hit the brick driveway, annoyed at how just the feel of her soft skin made him want to kiss her senseless.

She didn't seem to be as affected. Her attention was still riveted on the house. Usually during the holidays it was decorated with lights, a nativity scene, and Santa. But this year his mother had yet to call him to help with the decorations. As Rory's silver Lexus pulled in behind them, Patrick made a mental note to speak to his brothers and get the job done that weekend. He didn't decorate his condo, but he liked his parents' home decorated.

The arrival of Rory and Gerald finally pulled Jacqueline's attention from the house, and she hurried over to Gerald as he got out of the car.

"This is Patrick's parents' house," she said in a tight voice.

Gerald flashed Patrick a smile. "So I've heard. Beautiful home."

"Thank you." Rory came around the front of the car. "My father built it a few years after coming to Denver."

"Around the same time as he started M&M Construction?" Gerald asked.

Jacqueline turned to Patrick. "Your family owns M&M?"

Patrick shrugged and couldn't help teasing. "Just a bunch of beer-guzzling nail-pounders." She didn't seem to get the joke. In fact her face grew even paler. Concerned that the head injury was making her light-headed, he took her arm and guided her to the front doors. "Are you okay?" he asked.

She didn't have time to answer before the doors opened and the McPherson clan converged. Jake and his wife Melanie, Matthew and Ellie, Rory's wife Amy, Cassie and her husband James, and his horde of nieces and nephews. Jacqueline took a step back as Rory made the introductions, and Patrick couldn't blame her. The McPhersons en masse would intimidate an army. Especially Patrick's father, Big Al, who stood at the back of the group like a Scottish chieftain.

"Welcome to our home, Ms. Maguire," he said in his usual booming voice. "I had the pleasure of building a business complex in Chicago for your great-uncle Thaddeus when I first started M&M. I was sorry to hear of his passing. And your aunt's." He paused. "I hope my sons have taken good care of you after the unfortunate accident."

Jacqueline appeared to have trouble closing her mouth, even after Gerald gave her a nudge with his elbow. Patrick felt the same way. So her uncle wasn't just a blue-collar worker. This could complicate things.

"Mom, why don't you take Jacqueline inside?" Patrick said. "I'm sure she'd like to sit down."

His mother in all her Chanel glory slipped an arm around Jacqueline. "You're absolutely right, Patrick. I don't know what we were thinking standing here in the cold. Jacqueline, you and Gerald come on in by the fire, and I'll get you something warm to drink."

The group moved inside, but once they were there,

his father herded Patrick into his study. Of course his siblings followed. Along with his brother-in-law, James, who after marrying his sister had become a partner in the company.

Everyone crowded around the large desk as Big Al took the chair behind it.

"So what do you think, Patrick? Is she going to sue?"

Patrick had hoped that he could postpone this moment until after he'd talked with Jacqueline and had some time to think about what he wanted to do. Unfortunately, there was no way to talk about the incident without revealing the truth. And Patrick had never hedged around the truth.

"No." He sat down in one of the chairs in front of his father's desk. Before he could elaborate, his oldest brother, Jake, moved up behind him.

"I agree. Why would she sue when she has her aunt's billions?"

Billions? Patrick straightened. Jacqueline's family were billionaires? He didn't know why he was surprised. The statement about her mother had thrown him off, but now that he thought about it, Jacqueline had an arrogance that spoke of money. At least now she did. Back at the cabin, she'd been a different woman. Softer and much more friendly. Too bad that woman was long gone.

"We don't know for a fact that she inherited her aunt's money," Matthew jumped in. "She's not living on her aunt's estate. Although she does seem to be living the life of the rich and famous. She doesn't work, and her name popped up on numerous society pages. It seems she has a thing for parties, older men . . . and weddings."

"She's married?" Patrick's voice was deceptively calm. Especially when his emotions were so tumultuous.

"Apparently not," Matthew said. "She left both grooms at the altar. The second just this past Halloween."

At the moment Patrick really wanted to punch something. It appeared that Jacqueline had lied from the beginning. She hadn't been coming from a party as much as her own wedding. It turned out that her name fit her after all. Jacqueline was a manipulative little rich girl. A manipulative little rich girl whom he'd gotten pregnant.

Unwilling to beat around the bush a second longer, he dropped the bomb on his family. "She's pregnant with my child."

There was a long stretch of stunned silence before Jake flopped down in the chair next to him. "Holy hell," he said as the rest of his siblings stared at him in shock. His father didn't look shocked as much as pissed. His face flamed as he leaned forward and pounded on the desk.

"You impregnated a young woman and failed to mention it to anyone?"

Not willing to show his own agitation, Patrick leaned back and crossed his arms. "I didn't know about the baby until today."

"And you're sure it's yours?"

After all the lies he'd caught her in, Patrick should have had his doubts about the baby. He didn't. Not just because of the busted condom, but because there was no other explanation for why she'd shown up at his jobsite.

"I'm sure," he said.

"But how did it happen?" Cassie asked, which caused her husband James to lift his brows.

"After three children, you don't know, sweetheart?"

She swatted at him. "I know how she got pregnant. I just don't understand how Patrick met her. From the information Matthew gave us, she lives in an apartment in New York City. Are you traveling on weekends, Paddy?"

When Patrick didn't answer, Matthew spoke. "The wedding. Jacqueline's wedding was at the Gerhardts' estate. Which isn't far from Dad's old fishing cabin."

Cassie's eyes widened. "You had sex with her before her wedding?"

"No wonder she canceled," Rory said with a teasing twinkle in his eyes. "She was worn out."

"That will be enough from all of you," Big Al warned. He studied Patrick for only a moment before he asked, "Do you love her?"

Everything inside of Patrick tensed. He knew where his father was going, and Patrick wasn't about to go there. "I'm not marrying her, if that's what you're getting at."

There was a flicker of disappointment in his father's eyes before he leaned back in the chair and crossed his arms over his broad chest. "So I guess that leaves only one question." He turned to Jake. "Where does this leave the company?"

"In a bad place, I'm afraid," Jake said. "Since she had a good reason to be at the site, if she wanted to sue, a jury would decide in her favor."

Patrick's temper finally snapped, and he came up out of the chair. "She's not going to sue the damned company! In fact she didn't even plan on staying until you butted in and invited her to dinner."

"Sit down, Patrick," his father ordered. But Patrick refused to listen. His life was spiraling out of control, and he didn't need his father's two cents' worth. Or anyone else's. What he needed was some solitude to figure things out.

"For one second can you release control, Dad? Is that too much to ask? This isn't your problem or the company's. This is my problem." He jabbed at his chest. "Mine. And if you'll stay the hell out of it, I'll handle it."

There was a long stretch of silence, punctuated by the soft ticks of the grandfather clock in the corner. This wasn't the first time Patrick and his father had gotten into it, and as usual, his father had to have the last word.

"Fine." He got up and pointed a finger at Patrick. "But you had better handle it well. Not only because I refuse to hand over my company to some one-night stand but also because that's a McPherson she's carrying. And I don't ignore McPhersons—illegitimate or not." He moved around the desk. "Now let's go entertain our guests."

The room cleared, and on the way out, his brothers and James patted him on the back while Cassie gave him a tight hug.

"It's going to be okay, Paddy," she said. "Whatever you decide, we'll be behind you one hundred percent."

When his family was gone, Patrick sat down in the chair and massaged his temples. Whatever he decided? Hell, he was struggling to breathe. How could he possibly decide what to do?

"I'd say that you've had one hell of a day."

He looked up to see his great-aunt Wheezie peeking over the back of the leather couch that sat in front of the fireplace. From the looks of her mussed white hair, the old woman had been taking a nap. Or no doubt eavesdropping.

"I've had better," Patrick said as he joined her. She patted the spot next to her on the couch. He sat down and leaned his arms on his knees, staring at the fire that blazed in the fireplace. The heat and familiar crackling of the burning wood soothed his frazzled nerves almost as much as the feel of his aunt's hand, which came to rest on his back. Just like she'd done when he was a child and had gotten hurt or just needed a nap, she rubbed tiny circles in the very center until the tension eased from his shoulders.

"It's funny how life is so good at throwing curveballs," she said. "One second you're standing at the plate waiting to hit a ball out of the park, and the next that same ball hits you right between the eyes. It's happened to me more times than I can count. Each time I didn't know if I was actually hurt or just pissed off that I didn't see it coming."

"I sure didn't see this coming," he said.

"No, I guess you didn't. And like your daddy, you've always hated surprises."

Patrick *did* hate surprises. He liked his life like he liked his building plans, carefully drawn out and orderly. Then Jacqueline had shown up and scattered all his plans to the wind. Of course he couldn't blame her. He was the one who'd seduced her on Halloween night. The one who'd taken a chance on an old condom he'd found in a drawer.

He got up and walked to the fireplace. "It's my fault, Wheeze. I'm the one who made the mistake."

She snorted. "You aren't the first McPherson to make a mistake, and you won't be the last. It's how you handle your mistakes that counts. So quit beating yourself up about something you can't change and figure out where to go from here."

He turned and looked at her. "Since you've been shoving me at the altar for the last year, I'm going to assume that you want me to marry her. Like Dad."

"It's what people did in my day and age, but I'm not senile enough to believe that it's what people do today. After two wedding escapes, I'd say that Jacqueline doesn't want to be married either. So now all that needs to be decided is what to do about the pregnancy." She paused for just a moment. "Are you considering abortion?"

It had been one of the first things to pop into his head when he'd found out about the baby. But while he waited for the results of the tests, he'd realized that he feared for his child's life as much as he worried about Jacqueline. And he'd felt nothing but relief when the doctors had informed him that both were fine.

"No," he stated with finality, "she's not getting an abortion."

Aunt Wheezie looked relieved. "Then it seems to me that there's only one question left to answer. How can you be the best father you can be?" Just like that, his aunt cut through all his swirling emotions and got to the core of his fear.

He turned back to the fire and stared at the flickering flames. "And what if I don't know how to be a father? What if I don't have the father gene?"

"Now what would make you think a thing like that?"

The truth was hard to get past the lump in his throat. "Because I am just like Dad. I'm arrogant, hot-tempered, and addicted to my work." He glanced back at her. "And we both know, Wheezie, that Big Al hasn't been the best father in the world."

Much faster than he'd thought possible, Wheezie came up off the couch and slapped him hard across the face. "Now you watch the way you talk about your father, young man." She poked a gnarled finger at his nose. "Albert might be arrogant, hot-tempered, and addicted to his work, but he was the one who made sure you, and all your siblings, had food in your belly and a roof over your head. Yes, he's made a few mistakes over the years, but he loves his family more than life itself and don't you ever forget it." The anger in her face eased. "Now I realize you're scared. All new fathers are. But there's no such thing as a father gene. Jake, Rory, and James can attest to that. Like motherhood, fatherhood takes dedication and practice. And even then you're going to make mistakes that you'll come to regret. But you're an honorable man, Paddy, and you'll figure it out. I have faith in you."

As much as his cheek stung, it was hard not to smile at the tiny little drill sergeant standing before him. "You've always had faith in our family, Wheeze. That's what I love about you."

She smiled back. "You're damn right." She hooked an arm through his. "Now let's get to dinner. I want to meet this woman who has caused such a ruckus."

Chapter Twelve

Jac took a sip of water and tried to keep the passive smile on her face. It wasn't easy. Especially when she felt anything but passive. Beneath the facade of polite conversation and nice manners was a panicking woman who was moments away from losing it. The only thing that kept her in check was Gerald's warning looks and the tiny seed that grew inside her. Of course the seed was the reason behind most of her panic.

Patrick McPherson wasn't an uneducated blue-collar worker she and Gerald could intimidate with their wealth and status. He was an educated business owner with plenty of wealth and status of his own. In fact if anyone was intimidated, it was Jac. Not because the McPhersons' house was nicer than Aunt Frances's mansion. It didn't even come close to her aunt's auspicious home. Nor did the McPhersons have as many servants, acres of land, or outbuildings. But they did have something that Aunt Frances had never had...warmth.

The family room was filled with comfortable furniture that looked like it was actually used. The kitchen smelled like homemade bread. And once they were seated for dinner, the dining room rang with boisterous laughter and loud disagreements. Bowls were passed in a long assembly line, and the children weren't delegated to another room but sat in high chairs and booster chairs, most of their food all over themselves and the expensive designer rug.

"Aren't you hungry?"

The question came from Patrick's aunt, who sat next to her. *Sneezie?* No, Wheezie. It was a strange nickname, especially since the woman didn't seem to have any breathing problems. Just piercing green eyes that made Jac extremely nervous.

"Now's not the time to have a delicate appetite," Wheezie said as she took another drink of the amber liquid in her glass. If the fumes wafting over were any indication, it wasn't apple juice. "Pregnancy is one of the few times in a woman's life when she can get away with eating whatever she wants whenever she wants."

Jac wasn't surprised that Aunt Wheezie knew about the baby. Patrick wasn't the type of man to keep secrets. Damn him. Plastering on the same vacant smile she'd given all of Aunt Frances's friends, Jac picked up her fork and knife and cut into the chicken. The tender chicken and broccoli in the cheesy sauce was delicious, but not quite as delicious as Granny Lou's chicken divan recipe that was made with canned diced chicken and cream of broccoli soup.

"I never had any children of my own," Aunt Wheezie continued. "My plumbing wasn't set up for it." Jac choked, and Wheezie patted her on the back until she caught her breath. "Of course I had enough to worry about what with my nephew's family and bartending at the bar."

Jac turned to her. "You were a bartender? My mother was a—" She stopped just in the nick of time and tried to correct her slip. "Rosenblum."

The woman's eyes studied her. Like her nephew's, those green eyes seemed to drill right through her and ferret out all her secrets. "There's nothing wrong with being a bartender. As far as I'm concerned, bartenders are working-class psychologists. For the price of a drink, you'll get a good listener who's nonjudgmental."

It surprised Jac how much she wanted to believe the little old woman. Regardless of her mother's bad parenting, Jac wanted to believe that she'd had one redeeming quality. And she liked the thought of her mama spending her nights listening to people's troubles and trying to counsel them like Sam from the sitcom *Cheers*.

"My mom was a good listener," she said.

Aunt Wheezie studied her. "So how long has your mother been gone?"

"Seventeen years, three months, eleven days." Jac didn't know who was more surprised by the answer—she or Aunt Wheezie. Jac had had no idea that she'd kept such a running total in her head. She tried to come up with something to cover the uncomfortable moment and was thankful when Patrick leaned over and spoke.

"Are you finished eating, Jacqueline? I thought I'd show you around the house."

She nodded, and as Patrick made their excuses, she turned to the woman. "It was a pleasure to meet you."

Wheezie smiled. "The pleasure was mine."

The house tour consisted of walking down a hallway and into a room that looked like some sort of study. It had a large desk and a cozy sitting area. It smelled of tobacco, leather, and fathers. Jac didn't really know what fathers smelled like. But she thought it would be exactly like this room.

Patrick closed the door behind them and then moved over to the large stone fireplace where logs crackled and burned. He pointed to the brown leather couch with the glass of wine he'd brought with him. "Have a seat."

She complied only because she was tired. After the incident at the construction site, the hospital, and the huge meal, she wanted to lean back on the deep cushions and take a nap. Instead she perched on the edge with her knees pressed together and her hands folded primly on her lap. "I thought you were more of a beer—Scottish ale drinker."

"When in Rome." He toasted her with the glass of wine before downing it like a fraternity brother at a keg party. When he was finished, he set the glass on the mantel and stared down at the flames. The fire crackled as the clock ticked off the time. Never having been comfortable with silence, Jac grasped at any subject.

"I've never been to Rome."

He turned to her. "That's surprising. I would've thought that, with all your billions, you'd be well traveled."

She ignored his sarcasm. "My sister's afraid of flying."

"And what does that have to do with you?"

She shrugged. "I don't like doing things alone." Her gaze wandered to the tapestry of a crest that hung above the mantel. It had some kind of a Viking ship on it and an armored helmet with a cat sitting on top. She read the words printed over the cat: *Touch Not the Cat Bot a Glove*.

"I would heed the warning," he said, before his gaze settled on her stomach. "So what do you want to do?"

A stitch in her side had her leaning back against the soft cushions and slipping off her shoes so she could put up her feet. "I want to go to the hotel and have a nice hot bath. Then tomorrow morning I'm going back to New York." She decided to leave out the part about getting married so she could inherit her aunt's money.

He studied her. "And when will I get to see our baby?"

"Whenever you like," she said, confident that it wouldn't be often. It had been obvious during dinner that Patrick didn't take after the rest of his gregarious family. He was a loner. The black sheep. She couldn't see him wanting a crying baby hanging around.

"In New York, I'm assuming," he said.

"You'll love New York," she gushed. He would hate New York. He was the type of man who needed to see the horizon and drive his own transportation.

"And exactly what do you know about child rearing?"

The question annoyed her, probably because she'd been worried about the same thing. Which explained all the books she'd bought in the last week. Unfortunately, she'd been reading the prenatal books and hadn't gotten to the actual rearing yet. Still, she wasn't about to let Patrick know that.

"I'm sure I know more than you do," she said.

His arm dropped from the mantel. "Really? What do you do when a baby cries in the middle of the night?"

"Feed it."

"And if he's not hungry?"

"She," she stated firmly. "I'm not having a boy. I'm having a girl. Lulu Bay."

A look came over his face that could only be described as surprise mixed with a healthy dose of awe. "You know it's a girl?"

Something inside Jac did a crazy little flip-flop. She thought rough-and-tumble men always wanted boys. But if Patrick's expression was any indication, she'd been wrong. Which probably explained her snappy reply. "I won't know for sure until they do an ultrasound. But I refuse to have a boy who could turn out as arrogant as you."

He laughed. Not a small chuckle, but an out-and-out laugh that caused his eyes to crinkle and the stern lines of his face to relax with boyish charm.

"Fine," he said with a smile still on his face. "What will you do if our daughter is crying and she isn't hungry?"

Jac scoured her mind for possible alternatives to feeding and came up with zip. When she couldn't sleep, she called Bailey. Her sister talking about law worked better than sleeping pills. Unfortunately, Jac didn't think that talking law would work with a baby.

"Okay," she said, "so maybe I don't know a lot about babies. But I have seven months to learn."

His intense green eyes stared into hers. If he thought he could beat her in a stare down, he was right. She didn't stare people down. That was Bailey's cup of tea. Jac had always been more passive-aggressive.

Yawning, she stretched out on the couch and tucked a throw pillow beneath her head. It was a very nice house. So warm and cozy. Maybe, when she got her aunt's money, she would have the McPhersons build her one just like it on Aunt Frances's property. Then Gerald and Bailey could have the big house and she and Lulu could live in this snuggly home. It seemed like she closed her eyes for just a second, but when she opened them, the fire was lower and Patrick now sat in the chair across from her.

"I'm sorry," she said as she sat up. "I must've dozed off."

"I want joint custody."

She blinked and rubbed at her eyes, wondering if she was dreaming. When he continued, she realized it was more of a nightmare.

"If I'm going to be a father, I don't want to do it half-assed. I'll need to spend time with my daughter. And in order to do that, we'll both have to make some concessions. Since you don't have anything keeping you in New York, for our daughter's first couple years, you can live here. After that I'm willing to relocate. I'm thinking about starting my own business so that shouldn't be too difficult."

Jacqueline sat straight up as her Irish temper surfaced. "Have you lost your mind!"

He ignored her outburst. "I realize that it's not what you had planned. But it's the only intelligent solution if we both want equal time with our daughter."

"Intelligent?" She jumped to her feet. "But my home is in New York City, and that's where my daughter and I are going to live."

He stood. "Think about it, Jacqueline. In New York, you have no family to help you."

"I have a family!" Her voice rebounded off the high ceiling. "My sister and Gerald."

He lifted a brow. "Who probably know as much about raising a child as you do. Here we'll have more help than we need. You can live in the condo next to me that my brother and his wife just vacated."

Jac tried to breathe. Things were spiraling out of control, and she didn't know how to get them back. Patrick wasn't supposed to want the baby. Men like him didn't want babies. They wanted freedom. Maybe he was just bluffing—toying with her to see how far he could push her. Well, she'd been pushed far enough.

She tried to keep her voice steady and firm but it quivered with temper. "I'm not living next door to you, Patrick. Nor am I living in Denver. I'm sorry if you don't like it, but that's just the way it is." She turned to leave, but he stopped her with words that not only froze her feet but also her heart.

"Then I'll sue for full custody."

She slowly turned back around. "You'll never get full custody."

He shrugged. "Maybe not, but I certainly have enough lawyers in my family to take a shot at it."

With a sick feeling in her stomach, Jac realized that Patrick wasn't bluffing. He was going to fight for custody. And as Gerald had pointed out, there was a good chance that he might win. Unless…Jac smiled. Unless she brought in an experienced fighter. A fighter who could face an entire family of lawyers and still come out the winner.

It was time to call Bailey.

Chapter Thirteen

Wheezie hated snow. It made her bones cold and her arthritis kick up, and made a simple walk down her garden path to clean off her bird feeder a slippery and dangerous trek. She hadn't always felt this way. When she had lived in Chicago, she'd loved the mornings she'd awakened to find the ground covered in a pristine blanket of white. She'd loved strolling arm in arm with her husband through the throngs of people with their hats and shoulders dusted with sparkling flakes. And she'd loved opening the bar to those same cold people and offering them something to warm them on their journeys home.

But back then she hadn't had arthritis. Or bones as fragile as tortilla chips. Back then if she slipped and fell, Neill would've been there to catch her. Now there was no one to catch her. Which was exactly why she had no business being outside at nine o'clock in the morning, walking along the snow-covered pathway. But she wasn't about to let her sparrows go without breakfast just because she was a little scared about tripping and busting another hip.

Leaning on the broom she carried with her, she slowly made her way to the bird feeder. It took more than a few swipes to clean off the cylindrical stack of snow. Seeing that the feeder was empty, she headed to the shed where she kept the trash can full of birdseed. A few steps from the shed, a familiar voice drifted out the open door of the house.

"Aunt Wheezie?"

If it had been Mary Katherine or one of her children, she would've kept her mouth shut and ducked in the shed—they would tan her hide if they found her outside in nothing but her robe and slick-soled house shoes. Especially without her walker. But it wasn't her niece or great-nephews.

"I'm out here," she called back.

No more than a few seconds later, Rory and Amy's daughter stepped out the back door. Gabby was dressed like a typical teenager. She wore jeans that looked like they'd been painted on, a puffy ski jacket, and knee-high fuzzy boots.

"Oh, here you are." She glanced around the snow-covered yard. "What are you doing out here?"

"Feeding my sparrows." Wheezie waved her over. "Now come give me a hand so we can both get back inside."

Instead of getting after her for being outside in this weather, Gabby hurried down the pathway and used her shoulder to shove open the swollen shed door. Having helped Wheezie feed the birds before, she pulled off the trash can lid and reached inside for the scooper.

"So how did you get into the house?" Wheezie asked. "I thought you'd lost the key I gave you."

"The front door was unlocked."

Damn. It didn't bother Wheezie that the door was unlocked. What bothered her was that she could've sworn that she'd locked it last night before she went to bed. She shook her head as she followed Gabby back to the feeder. Getting old was the pits.

It took three trips for Gabby to get the feeder filled, but the teenager did it in a third of the time that it would've taken Wheezie. When she was finished she closed up the shed, and they walked back to the house, Gabby slowing her steps to keep pace with her.

"So what brings you here this morning?" Wheezie asked. "Shouldn't you be in school?"

Gabby held open the door. "We had a snow delay so I go in late and there's something I wanted to ask you."

Wheezie moved into the back porch and used the broom to brush the snow off her house shoes. "Then let me make us some tea."

Once she'd stomped off her boots, Gabby followed Wheezie into the kitchen. While Wheezie put the kettle on for tea, she helped herself to one of the oatmeal cookies in the jar on the counter. She devoured it in three bites and reached for another before she spoke. "Do you remember the Christmas that Mom and Dad got together?"

"Of course I do," Wheezie said. "That was the same Christmas Cassie met James."

Gabby nodded. "Well, remember how you helped me get what I wanted for Christmas that year?"

"The dirt bike?"

"Not just the dirt bike, but a dad I liked much better

than the guy Mom had planned to marry." She took a bite of cookie and chewed slowly before continuing. "Well, I was hoping that you could help me get what I want this year too."

Wheezie stopped in the process of getting the cups out of the cupboard and turned. "Seeing as how you have your father wrapped around your little finger, I would think you could ask him for just about anything and he'd get it for you."

The words seemed to make Gabby extremely uncomfortable, and she fidgeted with the zipper on her coat, sliding it up and down a couple of times before looking back at Wheezie. "But that's just it, Wheeze. Because he loves me so much, I can't ask Dad for this without hurting his feelings—or Mom for that matter." She paused for only a second before she dropped a bomb. "I want to meet my biological father."

It wasn't like Wheezie hadn't expected it. All children want to meet their biological parents sooner or later. She had just hoped it would be later, once Gabby was grown, and once Wheezie didn't have to be involved.

She forgot about the tea and shuffled over to the table and sat down, waiting for Gabby to join her before she spoke. "That's fair enough, but why now? Why don't you wait until this summer when you have time off from school and it will be easier to travel to Texas? If that's even where your father still lives."

"He does," Gabby said quickly. When Wheezie lifted her eyebrows, she shrugged. "A while back, me and my friend did some research on the Internet and found his address and phone number. This morning I kinda called him. I didn't tell him who I was or anything. I just acted like I was taking a poll for cable television. And he sounded real nice."

Nice? That wasn't a word that Wheezie would have used. The schmuck had never once tried to contact his daughter—something that pissed off the entire family. But for Gabby's sake, she hid her annoyance and allowed her to continue.

"I guess he lives alone," Gabby said, and Wheezie had no trouble figuring out why. "Which means that my...bio dad will be all alone for Christmas."

"And you want to go spend it with him?" Wheezie couldn't keep the surprise from her voice.

"Actually, I was hoping I could invite him here." Before Wheezie could say anything, she rushed on. "I know it's a weird thing to ask, but Grandma and Grandpa always have such a great Christmas Eve party and meeting him with all the family around would make it a lot less awkward."

At this point Wheezie should've mentioned the fact that Mary Katherine and Albert were going on a cruise and wouldn't be there for Christmas, but Gabby looked so excited by her plan that she didn't have the heart to burst her bubble.

"Well, it sounds like you've got it all figured out," she said. "So how do I fit into this?"

Gabby sent her a pleading look. "I was hoping you could bring it up to my parents—sort of like it's all your idea. You know, talk about how you think it would be good for me if I at least knew who he was—blah, blah, blah. Mom always listens to you, Wheeze. And that way Dad won't be hurt."

No, just ticked at Wheezie for butting her nose into

something that was none of her business. Of course it wouldn't be the first time.

"Okay, I'll see what I can do." The words were barely out of her mouth when Gabby jumped to her feet and gave her a big smacking kiss on the cheek.

"Thanks, Aunt Wheezie! I knew I could count on you."

Wheezie held up a hand. "Now don't be getting too excited. Christmas is a busy time of year for people. So even if I convince your parents, your dad might not be able to come here."

"My biological dad, Wheeze. Rory is my real dad." She unzipped her coat pocket and handed her a piece of paper with a number and address written on it. "I get that he might not want to come. I mean, he hasn't made the effort for sixteen years. But last night at Grandma and Grandpa's, I realized that even good people make mistakes. And maybe my bio dad wants to see me now, but just doesn't know how to go about doing it."

The pieces fell into place as Wheezie took the paper. "Ahh, so this has to do with your Uncle Patrick and Jacqueline."

Gabby shrugged sheepishly. "From what I overheard, Uncle Patrick isn't going to marry Jacqueline just like my dad didn't marry my mom. And everyone knows what a great guy Uncle Patrick is." She paused, and her eyes grew concerned. "He's not going to ignore his baby, is he, Aunt Wheezie? Uncle Paddy wouldn't do that...right?"

"Of course he wouldn't. And we don't know for sure that he's not going to marry Jacqueline."

Gabby shook her head. "I heard Dad and Mom talking on the drive home, and Dad said that Uncle Patrick has no intention of marrying such a snooty society snob. If he did, they'd be divorced in a month."

Wheezie had thought the same thing at the beginning of the evening, but rich society snobs didn't have bartender mothers. There was more to Jacqueline than met the eye, and Wheezie had every intention of finding out what.

The teakettle whistled, drawing Gabby's attention to the stove and the clock above it. Her eyes widened. "Crap! I gotta go." She leaned down and gave Wheezie a kiss. This one much gentler. "I'll call you later, Wheeze." She breezed from the room.

When she was gone, Wheezie got up and turned off the gas burner. After making herself a cup of tea, she carried it to the table and sipped it while she watched the sparrows flock around the feeder. She should probably call Amy and Rory and tell them about Gabby's desire to meet her father. But Wheezie couldn't bring herself to do it. The news would devastate Rory. He couldn't have loved the teenager more if she had been his flesh-and-blood daughter. No, she'd wait to call them until she'd talked to Gabby's biological father. There was a good chance that the man wouldn't even want to come.

But first there was another call she needed to make. Reaching for her flowered address book, she thumbed through it until she found the phone number she wanted. Marilyn Crane wasn't a close friend. In fact, Wheezie could barely tolerate the woman. Talk about a snooty society snob. But since Wheezie rated the Internet right up there with cell phones and walkers, she had little choice. She needed information, and Marilyn was better than the *National Enquirer* at collecting it. Since she had lived in New York City at one time, all Wheezie had to do was mention Jacqueline's aunt's name and the woman started rambling like a stock market ticker tape.

"Rosenblum? Of course I knew the Rosenblums. A friend of mine played bridge with Frances and said she was a cutthroat player. Of course I never cared for bridge myself. I prefer—"

"What was her niece's name?" Wheezie cut in, knowing that if she didn't, Marilyn would go off on a tangent.

"She has two, actually. I can't remember their names, but I remember the story of how they were dumped on poor Frances's doorstep. Two uncouth urchins from the backwoods of Louisiana—or maybe it was Mississippi. Anyway, their mother was killed in some kind of car accident. And Frances was the only relative they had left so she was forced to take them in when they were still relatively young. The oldest turned out okay and became a lawyer. But according to my friend, the youngest is a no-account just like her mother. She can't even hold down a job."

Wheezie rolled her eyes, already annoyed with the woman. "And why would she need to hold down a job if she inherited her aunt's money?"

"Oh, she didn't inherit it. At least not yet. There's some clause in the will that she has to meet before she gets Frances's fortune. And if she doesn't meet it, she gets nothing."

"So what was the clause?" she asked.

"My friend doesn't know exactly, but it must have something to do with getting married and settling down. Because from what I hear, the youngest niece has been chasing after men for the last year."

Wheezie took a sip of her tea as she mulled over the

information. So Jacqueline's failed weddings had something to do with her aunt's will. Some people might label her a gold digger, but those people didn't know what it was like to be poor—to go to bed hungry or watch your parents struggle to make ends meet. Wheezie knew. Her parents had come over on a boat from Scotland and worked and scraped for everything they'd gotten. If Jacqueline had been that poor, Wheezie could understand her desire to meet her aunt's stipulation.

"So why are you so interested in the Rosenblums, Louise?" Marilyn asked.

"The name was brought up in a conversation, and I was curious," Wheezie hedged, and then quickly changed the subject. "So how are your grandsons doing? I hear that Edward is engaged."

The ploy worked, and Marilyn spent the next thirty minutes filling Wheezie's ear with stories about her handsome and talented grandsons. When she finally stopped for a breath, Wheezie used the doorbell ringing as an excuse and ended the call. She sat for a moment digesting the information she'd discovered about Jacqueline before she reached across the table and grabbed her bottle of vitamins. She usually only took one, but this morning she popped two in her mouth and washed them down with her tea.

Between Mary Katherine and Albert leaving, Gabby's desire to meet her father, and Patrick's baby, this Christmas was shaping up to be as crazy as the last. Which meant that Wheezie would need all the extra energy she could get.

Chapter Fourteen

I think I see her," Gerald said as he looked over the heads of the travelers emerging from the airport security gates.

The fear in Jac's stomach ratcheted up a few knots. "Does she look mad?"

"Yep, she just shoved that security guy out of the way and kicked his bomb-sniffing dog." When Jac's hand tightened on his arm, he shot her a teasing look and laughed. "I'm just kidding. She looks fine. In fact she'll probably be all doped up from the tranquilizers she took so she could get on the plane."

Unfortunately, Gerald was wrong. As Bailey appeared with the black bag slung over her shoulder and her briefcase in one hand, she didn't look drugged. She looked feral. And her wild look wasn't all due to her fear of flying.

"Hi, Bay," Gerald said as he rushed forward and grabbed her bag from her shoulder. "How was the trip?"

Bailey shot him a nasty look before turning on Jac. Her gaze accessed her from head to toe before she lifted a hand and brushed back Jac's bangs to examine the bump.

"Are you okay?" she asked. When Jac nodded, she drew back a fist and slugged her in the arm. Jac had barely finished cringing before Bailey socked Gerald twice as hard.

"Really nice," Gerald moaned in pain. "That's going to leave a bruise."

"Good." Bailey fumed. "You deserve worse allowing my ditzy pregnant sister to talk you into coming out here on a vampire hunt. What were you thinking"—she poked him in the chest with one finger—"letting her get on a deathtrap of an airplane, wander around in a construction site without a hard hat, and get bullied by some macho construction worker? You deserve more than a sock in the arm. I should kick your ass from one side of this airport to the other."

"It wasn't his fault. It was mine," Jac jumped in. "If Gerald hadn't come with me, I would've come alone."

"Oh"—her sister turned on her—"believe me, I know exactly whose fault it is. But being pregnant, I can't very well kick your ass all around the airport, now can I? Besides, Gerald and I made a deal. I help him with his rent, and he keeps an eye on you." She glared at him. "Which doesn't include letting her make stupid decisions."

"It wasn't a stupid decision," Jac blurted out.

"Really? What would you call flying to Denver to see if your sperm donor is a vampire?" She lifted her eyebrows. "A rational decision?"

"No. And I didn't really fly out here to see if he was a vampire. I came because—"

"She's hot for him," Gerald said. "I can't say as I blame her, Bay. The guy is sweet man candy in work boots. A sexual fantasy in flannel. Naughty—"

Bailey cut him off. "I get the picture, Gerald." She looked at Jac. "Is he right? Do you like this guy?"

Jac took a moment to consider the question. There was little doubt that she liked Patrick physically. Whenever he was near, it was like pheromone overload. Every cell in her body clamored for a brush of his strong fingers, a sweep of his firm lips, or a thrust—

"Custody cases can get ugly." Bailey cut into her thoughts. "And the people involved don't usually end up friends. So if you're not sure you want this, you better tell me now."

Where Patrick was concerned, Jac wasn't sure what she wanted. Her body said, "More orgasms, please," but her brain knew that those orgasms would come at a price she wasn't willing to pay.

"I'm sure," she said. As soon as the words were out of her mouth, her sister's killer instinct took over.

"Okay, then." Bailey adjusted her grip on the handle of her briefcase and started walking. "I think I can get you full custody. Especially when you got hit in the head with a thermos on M&M's construction site. That gives us a huge bargaining tool. The McPhersons have a sterling reputation that I'm sure they won't want to tarnish with bad press about illegitimate children."

She quickened her pace so much that Gerald and Jac almost had to jog to keep up with her. "I couldn't dig up very much on Patrick. He graduated top of his class from the University of Colorado, where he played rugby until he got a knee injury. Other than that, he wasn't very newsworthy. Now his younger brother, Matthew, is a different story. The man's a dog."

"A dog?" Gerald huffed, struggling with the overstuffed carry-on. If Jac knew Bailey, it wasn't filled with clothing as much as work files.

"A hound dog," Bailey said. "The man has sex with so many women that he has his own blog page containing critiques on his performance in bed."

"But Matthew's married," Jac said, now as out of breath as Gerald.

"I know. Poor woman. Of course she should've known better. She's the psychologist who wrote that book about abstinence."

Gerald gasped. "That's why she looked so familiar. She wrote the best-selling self-help book *Virginal Love: Separating Lust from True Emotions*. I cut Jesse off from sex for an entire week because of that book, and the only thing it did for our relationship was end it. It appeared that good sex was all we had. And all I really wanted. Unfortunately, I found that out too late." He slowed his pace to catch his breath, and Jac followed suit.

"Did you think Matthew acted like a womanizer?" she asked him.

"Not with the way he doted on his wife." He shrugged. "Still, you never know about people. Maybe they have an arrangement."

Jac wasn't sure why the information about Matthew bothered her so much. Maybe because, during dinner, he and Patrick's other brothers had acted like perfect husbands and fathers. The type of men who could make happily ever afters. Obviously Jac had let her wild imagination get the best of her again.

Bailey stopped at the escalator that led to the parking garage and turned. "Are you two coming?" They hurried to catch up, and she waited until they were off the escalator and on their way to the car before she continued. "The oldest brother, Jake, is supposed to be one of the best corporate lawyers in the country. And I must admit that I'm looking forward to going head-to-head with him. I've set up an appointment with him and Matthew for two this afternoon."

"This afternoon?" Jac knew her sister didn't mess around, but she had been hoping to have a little time before she had to see Patrick again. There was something about the man that left her feeling disoriented and scattered.

"You don't need to be there," Bailey said. "In fact I think it might be better if you and Gerald stay at the hotel. It should only take an hour. I plan to be brief and straight to the point." Her sister stopped and waited for Gerald to place her bag in the trunk of the rental car before holding her hand out for the keys. Bailey never liked being a passenger. Which explained her dislike of flying.

Gerald grinned as he handed the keys over. "I say fifteen minutes, tops. No one can stand to be in the same room with you for longer than that."

They continued to verbally joust as Jac climbed in the backseat. Bailey's arrival had eased some of her fears. Patrick might have two lawyer brothers and a large arrogant family, but Bailey evened the playing field. People didn't expect a beautiful woman to be a cutthroat business shark.

The McPhersons were in for a big surprise.

* * *

The woman who sat at the other end of the long conference table from Patrick didn't look anything like her redheaded sister. Her hair was dark, her eyes hazel, and her body petite. Nor did she act like her. This woman in the cream-colored business suit was cool, direct, and logical.

She was also a ball-buster.

"I went to the jobsite today, Mr. McPherson. And I don't agree that you had the site adequately barricaded off." She tapped her pen on the table. "In fact I didn't even see any warning signs until I was inside. Of course, for my sister, that was too late."

Jake jumped in. "Do you wear glasses, Ms. Maguire?"

A dark brow lifted as she turned to him. "Twenty-ten, Mr. McPherson."

"What's your point, Ms. Maguire?" Matthew leaned up in his chair. "Why did you call this meeting? I thought this had to do with custody. Now suddenly you've switched the conversation to the incident at the jobsite. Are you planning on suing us?"

She looked mildly surprised, but Patrick knew it was all an act. Obviously Jacqueline was pissed about his giving her an ultimatum and had brought her sister in to even things up. Patrick had to admit that she was doing a good job of it. How could he possibly leave M&M after he caused a major lawsuit? And there wasn't enough in his account to cover both a lawsuit and starting his own company.

"Of course not," Bailey said in a syrupy voice. "What happened on Thursday was an accident. Although you might want to rethink some of your safety measures. Accidents can be prevented." She tipped her lips up in a bright smile, although, just as with her sister, it didn't reach her eyes. "But you're right, the reason I called the meeting is because of Jacqueline's baby."

"You mean our baby," Patrick interjected.

She cocked her head and studied him. The same way she'd studied him when they were first introduced—like he was a fungus she couldn't wait to get rid of. "I'm going to assume by that statement that you're willing to accept responsibility for your child. Not just verbally, but financially."

He had to wonder why a billionaire would worry about financial responsibility. Obviously Bailey just liked fucking with him.

"I am," he said. "But not in New York City."

Her hazel eyes drilled him. "I don't think you have that choice. New York City is my sister's home."

"My home is here. And Denver is a better place to raise a child than a smog-filled, overpopulated city."

"You should've thought of that before you had sex with a New Yorker."

Matthew coughed, no doubt trying to hide his laughter. "Ms. Maguire, I'm sure we can figure out a compromise. All my brother wants is an opportunity to get to know his child. He will pay all Jacqueline's expenses while she's here."

Bailey didn't hesitate to give her answer. "No."

Patrick had had enough. Bailey might be able to bully other men with her good looks and arrogant attitude, but she wasn't going to bully him. He got to his feet and rested his knuckles on the table. "Then I'll sue for full custody. Because you aren't the only one who did their homework, Miz-z-z"—he stretched out the word—

"Maguire. And I think I have a pretty good chance, considering your sister's love of partying and runaway bride antics."

Bailey's eyes narrowed. "Sue for full custody, and I'll sue your company for gross negligence."

"Start the process, Jake," he said.

Unlike Matthew, Jake was a man of few words. Even now he took his time before he spoke. "Ms. Maguire, I don't want to bring in the legal system, but I am starting to get the feeling that you want my brother to forget he has a child."

She pulled her gaze away from Patrick and directed her steely stare at Jake. "I don't expect him to forget he has a child. I just don't want him holding my sister hostage. If he wants to come to New York and visit his child, he's welcome anytime."

"Unlike your sister, I have a job," Patrick said. "It makes more sense for her to move here."

"For how long?" Bailey asked. "Until the baby's two months old? A year? Ten years? What exactly do you want, Mr. McPherson?"

His temper snapped. "I want to be a father!"

His outburst would've had his construction crew running for cover. Bailey seemed unfazed. She hesitated for only a moment before she spoke to his brothers. "I would like to talk to Patrick alone."

His brothers looked at him, and when he nodded, they got up from the table and excused themselves. Patrick was glad that he'd decided to tell just Jacob and Matthew about the meeting. Big Al wouldn't have left so easily.

"If you're planning on standing up during our conversation in order to intimidate me," Bailey said once the door was closed, "you're wasting your time. I don't intimidate easily."

"A family trait," Patrick replied as he sat back down, waiting for her to say what she wanted to say without his brothers around. It took a while.

"So you want to be a father?" she finally asked.

The question wasn't what he'd expected. He'd expected the woman to rake him over the coals. Instead her posture had relaxed, and she seemed much less intense. Late-afternoon light spilled in through the windows and shone off her mane of thick black hair, her dark eyes, and her olive skin. On closer examination, there was a family resemblance between her and Jacqueline. They both had a stubborn chin and the same cute little nose. Although, on this woman, *cute* wasn't an appropriate adjective.

"Yes," he said. "I want to be a father."

"What kind?"

"Meaning?"

She sat up and rested her hands on the table. "There are all kinds of fathers, Mr. McPherson."

"Patrick."

She nodded. "Patrick. Some fathers desert their children. Some display their children like trophies, but otherwise ignore their existence. Some prefer buying their children's love rather than spending quality time with them. And some fathers control their child's every move. Which kind do you want to be?"

"The kind who does the best he can."

"And what does your best consist of, Patrick?"

He hated to be patronized, and this woman could patronize almost as well as his father. He sat back and crossed his arms over his chest. "Since I've never been a father before, I'll have to get back to you on that. But it has to be just as good as what your ditzy sister brings to the table."

The composure she'd held in place during the meeting slipped. "I'd be very careful how you talk about my sister if I were you."

"Or what? You'll sue my company?" He laughed, starting to enjoy himself. "You and I both know how long and drawn-out that can be. Not to mention expensive. Although your aunt has made sure that you and your sister don't have to worry about that, hasn't she?" Her only answer was a slight lifting of her eyebrows as he continued. "I'm not asking Jacqueline to live here forever. All I'm asking is that, once the child is born, she gives me an opportunity to get to know her. And I can't do that if she's halfway across the country."

"Her?"

"Jacqueline is convinced that the baby's going to be a girl. Although she might've just said that because I accidentally used the word *he* and she loves to disagree with me."

For the first time, Bailey sent him a genuine smile. "She is contradictory. If you say *black*, she'll always say *white*."

"So I've gathered," he said dryly.

Her eyes seemed to narrow in on him as she rhythmically tapped the pen on her open file. It was extremely disconcerting, and he was sure that she knew it. "So why aren't you married?"

"I guess I prefer my own company to that of a chattering female."

Bailey burst out laughing. "And you were attracted to my sister?"

Patrick couldn't help it. He liked this woman. She might be a ball-buster, but she didn't beat around the bush or talk nonsense. If the circumstances were different, they could have been friends. He shrugged. "Circumstances."

The laughter faded from her eyes. "So you're not attracted to my sister?"

He didn't want to be. Jacqueline was everything he hated and more—rich, compulsive, and spoiled. Still, he couldn't deny that he was attracted to her. When she was in the same room, he couldn't seem to take his eyes off her. It could be because she was pregnant with his child. But he doubted it. Not when just a flash of her blue eyes made him rock-hard. Still, he wasn't ready to admit it. "What are you getting at?" He leaned up. "I thought we were talking about me being a good father. What difference does it make if I'm attracted to your sister?"

Ignoring the question, she got up and walked over to the wall of floor-to-ceiling windows. "You're wrong about her, you know. She isn't ditzy. She scored in the top seven percent on her SATs and barely opened a book. She is compulsive and a tiny bit materialistic. But you couldn't find a more kindhearted, generous, loyal human being." She glanced back at him. "I know you won't take my word for it, but she'll be a wonderful mother."

If Patrick took anyone's word, it would be this woman. He couldn't seem to help it. He liked Bailey and couldn't fault her for trying to protect her sister.

"One year," he said. "That's all I ask for. I give you my word that I'll take the best care of her and our baby."

She studied him for a long moment, and he really thought she was going to agree. Instead she dropped a bomb that had him reeling. "I'm going to assume that Jacqueline hasn't told you about getting married."

Married? Patrick felt like he had the time he'd been wrestling with Matthew and got kicked in the windpipe. Air wheezed out of him, and he couldn't seem to get it back.

Acting like she was completely unaware of his discomfort, Bailey walked over and sat down. "Being that Jac is a bit of a romantic, she wants the full Cinderella wedding complete with a Central Park horse-drawn carriage. And on Christmas day of all days." While Patrick struggled to breathe, she picked up the pen and started that annoying tapping. "But I can't really complain about the time frame. Not when the baby needs a father figure."

Air filled Patrick's lungs, followed by a whole lot of anger. "What do you mean a father figure? I'm the father." His hand came down hard on the desk. Bailey didn't even jump.

"Of course you are." She smiled in that patronizing way of hers. "But you certainly don't think that Jacqueline will remain single for the rest of her life."

Patrick didn't know what he thought. In fact he'd been so busy thinking about fitting into his child's life that he hadn't given much thought to how he'd fit into Jacqueline's. Now that he did, he discovered that the mere idea of Jacqueline being with another man pissed him off so much he couldn't sit still another moment.

He got to his feet. "Where is she?"

Chapter Fifteen

Jac didn't know what she'd expected when Bailey got back to the hotel after meeting with the McPhersons, but she certainly hadn't expected her sister to bring the most annoying McPherson with her.

All the questions Jac had been saving up fizzled as she stared in disbelief at the grumpy-looking man who followed Bailey into the room. Patrick was dressed in his usual construction uniform of work boots, faded jeans, and flannel shirt. But today he'd added a green ski jacket that turned his eyes a piercing emerald. His gaze took in Jac and then quickly narrowed on Gerald, who was propped up on the pillows next to her.

Gerald immediately clicked off the television and got to his feet. "Hi, Patrick. What a surprise. Jac and I were just watching *Property Brothers*—her new favorite show. And I must admit that construction brother Jonathan is drool-worthy when he knocks down walls with his big sledgehammer." His eyebrows lifted. "Do you have one?"

Bailey rolled her eyes. "Cut it out, Gerald. Patrick isn't here to talk about his tools. He volunteered to take us sightseeing. Now show me where the soda machine is so I can get a Dr Pepper before we leave."

Sightseeing? Had Bailey lost her mind? What happened to Killer Bailey who nailed guys' balls to the wall? Jac might've asked that very question if Gerald hadn't chimed in.

"Ooo." He clapped his hands. "You're going to show us around, Patrick? What fun." He sent Jac a bright smile before he headed out the door after Bailey.

For a second Jac thought about racing after them. Patrick did not look like he was in a good mood. Which could only mean one thing: Bailey *had* kicked some McPherson butt. The thought made Jac a lot less angry with her sister. Bailey was probably just trying to appease Patrick now that they were headed back to New York City.

Putting on a happy face, Jac got up from the bed. "It's so nice of you to show us around before we—"

"Do you love him?"

Jac blinked at the quick subject change. "What?"

He stepped closer. "The guy you're marrying. Do you love him?"

Jac tried to hide her shock. Bailey had told Patrick that she was getting married? Why would she do something like that? The light went on in Jac's brain. Of course, how stupid could Jac get? If Patrick thought she was getting married, he wouldn't expect her to stay here. Which meant that all she needed to do was tell him that she loved Renie's dad.

Unfortunately, with his green eyes pinned on her, that

was easier said than done. Try as she might, she couldn't seem to get the words out. "Yes, I...umm...I really..." She cleared her throat as his eyes narrowed.

She was about to skip the word *love* and go with *like a lot* when something behind her caught his attention. He stepped around her and walked to the other queen bed. Slipping a hand beneath the pillows, he pulled out his Scottish kilt. Since she'd left the cabin, the soft plaid had become a kind of security blanket for Jac. Something that soothed her when she couldn't sleep, almost as much as Bailey talking law. Of course she didn't want Patrick knowing that. And when he turned and stared at her in confusion, she tried to explain. "I must've gotten it mixed in with my wedding gown that night at the cabin," she said. "And the reason it's here is because I was going to bring it back to you. And the reason it was under my pillow is because..." She ran out of reasons as Patrick stepped closer. So close that she could smell the fresh outdoorsy scent that seemed to cling to him.

"And I think you're a really bad liar, Jacqueline." He lifted the kilt. "Not just about this, but about the man you think you're going to marry."

The word *think* should've set off a warning bell in her brain. But her brain would have had to be working in order for that to happen. And his nearness caused all coherent thoughts to vanish. She swayed toward him, and he rewarded her with a kiss that further fogged her mind. When he finally pulled back, his breath was as uneven as hers. He stared at her with those heated green eyes for what felt like an eternity before he spoke.

"If you're going to marry anyone, you're going to marry—"

Gerald came bustling back into the room. "Now that Bailey has her hit of caffeine, what are we waiting for? Let's go sightseeing!"

It turned out that Gerald didn't really want to sightsee as much as shop. Once Patrick pointed out the 16th Street Mall, all the tourist stops in downtown Denver were forgotten. Normally Jac would've been just as excited about shopping in a new city. But Patrick's kiss had left her feeling like she'd gone for a spin on a carnival ride. Or not the kiss as much as what he'd been about to say. Of course she must've misunderstood. There was no way that Patrick had been about to order her to marry him. Patrick wasn't the marrying kind. And yet she couldn't shake the thought, which left her feeling confused and disoriented.

She was relieved when Gerald finally finished shopping and they left the busy mall. While Patrick and Bailey helped Gerald with his multitude of bags, Jac headed to the bench across the street from the mall. She had just stepped off the curb when a car came zipping around the corner. It would've hit her if someone hadn't grabbed her from behind and pulled her to safety. Once she caught her breath, she turned to thank her savior. She was surprised to find the Santa street person standing there in his tattered coat and green stocking cap.

"Thank you so much," she said. "That car came out of nowhere." As she looked down the street after the car, a thought struck her. "Mr. Darby."

"More like someone in a hurry," Santa said. "People are always in a rush during the holidays. So how's that happily ever after coming?"

Jac would've continued to obsess about Mr. Darby if

she hadn't looked at Santa. There was just something about the man's twinkling eyes and peppermint scent that drained all negative thoughts right out of her. She smiled. "Not so well, I'm afraid, but I refuse to give up."

He took off the tattered stocking cap and scratched his head. "That's too bad. It would sure make things a lot easier."

Before she could ask him what he meant, Patrick came striding up with Gerald and Bailey close on his heels. He took her arms as his concerned gaze ran over her from head to toe.

"Are you okay?" he asked. She nodded, and his shoulders relaxed.

"Oh my God, Jac," Gerald said. "What were you thinking stepping out in the street without looking both ways?"

"She wasn't thinking," Bailey joined in. "What is up with you, Jac? You've been in a daze all day. Between you walking around like a zombie and Gerald in his silly rabbit hoodie—"

"It's not silly." Gerald stroked the fur that framed his face.

"I don't know what you'd call it," Bailey said. "You do realize that Peter Cottontail lost his life for your fashion, don't you, Geri?"

Gerald shot a glance at Santa. "Don't worry, Santa, it's only faux. I wouldn't want you putting me on the naughty boy list over a bunny hoodie."

"I wouldn't think of it, Gerald," Santa said. "Haven't you always gotten what you wanted?"

"Well, actually there was that underwear model—"

Bailey slapped a hand over his mouth as Patrick took a business card out of his wallet and tossed it and a hundred-dollar bill into Santa's hat. "Thank you for pulling Jacqueline out of harm's way. If you're interested in a job, call me." He took all the shopping bags from Gerald and Bailey. "I think we've had enough sightseeing for one day. Why doesn't everyone stay here and I'll go get my truck?"

When he was gone, Gerald spoke. "So? Are we having fun yet?"

"No," Jac said. "I'm not having fun. First my sister brings home the enemy, and then Mr. Darby almost runs me over." Suddenly, worried about airing her dirty laundry in front of strangers, she glanced over at Santa. He was gone. No doubt on his way to the liquor store with Patrick's money. Except the image of a drunk didn't fit with the jolly old guy. She'd rather think of him using the money to feed his reindeer.

"For the love of Pete, Jac, enough about Mr. Darby." Bailey sat down on the cement wall that bordered one of the trees lining the street and pulled off her sensible pump. "You were the one who stepped out in the street without looking. And I don't think that Patrick's the enemy."

Gerald sat down next to Bailey. "So I gather that Patrick wasn't intimidated by the threat to sue his company."

Bailey shook her head. "I doubt that the man is intimidated by much. Although I think you overreacted, Jac. Patrick isn't trying to steal your baby as much as spend time with his kid."

"I don't know what you'd call it. Patrick threatened to sue for full custody if I didn't move here."

"Only because he thinks it's the most logical plan," Bailey said as she replaced her shoe. "And I'm starting to wonder if he isn't right."

"What?" Jac stared at her sister. "Please don't tell me that you're taking Patrick's side?"

Always one to avoid a sister fight, Gerald got to his feet. "If you ladies will excuse me, that scent of peppermint has me craving peppermint hot cocoa, and I'm going over to that coffee shop and see if they have some."

Once he was gone, Bailey continued. "I'm not taking Patrick's side, Jac. I just want you to use common sense instead of hormonal emotion. What's wrong with moving to Denver for a year? It's not like you have a job or any responsibilities in New York."

Jac's eyes widened. "Move away from a family I love to live with a man I don't even like?"

"Isn't that what you are planning on doing with Renie's dad? And be truthful, Jac. Do you really dislike Patrick that much?"

Jac took a moment to consider the question. She did dislike his arrogance and bossiness. And the way he could have a civil conversation with Bailey but not with her. But there were some things she didn't dislike. Like his long blond hair, the spring green of his eyes, and the way the soft fabric of his flannel shirts molded to his broad shoulders and muscled chest.

"No," she said as she sat down next to her sister. "I don't dislike him that much."

"And you certainly desire him."

"So what? I've lusted after lots of guys."

"Really? Name one."

Jac tried to come up with a name, but it wasn't easy. She had dated a lot of men, but lusted after very few. "When I was seventeen, there was Damon Jackson."

"You didn't lust after him. You lusted after the shiny new Jaguar his dad bought him for Christmas."

"What about Mikey Hall?"

Bailey rolled her eyes. "Geez, Jac. You were ten, and he was twelve. Don't tell me you had the hots for him?"

No. More like his mother's homemade chocolate chip cookie recipe.

"Richard Gere!"

"Only because you wanted to be his pretty woman. Besides, movie stars don't count." Bailey glanced up at the overcast skies, no doubt already worrying about the return flight home.

"Okay," Jac said. "So I haven't lusted after a lot of men. What difference does that make?"

Bailey looked at her. "Did you ever think that maybe you were saving yourself for the right one?"

"Patrick?" She snorted. "Not hardly."

"Why not?" Bailey said. "Patrick is young, intelligent, good-looking, and wealthy. You could do a lot worse for a husband."

"A husband! Have you lost your mind?"

"Think, Jac." Bailey tapped her head. "The stipulation in the will says that your husband must be from Aunt Frances's social circle. Well, Patrick's wealthy, and his father knew Uncle Thaddeus. And if you're willing to marry some old men for Aunt Frances's money, why not a young, good-looking man who is the father of your child? Maybe if you look forward to the honeymoon, you'll stick around for the ceremony."

Jac started to argue, but then realized she couldn't. Bailey was right. If her plan was to marry for her aunt's money, why wouldn't she choose a man who made her sizzle? And there was little doubt that the man made her sizzle. As Patrick pulled up to the curb in his big mud-splattered truck, her heart did a crazy little flip, and her face filled with heat.

"But I couldn't live away from you and Gerald for a year," she said. "At least Renie's dad lives in New York so I'll be able to see you every day."

Bailey took her by the arms and gave her the serious sister look. "I think it's time you experienced life without me and your sidekick Gerald." She paused for a moment. "And if you married, you wouldn't have to worry about Mr. Darby trying to kill you—"

"Patrick!"

Jac glanced over her shoulder to see a beautiful dark-haired woman heading toward them. She wore designer jeans that hugged her trim hips and a sweater that molded to her curvy breasts. Curvy breasts that she pressed against Patrick as she launched herself into his arms. Patrick didn't register any signs of surprise at the woman's aggressive behavior. In fact his hands came to rest on her waist as if they'd been there before.

Heat filled Jac's face once again, but this time it wasn't from desire as much as anger.

"It was the strangest thing," the woman gushed as she pulled back and ran her hands over Patrick's chest like she was reading Braille. "I came out of this store and stopped to put money in this cute little Santa's stocking cap when I saw your business card. I asked him where he had gotten it, and he said you were just outside. So I figured that it had to be fate—you know, just like that movie *Serendipity*."

Serendipity? Jac had seen the movie, and this was

nothing like it. Especially when she was cast in the role of single sidekick. Before she could stop herself, she jumped up and changed the script.

"I just loved that movie." She hurried over and hooked an arm through Patrick's, forcing the woman to step back. "So aren't you going to introduce us, Patrick?"

He didn't look thrilled by the idea. "Jacqueline, this is..." His brow knotted. "Brittney?"

The woman's eyes widened. "Bridget."

Patrick nodded. "Right. Bridget, this is Jacqueline."

The fact that he didn't remember Bridget's name made Jac feel a little better. But only a little. "It's so nice to meet you, Brittney," she said. "And I hate to rush off. But our baby"—she looked at Patrick and patted her stomach—"is making my tummy a little queasy, and I think I need to lie down."

Bridget looked at Jac's flat stomach and then at Patrick. "Our baby?"

Jac thought Patrick would try to explain. He didn't. Without one word he took Jac's arm and helped her into the truck. Once she was tucked inside, he slammed the door, gave the woman a brief nod, and headed around to the driver's side.

Gerald hopped in the backseat with his peppermint cocoa. "What was that all about, Jac? For a second I thought there might be a catfight. And wouldn't it be better if Patrick had a girlfriend?"

Gerald was right. If Patrick had a steady girlfriend, there was a much better chance that he'd forget all about the baby. Except suddenly Jac realized that she didn't want him to forget about Lulu. She wanted Lulu to have what she and Bailey hadn't. She wanted her to have a father who would never forget her. A father who would bring her a present on her birthday and flowers on her graduation, and walk her down the aisle at her wedding.

Slightly stunned by the epiphany, she watched as Patrick climbed into the truck. The wind had ruffled his hair, added a blush to his cheeks, and made his lips chapped. Without thinking she pulled some lip balm from her purse and unscrewed the lid. She dabbed some ointment on the tip of her finger, then leaned over the console. She only meant to quickly spread the balm on his lips. But at the first touch of his mouth, her finger froze, and she found herself melting into clear green eyes as another epiphany hit.

She was going to marry Patrick McPherson.

Chapter Sixteen

"What do you mean you're skipping Christmas?"

Cassie's shocked look almost caused Wheezie to chuckle. Or maybe what she found so amusing was the other shocked faces in the room. McPhersons didn't like change. And having traditions altered was even worse.

"We're not skipping Christmas, Cassandra," Mary Katherine said in a soothing voice that was the exact opposite of her daughter's high-strung one. "We're simply celebrating it on a cruise ship." She glanced at her husband, who sat right next to her on the couch. "Isn't that right, Albert?"

Big Al looked like he was having trouble swallowing a hard pill. His Adam's apple bobbed a couple of times before he cleared his throat. "If that's what you want, Mary."

"Are you saying that you don't want to go, Albert? Because if you don't—"

"No. No." He put an arm around her and pulled her

close. "A cruise will be just another opportunity to spend time with my lovely wife."

It was strange, but as he pulled her close, Mary looked about as happy as her husband. If Wheezie hadn't just heard it from the horses' mouths, she would think that neither one of them wanted to go on a cruise. Or spend more time together.

"But Christmas?" Cassie continued. "Why not wait and go on a cruise after the holidays?"

"It's not that big of a deal, Cass." Matthew came in from the kitchen, munching on some of the gingersnaps Wheezie had brought. "As it turns out, Ellie and I won't be here either. Her parents have decided to renew their vows on the day before Christmas. So we're driving to Kansas."

"Oh no," Mary said, before she seemed to catch herself. "I mean, how wonderful for your parents, Ellie. I'm sure you and Matthew will enjoy spending time with them."

"Well, if you guys are heading out of town," Jake said, "Melanie and I might just take the kids skiing. The twins and Chase have been dying to get on the slopes." He lowered his voice to a whisper. "And since we got them skis this year, it will work out perfectly." He glanced at Rory. "What about if you and Amy join us? We could get tickets on the Polar Express for Douglas. And I'm sure Gabby would love to get in some skiing."

Wheezie doubted it. Especially when Gabby had her heart set on meeting her biological father. Not that it was going to happen. The man had turned out to be as big a horse's ass as Wheezie had thought. He had no desire to come for Christmas to meet his daughter. In fact he'd made it perfectly clear during their phone conversation that he had no desire to meet Gabby ever.

Now Wheezie had to figure out how to break the news to her niece.

"Great," Cassie fumed. "Everyone just run off on your cruises and ski trips and leave the rest of us here alone."

James reached out and took her hand. "With the size of your extended family, Cassandra, I wouldn't really call it being alone. Besides, my dad and his wife have been bugging us to come to Pittsburgh for Christmas. Why don't we do it this year?"

"But what about Wheezie and Patrick?" Cassie said.

"Don't worry about me." Wheezie flapped a hand. "I have no desire to travel anywhere. After the excitement of last Christmas, it will be nice to have some peace and quiet." She glanced over at her Nordic-looking nephew. "Paddy and I will keep each other company."

Patrick wasn't listening. He sat on the other side of his mother, staring at the fire that crackled in the fireplace, completely lost in thought. Wheezie figured she knew what occupied his mind. According to Matthew, Jacqueline's flight back to New York had been scheduled for that morning. If the look on her nephew's face was any indication, Patrick wasn't exactly happy about it. Wheezie wasn't either. After doing a little more research, she'd decided that fate had picked the perfect match for Patrick. Now all she had to do was figure out how to get Jacqueline back to Denver.

"So you're not going to put up decorations?" Cassie looked around the room. "No Christmas trees, no lawn Santas, no lights? And what about the annual Christmas Eve party? You know how all the relatives look forward to it."

There was a hint of sadness in Mary's eyes as she organized the magazines on the coffee table. "You can still have outside decorations and Christmas trees at your own houses. And I'm sure someone else will volunteer to have the Christmas Eve party. If not, the family will still meet up for midnight mass."

"I don't mind having it at my house," Wheezie volunteered. There was a long stretch of silence punctuated by the family's exchanged looks of uncertainty. Looks of uncertainty that really irked her. "Unless you think I'm too old and senile to handle a party on my own."

"Of course not, Louise," Mary Katherine said. "We just don't want to burden you with such a big project. And didn't you just say that you were looking forward to a less stressful Christmas?"

"Stressful?" She snorted. "Since I pretty much put on a party at my bar every night for almost forty years, I can plan a family get-together with my eyes closed." She got to her feet, thankful that her knees didn't stiffen up like they normally did after an extended amount of sitting. "Now if you'll excuse me, I'm going to do some planning."

With everyone's eyes glued on her, Wheezie shuffled from the room. In the study she sat down on the couch and massaged her legs. Beneath the black pants, they felt shriveled and like they didn't belong to her. In Chicago she had walked miles every day. Now she could barely walk five feet without stumbling. It was embarrassing, it was humiliating, and it really ticked her off.

Lying back, she adjusted a throw pillow beneath her head and crossed her hands over her chest. It seemed that lately she'd done her best sleeping in the coffin pose. Obviously her body was preparing for the end. With a disgusted snort, she rolled to her side. But she had barely gotten comfortable when the door opened and Gabby came charging into the room.

"Aunt Wheezie?"

Wheezie thought about not answering. She knew why Gabby was looking for her, and she wasn't ready to break the bad news about her father. Of course she had to do it sometime. She peeked over the couch to find Gabby already heading out the door.

"I'm here."

Gabby turned, and her eyes lit up. It was a shame that Wheezie was going to douse that light. Gabby closed the door and hurried over to the couch. "So? Did you talk to him? What did he say? Is he coming?"

Wheezie sat up and tried to find the right words. Unfortunately, there wasn't a good way to break the news that your father was an asshole. "Yes, I talked to him," she said.

Gabby studied Wheezie for only a second before her face fell. "Oh. I guess he doesn't want to meet me." She lifted her shoulders in the most pathetic shrug Wheezie had ever seen. "That's okay, Wheeze. I mean, why would he want to meet me after all these years?" She swallowed hard. "It was really a stupid idea—"

"He's coming." The words popped out of Wheezie's mouth without her brain being involved. Just her heart. And the pure elation that washed over Gabby's features made Wheezie's mouth keep flapping. "In fact, he sounded very excited to get to meet you. No doubt he's been wanting to meet you for a while and just didn't know how to go about initiating it."

"I knew it!" Gabby did a little jump and punched the

air with her fist. "I knew he was having second thoughts and all he needed was an invitation." She flopped down on the couch while Wheezie scrambled to find a way out of the hole she'd dug for herself. Thankfully, God gave her a ladder. "So did you already tell Mom and Dad that he's coming to Grandma Mary's Christmas Eve party?"

"I was going to." Wheezie tried to look upset. "But then I found out that your parents are planning on taking you on a ski trip for the holidays." She held up her hands. "So I guess we should plan your father's visit for another time."

"A ski trip?" Gabby shook her head. "You must've misunderstood, Wheezie. My dad and mom wouldn't want to leave the family at Christmas."

"It seems that the family all have other plans. Your grandmother and grandfather are going on a cruise, Matthew and Ellie are going to see her parents, and Cassie and James are going to see his. And Jacob, Melanie, and the kids are going skiing with your family."

"No!" Gabby jumped up. "I don't want to go skiing. I want to stay here and meet my bio dad." She got a determined look in her eye. "I'll take care of my parents, Aunt Wheezie. You just make sure that my bio dad gets here for Christmas." Before Wheezie could say anything, she headed for the door. She had just reached it when Patrick stepped into the study, looking even unhappier than he'd looked before.

"Hey, Uncle Paddy," Gabby said. "I can't talk now, but I'll see you in the morning to go motocross riding." She gave him a quick kiss on the cheek as she sailed past. When she was gone, Patrick closed the door and turned to Wheezie.

"Okay. What's going on, Wheeze?"

Exhausted from all the lies she'd told Gabby, Wheezie flopped back down on the couch. "If you're talking about your parents going on a cruise, I don't have a clue what's going on. Especially when neither one of them seem real happy about it."

Patrick walked around the couch and stood over her. "I'm not talking about my parents' cruise. I'm taking about Gabby's biological dad coming for Christmas."

Wheezie's eyebrows lifted. "Eavesdropping?"

"It seems to run in the family." Concern filled Patrick's eyes. "Does Rory know?"

"No. And I don't think that there's any need to tell him. Not when Gabby's father has refused to meet her."

Patrick's concern quickly turned to anger. "He doesn't want to meet her?"

Wheezie shook her head. "He claims he's too busy with work."

"Asshole." Patrick sat down next to her.

"That's exactly what I thought. Which is exactly why I didn't tell Gabby. It would only hurt her. I'm hoping she'll go on the ski trip with her parents, and I'll be able to delay telling her until after the holidays."

Patrick ran his hand through his hair. "Why now? She's never expressed any interest in talking to her father before." When Wheezie didn't answer right away, he drew his own conclusions. "The baby," he whispered. "This is all because of my irresponsibility."

"There's no reason to blame yourself, Patrick. All kids want to know who their biological parents are. So it would've happened sooner or later." She studied his stern profile. "So I heard that Jacqueline went back to New York. I guess you couldn't convince her to stay."

He hesitated for only a moment before giving Wheezie an early Christmas present. "She didn't leave."

"Oh, really? So she's decided to take you up on your offer and move into the condo next to you?"

"No. She's as stubborn as her sister. But at least Bailey thinks logically. Jacqueline doesn't have a logical bone in her body. She lives in some kind of a dream world." He got up and walked to the fireplace. "Damn, the woman drives me crazy."

"And yet you're attracted to her."

His shoulders tightened before they relaxed. "Yes, I'm attracted to her. God only knows why."

Wheezie smiled. "We're often attracted to qualities in other people that we have trouble finding in ourselves. You're too logical, Patrick. Maybe a dreamer is exactly what you need."

"Whether I need it or not, that's what I'm going to get." He paused for a moment. "I've decided to marry her."

Wheezie had the sudden urge to jump up and punch the air like Gabby had done. "What made you change your mind?"

Patrick shrugged. "I want my child to have my name, live in my house, know me as her father." He ran a hand through his hair. "And I want Jacqueline. More than I've ever wanted a woman. It's not love, but, unlike my siblings, I've never believed that the love of my life would drop out of the sky. Instead I got a woman pregnant. I don't know why it happened. All I know is that the deed is done, and now I need to make the most of it."

Wheezie wasn't so sure that the love of his life hadn't dropped out of the sky on Halloween night, but she kept her mouth shut. "So when's the wedding?"

"Tomorrow. I already called Judge Murdock." He turned to her. "We're getting married at the courthouse."

It was much more than Wheezie could've asked for. Time was not on her side. "When do I need to tell Barkley to have me there?"

An uncomfortable look settled over his face. "I'd prefer that you didn't come, Wheeze. If you come, the entire family will be mad that they weren't invited. And once Mom finds out, she'll want a church wedding and a big reception, which would cause her to cancel her cruise and everyone else to cancel their holiday plans. And I don't want to ruin Christmas for everyone. So I'd like you to keep it under wraps until we're married."

Wheezie didn't think it had as much to do with ruining everyone's Christmas plans as with Patrick wanting to keep things simple. Unfortunately, Wheezie had a sneaking suspicion that there would be nothing simple about Patrick and Jacqueline's marriage.

Chapter Seventeen

Jac's third wedding was nothing like her first two. There were no sprays of beautiful flowers or poufy puffs of tulle. No pretty bridesmaids or cute flower girls. No expensive wedding gown or tuxedoed groom. Just a cold judge's office with Gerald standing at her side holding a grocery store bouquet and Bailey standing behind her ready to tackle her if she panicked and headed for the door.

Surprisingly, even though the wedding wasn't anything like her dreams, Jac had no desire to escape. A strange calm settled over her the moment Patrick took her hands in his. Her calm could've come from the heat of his skin or the strength of his grip. Or perhaps it came from the clear, steady green of his eyes. Whatever the reason, her voice didn't quaver when she repeated her vows, and her hands didn't tremble when Patrick slipped on the simple gold band. In fact Jac didn't show any signs of nerves until the judge spoke his final words:

"I now pronounce you man and wife."

Then Jac promptly leaned over the trash can by the desk and threw up the Western omelet she'd had for breakfast. When she finished, she lifted her head to find Gerald looking like he was ready to lose his breakfast, the judge calling the janitor, and Patrick holding out a red bandanna that didn't go with his blue dress shirt.

"Better?"

She nodded weakly as she took the bandanna. Although a few minutes later, when Patrick had gone to get the truck and she was standing out in front of the courthouse saying her good-byes to Bailey and Gerald, she didn't feel better. She felt like she'd made the biggest mistake of her life.

"Maybe I should come to New York with you," she said against Bailey's shoulder. "Patrick won't care as long as I come back before the baby is born."

Bailey awkwardly thumped her on the back before pulling away. She had the hard lawyer look she always got when she'd made up her mind about something. "It's going to be okay, Jac." She shot a glance over at Gerald. "Tell her, Geri."

Gerald smiled weakly as tears filled his eyes. "Of course it's going to be okay." A sob broke loose as he pulled Jac into his arms. "What will I do without you, Jac? Who will make me stuffed French toast in the morning and flavored popcorn at night?"

"Good Lord," Bailey groaned. "Stop your dramatic whining, Geri. You don't see Jac and me crying, do you?"

He continued to hold on to Jac in a death grip. "Only because you two are the ice princesses and don't cry at anything."

"It's a Maguire thing," Bailey said. "Besides, it's not like you won't be coming back for Christmas."

Jac looked over Gerald's shoulder. "You're coming for Christmas too, Bailey, aren't you?"

Her sister nodded. "Of course I am. But with work, I might have to take a later flight." She pried Jac away from Gerald. "Remember to take your prenatal vitamins every day. And don't eat too many sweets. And you need to find a good obstetrician and get an appointment as soon as—"

"I already have one picked out." Patrick walked up. "He's a friend of the family and one of the best in the city."

Bailey turned and gave Patrick her version of a smile, which pretty much was just a baring of teeth. "Remember our bargain, McPherson." Then she gave Jac another quick hug and grabbed Gerald's arm, tugging him toward the parking garage.

As she listened to Gerald's sobs, there was a brief moment when Jac wanted to burst into tears. But Bailey was right. Maguire women didn't cry. They just sucked it up and moved on. Accepting her fate, she followed Patrick to the truck he'd parked next to the curb. For once it was clean, and she had to wonder if he had washed it for the occasion. It was doubtful. Especially when he hadn't exactly dressed for it. The cotton button-down shirt was an improvement over flannel, but dress pants instead of jeans would've been nice.

"Are you still feeling sick?" he asked as he helped her up into the truck. "Should I take you to the doctor?"

"No, I usually feel much better after I..."

"Toss your cookies?" A smile flashed over his face, making her realize that, regardless of his inappropriate clothing, she'd married a devastatingly handsome man. "I don't think Judge Murdock will ever forget it."

She laughed. "He did look appalled, didn't he? I'm just lucky that your family wasn't there to witness it." She paused before adding, "I guess they were pretty upset with the news."

His smile faded, and he handed her the seat belt before closing her door. He waited until he'd gotten in and pulled out into traffic before he answered. "I haven't told them yet. But once they've had time to think about it, they'll accept it. They've been wanting me to get married for a while."

"And why haven't you?" she asked.

It took a while for him to answer. "Maybe because I never found the right girl."

The right girl. Since she was marrying him for money and he was marrying her for the baby, Jac couldn't really claim the title. Which suddenly made her feel extremely sad and kept her from continuing the conversation.

It didn't take them long to reach Patrick's home. He pulled into a parking lot behind three modest condos, proving once again that Patrick wasn't the type to flaunt his money. He reached above his head and pushed the remote clipped to his visor. The garage door of the first condo slowly lifted, revealing a leather-pimped-out, shiny-chromed Harley motorcycle parked on one side, along with a mountain bike, numerous tool chests, and a beer keg.

Once he'd squeezed the big truck into the space that was left, he hopped out and came around to her side to open the door. She hadn't expected him to carry her over the threshold, but she hadn't expected him to grab her luggage from the bed of the truck and head inside without her either. She followed him through the door and up the stairs. When they reached the top, a whirl of fur came barreling toward them. Jac backed toward the stairs while Patrick greeted the pit bull with thumps and ear scratching.

In Mississippi one of their neighbors had owned a pit bull named Kong. The dog had had two mismatched eyes and a set of teeth that rivaled a gator's. Every day, on their way to school, Bailey and Jac had had to pass Kong's house. And every day the dog had tried to eat through the chain link fence to get to them. The pit bull that suddenly took note of Jac didn't have a chain link fence containing it. In fact there was nothing to stop the dog when it charged toward her with teeth flashing and slobber flying.

A scream swelled up in Jac's throat. But before she could release it, Patrick gave one command.

"Stay."

The dog immediately dropped to its haunches, its eyes trained on Patrick for the next command. Instead Patrick picked up the suitcases and headed for the stairs that led to the third level. Before he disappeared, he called over his shoulder, "I hope you like animals."

Jac stood with her back plastered against the wall, staring at the dog, who continued to sit, but still looked at her like she was a leg of lamb. An overweight basset hound appeared out of nowhere and waddled toward her, sniffing around her heels before leaving a wet trail of slobber on her shoe. A calico cat joined him, rubbing against her legs. But the cat soon grew bored with the statue of a woman and meandered back into the living room, where it jumped up on the pool table with two other cats.

A pool table.

Suddenly Jac forgot all about the zoo of animals as she took in her surroundings. The pool table took up the entire living room, the only wall filled with a pool cue rack, a wide-screen television, and a multitude of neon beer lights. Next to the living room was a small dining room that held a dart board, a neatly organized desk with a computer, and a desk chair with a blow-up doll sitting in it. The doll wore nothing but lacy panties and a red feather boa that pooled between her spread legs.

As she stared at the placid smile on the doll's face, Jac felt like throwing up again. This had to be some kind of a joke. Somehow Patrick had discovered that she hated pool tables and pit bulls almost as much as she hated motorcycles, and he had pulled all of these things together to make her go racing back to New York.

"Sorry. In my hurry to pick you up at the hotel this morning, I guess I forgot to put Miss Featherbee away."

Jac pulled her gaze away from the blow-up doll and found Patrick standing at the bottom of the stairs wearing one of his signature flannel shirts. He patted his thigh, and the pit bull raced over for a head scratching. With the dog's attention elsewhere, Jac eased into the kitchen, putting the breakfast bar between her and the sharp-toothed animal. The kitchen seemed to be the only normal space in the house. Although it didn't appear to be used much. The stainless steel stove looked brand-new, and aside from a coffeemaker, there were no small appliances on the granite countertops.

"I'm assuming that you don't cook," Patrick said. When she didn't say anything, he moved into the kitchen and opened the refrigerator. "And since I haven't gone to the grocery store, it wouldn't do you any good anyway. I'm afraid that you'll have to order in for lunch."

"Order in?" She was too stunned by her new home to do more than repeat what he said like a parrot in a cage.

Patrick pulled a bottle of water from the fridge. "Although if you don't mind walking, there's a grocery store and some good restaurants within blocks. And I'll pick up dinner on the way home from work."

"You're going to work?" Jac hadn't expected a true honeymoon, but she had expected to spend the rest of the day in bed naked with Patrick. It didn't look like that was going to happen.

"I've been thinking about starting my own business, but before I do, I want to make sure everything is running smoothly at M&M." He unscrewed the cap on the water bottle and took a deep drink.

"And what do you expect me to do while you're gone?"

He lowered the bottle, a drop of water clinging to his bottom lip. "Whatever women do—shop online, text your friends, do your nails." He chugged down the rest of the water, then screwed on the lid and tossed the bottle at the overfilled trash can. "I'll be back around six or seven." He took a jacket off one of the hooks and reached into the pocket. "If you need me, you can reach me at either number." He handed her his business card.

She was so stunned by his callous desertion that he was halfway down the stairs before she remembered the pit bull. "But what about the dog? You can't leave me alone with a vicious animal."

He stopped and turned. "Gomer's a pussycat. Just give him plenty of dog treats and he'll love you forever. The dog walker usually comes by at noon to take him and Gilbert to the park. Cynthia…no, Carrie. Or maybe it's Candace. Anyway, she called and said she couldn't come today. So if you can let them out to pee every now and then, that would be great." He clomped the rest of the way down the stairs, and the door slammed closed behind him.

Jac might've run after him if Gomer the pussycat hadn't blocked the stairs. The pit bull didn't growl exactly. It just sort of bared its big teeth.

"Easy, Gomer," she said as she backed toward the kitchen, hoping that's where she would find the doggy snacks. The dog followed her. In fact all the animals followed her. The pit bull, the basset hound, the three cats. They converged on her like a pack of wolves. She quickly opened one cupboard after another, looking for anything that resembled dog or cat treats. Finally giving up, she grabbed a box of Cheerios and poured the entire box out on the floor. The mass feeding frenzy that ensued gave her time to grab her purse off the counter and race up the stairs. Choosing the first bedroom she came to, she slammed the door and locked it.

The bedroom was as sparsely furnished as the rest of the house. A nightstand, a single chest of drawers, and a bed. And it made her realize that no one would go to these lengths for a joke. This sparsely furnished pool hall was how Patrick lived. A wall of panic rose up inside her, and she pulled her cell phone from her purse and dialed Bailey. When she didn't answer, she looked up a cab service with every intention of heading to the airport. But the strange flutter in her stomach stopped her. It wasn't nausea. It felt more like the flapping of a butterfly's wings— a brief sensation that was gone as soon as it came.

Jac placed a hand over her stomach. The baby? It couldn't be. Not this soon. Yet she had felt something.

Moving over to the bed, she pulled up the Web browser on her phone. She had her answer within seconds. Flutters or quickening aren't felt until thirteen weeks from the start of your last period. Which meant it was more than likely gas. The answer didn't disappoint her as much as intrigue her. And as she scrolled through different articles on pregnancy and studied pictures of growing fetuses, something did happen inside of Jac. The baby became something more than just a fantasy. Lulu became real.

For the first time in her life, Jac realized she was responsible for someone other than herself. She was responsible for the tiny seed that grew inside her. It wasn't just about dressing Lulu and taking her for walks, it was about making sure she was happy and healthy...and felt loved. Wasn't that why she'd married Patrick in the first place? Not just for her aunt's money, but also so her daughter would have what Jac hadn't? A father who loved her? If that meant living in a man cave for a year, so be it.

Her cell phone rang, and she answered.

"Please tell me that you're not somewhere in the airport," Gerald said. "I know I was upset about leaving you, but I think that Bailey is right. Everything is going to be okay, Jac."

She leaned back on the pillow and rested a hand over her stomach. "That's easy for you to say. You didn't marry a Neanderthal."

"Are we talking in the bedroom or out? Because there's nothing wrong with a little cave-like behavior in the bedroom. Like hair tugging. Maybe a little over-the-shoulder tossing."

"I wish," Jac said. "I'm talking more about his frat house with its motorcycle, pool table, and pit bull."

"What did you expect? Your husband is very alpha."

The word *husband* made her pause before she continued. "So alpha that he left his wife on their honeymoon to go to work. No doubt because Bailey refused to tell him about Aunt Frances's will and instead informed him that I was flat broke."

"She told him that before he married you, so I don't think that had anything to do with it. Maybe after your puking session at the courthouse, Patrick just thought you needed some rest."

She flung her arm over her eyes. "I don't want rest. I want another orgasm!"

Gerald laughed. "Then let him know."

"Just blurt it out during dinner?"

Gerald released an exasperated sound. "I was thinking of something a little more subtle. Like wear one of his shirts without any underwear—men like Patrick love that. It's a possessive thing." He moved his mouth away from the phone. "Give it a rest, Bailey." He returned to Jac. "Listen, I've got to go. Your sister has decided to have an argument about discrimination with one of the security guys. I'll talk with you later."

Once Gerald hung up, Jac thought about what he'd said. Maybe Patrick was just thinking she needed rest. Maybe all he needed was a little seduction. Kicking off her shoes, she reached for the remote and turned on the television. After surfing through the channels, she giggled with delight when she found the movie *Pretty Woman*. It was just the inspiration she needed.

If anyone could do seduction, it was Julia as a hooker.

Chapter Eighteen

It had been a long day, and by six o'clock Patrick was dead on his feet. It hadn't helped that he had spent a sleepless night thinking about his upcoming marriage or that, at four in the morning, he'd finally given up on sleep and gone for a long run on the icy streets of Denver to clear his head. Exercise hadn't helped. He still felt like he was walking around in a fog. Only now it was a married fog.

He didn't blame Jacqueline for his predicament. He blamed fate. It was fate that had brought her to the cabin on Halloween night. Fate that had made the condom bust. Fate that had turned a content single man into a miserable married one.

"Fate can be your friend or your enemy. I guess it all depends on your viewpoint."

Patrick lifted his gaze from the blueprints he'd been staring at, but not seeing, and turned to find the little old street bum standing in the shadow of the overhead steel beams. His cheeks were flushed from the cold, and his eyes twinkled merrily. The coat he wore didn't seem warm enough for the weather, but at least someone had given him a hard hat. It sat at a jaunty angle on top of his thick white hair.

Since there was no way the old guy could've read his mind, Patrick figured that he'd been thinking out loud. Which showed exactly how tired he was.

"So I'm assuming you're here for a job." Patrick picked up his cup of coffee and was thoroughly disappointed when it turned up empty. "Jimmy's already left for the day. But if you come back tomorrow, I'm sure he can find you something."

The man stepped closer. "Actually, I'm not here for a job. I already have one that takes up all of my time."

As far as Patrick was concerned, begging didn't qualify as a job. But since the man had to be close to Wheezie's age, if not a little older, Patrick refrained from pointing that out and pulled out his wallet.

The old guy held up a hand. "Thank you, but I didn't come for money either." He paused for only a second before adding, "I came for you."

"Me?"

"Yes. The other day I forgot to ask you what you wanted for Christmas."

Patrick realized why the man was living on the streets. He was a few cards short of a deck. Which made Patrick pull even more money out of his wallet. "Here. Try not to spend it on booze."

The man's whiskers lifted in a smile. "I'm not much of a drinker. Although occasionally I do like a hot toddy."

He ignored the money Patrick held out. "It's a simple question, Patrick. What do you want?"

There was something in his blue eyes—a familiarity and kindness that had Patrick answering truthfully. "My own life."

Instead of questioning him, the old guy nodded as if he understood perfectly before looking around at the skeleton frame of the building. "Sometimes when you're born into things, it's hard to grow out of them."

"I don't want to grow away from my family. I just want to grow. To have the experience my father had of starting a business from scratch." He looked around. "Nothing this big—but something that is mine from start to finish." He shook his head. "But now with the baby on the way..." He let the sentence trail off.

It was a truth Patrick had been avoiding, but he couldn't ignore it anymore. How could he possibly start a new business with a wife and baby to take care of? And he didn't doubt for a second that, once Jonesy found out, the offer would be off the table. Jonesy didn't want a family man. He wanted a builder who would concentrate solely on building his sports bars.

Suddenly too tired to continue the conversation, he held out the money. "Look, I need to finish up and get home. Please take this. Do you have a warm place to sleep tonight?"

The old guy hesitated for only a second before taking the money and pocketing it. "Don't worry about me. I love the cold weather." He leaned over and picked up the candy-striped thermos that had hit Jacqueline in the head. "But I will take my thermos. It keeps my hot cocoa nice and toasty."

Patrick's forehead knotted as he stared up at the steel girders. "But how did it get—" He cut off when he glanced over and saw that the man was gone.

Patrick spent the entire drive home thinking about the little old bum and his thermos. The only explanation he could come up with was that the man had somehow gotten on the lift and ridden to one of the top floors. While it was a relief that one of M&M's employees hadn't been negligent after all, it also made Patrick realize that he needed to stiffen up security around the lifts.

But all thoughts of security and the street bum dissolved when he pulled into the back parking lot of his condo. Instead of opening the garage, he sat right outside staring up at the glowing windows. He had always thought of his home as a refuge from the outside world, a place where he could drink a cold ale, shoot a game or two of pool, and then fall asleep on his pillow-top mattress. No more. Now it held a woman. A woman he couldn't even begin to understand.

Unfortunately, Patrick never reneged on an agreement. Resigned to his fate, he pushed the opener and slowly pulled into the garage. When he stepped inside the condo, he expected to be greeted by his herd of pets. Instead he was greeted by the succulent scent of food. Since he had eaten little breakfast and skipped lunch, he was starving and could only hope that Jacqueline had ordered some takeout for him.

"Where are the dogs—" His words fizzled when he came up the stairs and saw Jacqueline standing at the stove surrounded by a circle of sitting cats and dogs. Her designer dress had been replaced with one of his flannel shirts, the tails hanging over her curvy bottom. Her legs and feet were bare. Her hot pink toenails stark against the solid oak floor. Steam rose up from the multiple pans that simmered and boiled on the burners, encircling a head of auburn waves.

When she saw him, her eyes softened, and she smiled. Not the fake, superior smile she normally wore, but a warm smile that caused her entire face to light up. While he stood stock-still, she wove through the animals and placed a kiss on his lips. As far as kisses went, it was nothing more than a quick brush. Yet it left a residual heat that went straight to the crotch of his jeans.

"How was your day at work, dear?" she asked, her voice tinged with a soft Southern drawl. When he didn't answer, she walked to the refrigerator and took out a bottle of Scottish ale. She pulled a bottle opener from her shirt pocket and opened it before placing it in his hand. The feel of the cold bottle brought him out of his daze.

"That's my shirt." It was one of the stupidest things he'd ever said, but the scent of food and woman had woven a spell around his brain as much as it had around his dogs and cats.

She smoothed the shirt over the gentle slope of her hips. "I didn't think you'd mind."

He cleared his throat. "Just don't get anything on it."

"If I do, I guess I'll have to take it off." She moved back over to the stove, while the visual of her cooking naked made the crotch of Patrick's jeans even tighter. He took a deep pull of ale and tried to act like he wasn't on fire.

"So what did you do to win them over?" He tipped the bottle at Gomer, who had yet to even notice Patrick.

His canine eyes followed Jacqueline's every move with a glassiness that was duplicated by his friends.

"Just gave them treats like you told me to." She lifted a lid off the large pot and a wonderful smell filled the air. "I hope you like pot roast. I thought it was the manly type of food a big construction worker like yourself would enjoy."

Patrick did love pot roast, but at the moment, it didn't appeal to him as much as the woman cooking it. There was something about this domestic Jacqueline that made his heart thump crazily and his mouth go dry. He took another drink. "I thought you didn't cook."

She dipped a spoon in the pot. Holding a hand beneath it, she walked over and stopped in front of him. "I didn't tell you that. That's just what you assumed." She held the spoon to his mouth. "Be careful. It's hot." The word *hot* came out in a puff as she blew on the gravy before slipping the spoon between his lips. "Is it yummy?" she breathed.

It was yummy, but no yummier than the moist mouth that was only inches from his. The desire for her body quickly outdistanced the desire for food. He reached for her, but she stepped away.

"Why don't you change out of your work clothes while I get dinner on the table?"

Table? He glanced behind him. Sure enough, she had turned his desk into a table with a sheet for a tablecloth and the candle his mother had given him for a centerpiece.

"Where the hell is my computer?" he asked, right before the aroma of fresh-baked bread assailed his nostrils. He turned to the delectable sight of golden-topped rolls being pulled from the oven.

"Don't worry," she said, "I put it in the bedroom so you

can be more comfortable while you work." She pulled
one fluffy bun from the rest and smeared it with a liberal
amount of butter, then held it out to him. "Now these are
my Granny Lou's special recipe. She could cook like no-
body's business."

The warm, yeasty bread melted on his tongue, and he
closed his eyes in ecstasy. He couldn't remember the last
time he'd had bread straight from the oven. It reminded
him of his Aunt Wheezie and the cold winter days of his
childhood.

The brush of warm skin against his bottom lip caused
his eyes to open. He found Jacqueline licking her finger.
"Mmm"—the sound came from deep within her chest—
"that is good." Then before he could replace her finger
with something else—like his tongue—she placed a hand
on his chest and pushed him from the room. "If you don't
hurry, your dinner will get cold."

Dazed and confused, Patrick climbed the stairs to the
third level. It was only after he stepped beneath the
shower spray of hot water that his brain began to function
again. What the hell did she think she was doing? He
didn't want his computer in his bedroom reminding him
of all the work he needed to get done. He wanted it back
out in the dining room with his dart board. His dart board.
What had she done with his dart board?

He quickly finished showering and pulled on a T-shirt
and a pair of sweats with every intention of finding out.
But when he reached the dining room, dinner was waiting. And the sight of the tender roast beef, fluffy potatoes
and tiny little carrots all swimming in rich gravy wiped
out all thought of dart boards. He sat down and dug into
his dinner with a relish he hadn't felt in years. He used to

go over to his parents' for this type of comfort food. But since his mother had started working at the domestic violence shelter, she'd stopped cooking big meals. Until this moment he hadn't realized how much he'd missed them. Paying little attention to Jacqueline or the dogs and cats that encircled his feet, he ate his way through two helpings. Finally he leaned back in the chair and sighed with contentment. Now that his stomach was full, he needed to get some things straight.

"I want my computer back on the desk."

Carrying a bowl, she sat down on the barstool next to him. "What do you have against tables?"

"Nothing. But I like my house the way it is—or the way it was."

"Bite?" She spooned up brownie and ice cream dripping in chocolate syrup. When he shook his head, she took the bite.

Patrick didn't care for sweets, but if the dessert was as good as she made it look, he might have to reconsider. As soon as her lips closed around the spoon, her eyes closed and her head tipped back, displaying the soft skin of her throat. She seemed to suck more than she chewed, as if trying to get every last bit of flavor from the dessert. A pink tongue flicked out to catch a dollop of wayward chocolate, and her lips pressed together as that little sigh/moan she made during sex escaped her throat. Then she opened her eyes and smiled at him before scooping up another bite and starting the entire process all over again. After she finished the second bite, Patrick's dick could've hammered three-inch nails.

"Don't you want some?" she asked, her blue eyes dreamy and her full lips glossy with chocolate.

"Oh, I want some," he rasped out, before coming out of his chair so quickly he knocked it over. But he didn't care. He wanted his wife, and he wanted her now.

Lifting her from the barstool, he kissed her the way he'd wanted to since he'd found her in the kitchen— with a deep, tongue-tangling kiss meant to take her breath away and leave her as horny as he felt. However, her sweet mouth and exploring tongue ended up taking his breath away, forcing him to pull back as he fumbled with the buttons on her shirt.

When he couldn't seem to get his fingers to work, he gave up and, in one yank, sent all the buttons flying. Jacqueline's eyebrows lifted for a fraction of a second before she shrugged and the shirt slipped off her shoulders to reveal creamy breasts swelling over a pink lacy bra. The scoops of tempting flesh rivaled any culinary treat he'd been offered that evening, and he pushed down the satin straps and dipped his head to one breast.

Jacqueline moaned and slid her fingers through his hair as he pulled one pretty nipple into his mouth. While he feasted on her breast, he caressed his way down to her lace panties, his fingers trailing along the edge of the waistband before dipping inside. She was hot, wet, and more than ready. But before he could even test her inner sweetness, her hand slipped between them and released him from his sweatpants.

The feel of her fist around his rock-hard cock almost brought him to his knees. He released her breast and moaned as her other hand joined the first, cradling his testicles with soft caressing squeezes as she stroked him from base to moist tip. He endured the torture until every cell in his body clamored for release. Then he covered her hands and halted their play. Even then, climax was only seconds away.

Possibly milliseconds.

Realizing he'd never make it to the bedroom, Patrick moved her away from the desk and, with one swipe, cleared off the dishes. After he picked her up and set her down on the sheet, she glanced at the mess on the wood floor and smiled.

"Good thing there's no carpeting." Then she kicked off her panties, and he was lost.

He stepped between her legs and drove into her moist heat. He threw his head back as a tremor of pure pleasure rocked his body. It had been a long time since he'd felt the inside of a woman without a condom. It felt good— so damned good. Like stepping into a steamy hot shower after a cold winter run. The warmth enveloped him and seeped in through his pores. Then the internal muscles of her body tightened, and the pleasure increased to epic proportions.

"Patrick, please move," she ordered in a breathy voice.

Unfortunately, he was afraid to, afraid that if he did, it would all be over too quickly. Of course, even if he didn't move, it might be over too quickly. The feel of her warm, tight body was as close to heaven as a man could get.

With his eyes squeezed closed, he pulled out, then slowly pushed back in as he went through every baseball statistic he knew. It didn't help. His cock was locked and loaded, and no batting average was going to keep his bat from hitting it out of the park. Especially when she wrapped her legs around his hips and pushed up against him. That was all the prompting he needed. His hips picked up speed, thrusting deep and deeper still. He tried to hold off, he even opened his eyes hoping it would distract him from the tight, amazing fit of her body. Unfortunately, the sight that greeted him only made him hotter.

Jacqueline leaned back on his desk with her back arched as she met him thrust for thrust. The straps of her pink bra hung down around her arms, the cups pushed underneath the soft swelling flesh and distended nipples. Above those perfect breasts, she watched him with a sultry desire that sent him right over the edge.

The climax rocked his body and his world. It burst upon him like a thousand welding sparks. Singeing his nerve endings. Frying his brain. When he came back to earth, he realized two things:

Jacqueline hadn't reached orgasm.

And she didn't look happy about it.

"Sorry," he said. It didn't seem like enough, but it was all he could get out. After the satisfying meal and the more-than-satisfying sex, he felt drained. Not to mention the sleepless night and ten-mile run. But that didn't mean he wouldn't make amends. Just not standing in the dining room with his legs quivering with exhaustion.

"Maybe we should finish this in the bedroom." He untangled her legs from around his waist.

She lifted her eyebrows. "I thought you were finished."

For the first time that he could remember, Patrick actually blushed. He cleared his throat. "Not yet."

Suddenly Jacqueline looked a lot less angry. She pushed up the straps of her bra and climbed off the desk. He thought about carrying her up the stairs, but he didn't trust his legs. So instead he picked up the flannel shirt and handed it to her.

She looked at it in confusion. "Am I going to need this?"

Feeling like a complete fool, he jerked it back. "No. I just thought... never mind." Obviously, if he was going to have sex every night with his eager young wife, he needed to get a good night's sleep and cut back on his running. His brain had turned to mush, and it was more than a little emasculating. For a moment he wondered if he should run to the store for some Red Bull. But then she flashed him a sexy smile over her shoulder as she moved up the stairs, and he figured he had enough endurance to last him.

He followed her to the bedroom, shoving the animals out with his foot before closing the door. As she headed to the bathroom, he slipped off his T-shirt and sweats and got into bed. The sheets were clean and smelled like detergent and chocolate brownie. It was a nice, soothing scent that suddenly made him realize that being married wasn't so bad.

Patrick inhaled deeply and closed his eyes.

Not bad at all.

Chapter Nineteen

"You want me to hire a dad for your niece?"

Wheezie ignored Barkley's shocked look and pulled on her knit gloves. "No. I want you to hire an actor to play Gabby's dad. There's a big difference."

Barkley shook his head. "Not in my book. You're still tricking a sweet kid."

Annoyed, Wheezie turned on him. "Well, just what do you expect me to do when she talked her parents into letting her skip the ski trip and stay and help me with the Christmas party—all so she could meet her real dad? A dad who has no desire to meet her."

"I don't know why you just didn't tell her that her father couldn't make it."

"That might work for now, but what about later?" Wheezie tugged on the other glove. "There's little doubt that Gabby will try again—or want me to. No"—she shook her head—"this way works better for everyone concerned. Rory won't have to find out and be hurt. And

Gabby will think that her biological dad is a good guy who just can't see her again because he's going to Africa to do missionary work." Barkley snorted, and she shot him an annoyed look. "What's wrong with that excuse? You did missionary work in Africa."

"True. But few people believe it."

She arched a brow. "More than likely because it's hard to believe an ex-criminal turned street boxer would have the time, or inclination, to do charity work."

"Maybe my troubled past is why I did missionary work."

"And why you've never settled down with one woman or one job. Makes me wonder why you've stayed so long with me."

He flashed her a smile, and she was again reminded that, despite the broken nose, Calvin Barkley was a handsome man. He looked a little like Cary Grant if he'd been a big brute of a pugilist. She smiled at the thought of Barkley replacing Cary in the movie *To Catch a Thief*. With his background, Barkley would make an excellent cat burglar.

"Because, like a barnacle, Wheezie," he said, "you've grown on me." He nodded at the stack of books on the seat between them. "Besides, it gives me time to read."

"Which means that you should have plenty of time to locate an actor who will keep Gabby's heart from breaking."

After only a brief second, he conceded. Just like she'd known he would. The man might look like a brute, but he had a heart the size of his Volkswagen.

"Fine. But I still think you should tell Gabby the truth. Disappointment is just part of childhood. The sooner she learns that, the easier it will be for her."

It wasn't the first time Barkley had made reference to his troubled childhood. But given that the man was as tight-lipped as a jar of pickles, he wasn't going to fill her in.

"I shouldn't be very long," she said. "Mary Katherine just wants to go over the plans for the Christmas party with me so I don't forget anything. Obviously she thinks dementia has already set in."

Barkley laughed. "That's doubtful. Especially when you just whupped my butt at pinochle."

"That doesn't take much," she teased. "So are you bringing someone to the Christmas party this year?"

"No."

"Are you sure you're not gay? Because seven years without a date is extremely suspicious." It was a game they liked to play as much as pinochle. Wheezie had worked in a bar long enough to figure out a man's preferences. And Barkley liked women. Even if he'd yet to bring one to meet her.

With only a slight lift of an eyebrow, he got out and came around the front of the car to open her door. It hadn't snowed in days and the sun was out, but the temperature was still frigid. She hunched her shoulders against the wind and continued to tease him.

"What about Jacqueline's friend Gerald? And don't tell me that you're not interested. I saw you eyeballing his scarf."

He laughed. "Maybe you can get me one for Christmas—a scarf, not Gerald." He tucked her hand in the crook of his big arm. "I'd ask you if you wanted me to get your walker from the back, but I already know your answer."

"Didn't I threaten to fire you the last time you brought that up?"

He guided her up the path, then paused, allowing her time to climb the step. "You did, but since Big Al is the one who hired me, I'm not too worried." He shook his head. "One of these days, Wheezie, you're going to fall and break a bone. And then you're not going to have a choice in the matter."

"Well, that day's not here yet," she said just as the door opened.

"There you two are." Mary Katherine stepped back. "Come on in out of the cold."

"Actually"—Barkley glanced at Wheezie—"I've got a few errands I need to run. But I'll be back in about an hour."

Mary ushered Wheezie into the house and helped her off with her coat. "I'm glad you were able to come over, Louise. Not only did I want to give you a list of things Barkley needs to pick up for the Christmas Eve party, but I wanted to give you some news."

Wheezie figured she knew what the news was, but she kept her mouth shut and followed Mary into the family room. A fire was going, but the large room sure looked empty without the big Christmas tree that always resided in the corner during the holidays. Rather than sit on the soft couch that was hard to get up from, Wheezie took a seat in the wingback chair and waited for Mary to share her news.

"Patrick called me this morning," Mary said as she sat down on the couch. She smoothed out a crease in her pants before she took a deep breath and slowly released it. "It seems that he and Jacqueline have gotten married." When Wheezie didn't say anything, she continued. "Judge Murdock performed the ceremony yesterday, and the reason Patrick didn't tell us is because he didn't want us making a big deal." She shook her head. "As if marriage isn't a big deal."

"So I'm assuming you're upset by the news," Wheezie said.

Mary sighed again. "No—yes. Part of me is proud that my son did the responsible thing, but the other part of me is worried that he's made a huge mistake. When I asked if he loved her, he said no. How will their marriage work if they don't love each other?"

Wheezie smiled. "The same way yours did."

Mary looked shocked. "What? Albert and I were madly in love with each other."

Wheezie shook her head. "Not before you were married. I was there and witnessed your entire two-month courtship. And it had more to do with hormones than it did with love. You two were so physically attracted to each other that the entire room heated up when you were in it. But being the good Catholic girl you are, you couldn't have sex with Albert without a wedding ring. I would say that the madly-in-love part didn't come until you'd been married for a few months and got to know one another. Neill and I were the same way. We were two young, hormonal kids who didn't have a clue what love was. It took us being married for a few years—living through hard times and good times—before we figured out the difference. Lust is an immediate reaction brought on by physical attraction. Love is a strong emotion developed over time."

Mary thought for a moment. "So you're saying that Patrick and Jacqueline have a chance?"

"A good chance," Wheezie said without any doubt whatsoever. "Not only do they almost catch fire whenever they look at each other, Jacqueline is the first woman whose name Patrick actually remembers. I take that as a good sign."

Mary's shoulders relaxed, and she smiled. "You do have a point. Maybe he will find happiness with Jacqueline. So what do you think we should get them for their wedding gift? I wanted to cancel the cruise and throw them a reception party, but Patrick flat-out refused." A frown settled over her face. "It would've been such a good excuse."

Before Wheezie could ask what she meant, Albert strode into the room looking none too happy.

"So I guess you've told Wheezie the news. So what do you think of Patrick tying the knot without one word to his family, Wheezie?"

"I think he's smart. Those two have enough to deal with without throwing our entire clan into the mix." She pointed a finger at him. "And I hope you're not going to make a big fuss over this, Albie, or I'll have to take you over my knee like I did the time you threw rocks at the neighbor's cat and broke their front window."

Albert scowled and sat down next to Mary. "That cat deserved to have rocks thrown at him. He scratched me every time I tried to pet him."

"Maybe he wasn't in the mood to be petted," Mary said.

Albert gave her a loving look. "Unlike my sweet wife who loves her husband's pets." He pulled her close and gave her a resounding kiss on the cheek. "So what are we doing today, ladies? Do you want me to take you to lunch? Shopping? Hair salon—?"

"No!" The word came out of Mary's mouth loudly and adamantly. When both Albert and Wheezie looked at her in surprise, she blushed brightly. "I mean Wheezie and I were just going to talk about the Christmas party. So why don't you hop online and order yourself a new pair of swim trunks for the cruise?" Her eyes turned hopeful. "Unless you no longer want to go on the cruise."

"Of course I want to go." He gave her an overly bright smile. "Anything to please my dear wife. But I do need some swim trunks. And since I worry about them getting here before we leave, I better head to the office—I mean the mall." He gave Mary another kiss and then kissed Wheezie on the cheek before heading for the door. "I promise not to be long, my love."

"Take your time, sweetheart," Mary called back with a simpleton's smile on her face. Once the door slammed, the smile faded, and she burst out in tears. "God forgive me," she sobbed. "But I can't take it for a second more—not one second more."

Since Mary was the backbone of the McPherson family and rarely cried, Wheezie got up and walked into the kitchen, where she pulled the bottle of rum that Mary kept for rum cake out of the cupboard and poured some in a glass before taking it, and a box of tissues, back into the family room.

"Take a stiff drink," she said as she handed the glass and box to Mary. "Then tell me what's going on."

Mary took a big gulp of rum before shivering. "It's Albert, Louise. He's driving me crazy. Every time I turn around, he's right here in front of me."

Wheezie had to bite back her smile. "But isn't that why you kicked him out of the house last Christmas, Mary

Katherine? Because he wasn't spending enough time with you?"

With tears welling in her eyes, Mary nodded. "Albert has given me exactly what I wanted. Except now I realized that it wasn't what I wanted at all." She sniffed. "Which makes me the most selfish, spoiled wife ever."

Wheezie patted her back. "Or just a normal one. Every woman goes through the same thing when her husband retires—especially if she's an independent woman who is used to doing things for herself. You went from no company to having a man around all the time. That's enough to make any woman crazy."

Mary studied the rum in the glass. "I just thought it would be different. I wanted us to have more time together, but not every second of every day. He goes with me to the grocery store, to the hair stylist, to the women's shelter. The other day he even went with me to get a pedicure. And I've got to tell you, Louise, there was just something about seeing my husband getting his toenails buffed that didn't set well with me. I never thought I would say this"—she took a deep breath and released it—"but I want my arrogant, selfish, alpha-man husband back!"

Wheeze tried to keep the smile from her face, but it was difficult. "Meaning you want him to go back to work at M&M?"

"Yes. And the sooner the better."

"But what about the cruise?"

"How was I supposed to say no when I've been begging to go on a cruise for years?" Mary shook her head. "But not at Christmas. I want to be with my family at Christmas. I want to decorate my house, bake cookies with the grandkids, and shop for toys instead of ridiculous swimming suits."

"So tell him." Wheezie said.

Mary downed the rest of the rum in one gulp. "How can I back out now without hurting his feelings—or worse, him wanting a divorce? And I wouldn't blame him a bit." She shook her head. "No, Albert was nice enough to arrange a cruise for my Christmas gift, and I'm going to enjoy it come hell or high water." She got to her feet and walked into the kitchen, where she pulled a tablet and pencil from a drawer. "Now let's go over what you'll need to get for the Christmas Eve party."

Thirty minutes later Wheezie was ready for a shot of rum. Not only was Mary stubborn, she was more than a little anal.

"That should do it." Mary tore off the five sheets of paper and held them out to Wheezie. "And if I think of anything else, I'll be sure to call."

"You do that, Mary Katherine." Wheezie took the lists and got up from the couch.

Mary followed Wheezie to the front door and pulled her coat from the hall closet. "We probably should meet again before I leave. Not only to go over the last-minute details for the Christmas party, but also to plan Patrick and Jacqueline's wedding reception. I understand that Patrick doesn't want to ruin our cruise, but he can't complain if I throw them a party after we get back. Because they're newlyweds, I thought I'd wait a while before I called and planned it with Jacqueline."

"I think that's a good idea. Best to let the newlyweds get to know each other without family interference." Not that Wheezie hadn't done her share of interfering. But now it was up to the two of them to sink or swim. Since Patrick had always been a good swimmer, she had high hopes.

Barkley was waiting in the car when Wheezie stepped out the door. As soon as he saw her, he hopped out and helped her into the front seat. Wheezie waited until they pulled away from the curb before she spoke.

"So did you find someone to pose as Gabby's father?"

Barkley shook his head. "It's not as easy as you think finding someone to work on Christmas Eve." He glanced down at the lists in Wheezie's hand. "What's that?"

Wheezie wadded up the paper and stuffed it in her coat pocket. "Just trash. Now let's get back to finding you someone to bring to the Christmas Eve party. What about the pest control guy? He looks nice and has a way with an insecticide wand."

Chapter Twenty

I hate FaceTime," Gerald said as he smoothed a hand down his neck. "I always end up looking at myself in the corner of the screen more than I look at the person I'm talking to. And electronic screens always make you look so old and haggard."

"Do I look haggard?" Jac studied her tiny picture in the right corner of her phone.

"No. You look depressed. So I'm guessing that Thor didn't want to use his hammer on you."

"He used his hammer all right. It was just so lightning-quick, I didn't get a jolt." She leaned back in the chair, annoyed that Patrick had turned her table back into a desk. What kind of a man didn't have a table? Or more than one chair and a couple of stools? Obviously, the kind who didn't want company. One of the cats jumped up on the desk—at least not the human kind of company. As soon as the cat was settled in a ball of fur, Gomer came up and rested his head on Jac's leg. Ever since she'd given him the roast beef bone, the pit bull had become her best friend. Obviously all males caved at the sight of beef.

"So you got a wham-bam-thank-you-ma'am?" Gerald examined the pimple on his chin.

"Followed by loud snores."

Gerald laughed. "Maybe your sexual prowess sapped all his strength."

"Doubtful." Bored with watching Gerald's grooming, she opened a desk drawer and searched through it. "I think it was the pot roast and Granny Lou's pull-apart buns."

"I would've loved to meet your grandmother. She sounds like she had a quirky sense of humor. What are you doing?" Gerald asked. "Are you snooping through Patrick's stuff?"

"Since we're married, it's not snooping. His stuff is my stuff." She went through the stack of bills on the desk.

"Somehow I don't think Patrick would agree."

She pulled out a credit card bill and looked at the list of charges. "This is pathetic. A hundred-thousand-dollar limit and all he charged last month was a couple hundred in takeout and Levi's. The man obviously needs someone to show him how to spend his money." A thought struck her, and she lowered the statement and glanced around the apartment. "And how to decorate his home."

"Ja-a-ac." Gerald's voice held a warning and fear. "Please tell me that you're not thinking what I think you're thinking." She set down the phone and turned on the computer. "Jac!" he yelled. "Look at me. Remember how quickly you can go through money. And Patrick looks like a saver, not a spender."

"Which is exactly why he needs my help." She typed

"furniture" into the search engine. "And stop worrying. I'm only going to spend a little and only on things he needs. And once I get Aunt Frances's money, I'll pay every cent back. Turning his house into a livable space will be my parting gift to him."

"Somehow I don't think he'll see it as a gift."

"Maybe not at first. But after he enjoys eating at a dining room table and lounging on a comfortable couch, he'll change his mind. And I'm not letting my child live in a man cave—or come to visit it." She glanced down at the phone to find Gerald looking frightened. Feeling guilty, she picked it up. "Stop worrying, Geri. All he can do is yell at me and make me return it, which is nothing that Bailey hasn't done when I overspend."

"But Bailey loves you."

Jac scowled. He did have a point. Unfortunately, an enormous pool table beat out logic. "All I can say is that if Patrick expects me to stay cooped up in his condo without a car, than I'm going to need something to sit on besides an uncomfortable desk chair. And since you're my friend and so good at decor, you're going to help me pick it out."

Even on the small screen, it was easy to see the resigned look that came over Gerald's face. "I was afraid you were going to say that."

It only took a few hours to find furniture for the dining and living rooms. Gerald was reluctant at first, but once he turned on his computer and started shopping, his creative nature took over.

"No pinks or purples or flowery prints," he said as he clicked through pictures online. "We need strong, manly colors if we want to win Patrick over. Roasted chestnut, forest greens, navy blues, perhaps a splash or two of burnt orange and rusty reds. Dark woods and no leather. Leather is cold and uninviting. We want soft material and deep cushions. And as much as it goes against every decorating gene in my body, we probably should get him a recliner."

Jac didn't care if Patrick had a recliner as long as she got a dining table, a couch, and an extremely feminine vanity table with a cute little stool. The only hitch in their furniture shopping came when she tried to order and the purchasing form wanted the security code on the back of the credit card. Jac would've had to abandon her plan if she hadn't stumbled on a spare credit card in the desk drawer.

By lunchtime the furniture was ordered and delivery times confirmed. Exhausted and starving, Jacqueline finally ended the call with Gerald and heated up some of the leftover pot roast. While she sat at the counter eating, she glanced over at the pool table. It was the only thing left to deal with. The desk she could have moved into the spare bedroom with Patrick's treadmill until they needed to buy baby furniture. But that wouldn't work for the pool table. She thought about giving it away, but figured that was pushing it.

A whine had her looking down at the dogs. It was hard to ignore such pleading eyes, so she shared the rest of her roast beef with them before giving some to the cats. She didn't have a clue what the cats' names were or whether they were boys or girls so she called them Hairball One, Two, and Three. She had just finished feeding Hairball Three when she heard the rumbling of the garage door.

Patrick?

She smiled. Obviously he felt guilty and had come home for lunch to give her what he hadn't last night. Quickly she released her hair from the ponytail holder and shook it free. She wished that she had time to put on makeup and change into something a little sexier than leggings and a sweater, but the door opened before she had even slid off the barstool.

The dogs and cats brushed past her on their way to greet the person coming up the stairs. Unfortunately it wasn't Patrick. It was a beautiful skinny blond woman holding two leashes.

"Oh!" She looked as surprised as Jac. "I'm sorry. Patrick didn't mention that someone was staying with him."

Nor had he mentioned that his dog walker looked like Heidi Klum. The blonde was even prettier than the petite brunette they'd run into downtown. Jac felt the same annoying ball of anger settle in her stomach that she'd felt before. But this time the ring on her finger gave her a little more leverage.

"You must be the dog walker. I'm Patrick's wife, Jacqueline." She held out a hand, but the woman ignored it as her eyes widened.

"Wife?" Her gaze swept over Jac from head to toe before her shock melted into laughter. "That's a good one." She pointed a finger at her. "You had me going there for a second. Are you the new maid? Patrick said he was going to get one, even though I told him that I'd be happy to clean for him."

The way she said "clean" didn't sound clean at all to Jac. Jac held her temper in check and smiled. "No, I'm not the maid. Although if you don't mind cleaning, I'd love to hire you. Patrick doesn't like me lifting a finger."

She held the hand with the wedding band to her chest and giggled. "Silly, protective man."

The woman's gaze narrowed in on the ring, and all humor faded. In fact she looked like she was about ready to explode. "Are you kidding me? I've been humping my ass to walk his dogs during my lunch breaks all for a chance to marry a hot millionaire, and he went and married some fat redhead." She threw the leashes on the floor. "That's bullshit!" She was down the stairs and out the door before Jac and the animals could do more than blink. Which was probably a good thing. If she had remained, Jac might've shown her the knuckle side of a fat redhead's fist.

The dogs started to whine, leaving Jac no choice but to pick up the leashes. "Fine, but only this once. I don't like animals."

Walking dogs wasn't as easy as it looked. Gilmore was a sniffer who refused to keep up, and Gomer was a puller who refused to slow down. Being tugged in two different directions made Jac feel like a tug-of-war rope. A walk around the block took more than an hour. And she was relieved when she neared the condos.

As she stopped to let Gomer lift his leg on a tree, she noticed the beat-up car across the street. The hood was up, and a man worked on the engine while his wife stood on the sidewalk, cradling a baby and keeping an eye on the two little kids who played a game of chase.

Jac didn't know why the family bothered her. Probably because she had been in a similar situation more times than she could count when her mother had been alive. Her mother had always been buying some piece-of-crap car that would break down. And she had always called some loser boyfriend to fix it.

"It looks like you've got your hands full."

Jac pulled her attention away from the family and turned to find Santa sitting at the bus stop. After being cooped up in the condo with only grumpy Patrick as company, it was nice to see a friendly face.

"Hello," she said as she tried to pull the dogs over to the bench. "We just keep running into each other."

Santa smiled. "It's a small world. Which works out nicely for me." He made a clicking sound and the dogs stopped their tug-of-war and trotted over to him. But instead of jumping and covering him in doggy slobbers, they calmly sat down and waited for him to scratch their heads.

Glad for a reprieve, Jac took a seat on the bench next to him. "So it looks like you're as good with dogs as you are with people."

Santa's eyes crinkled at the corners. "Love is a language every animal seems to understand."

The man's wisdom was truly amazing. Of course he couldn't be too wise if he was living on the streets. Since it appeared that they were destined to be friends, she couldn't help asking, "So what happened? Did you lose your home?"

"No. I have a home. I just decided to do a little traveling."

It was obviously a lie. One his tattered clothes attested to. But Jac knew what it was like to lie in order to save face. She had spent her life pretending to be someone she wasn't so she would fit into her aunt's social group. It was exhausting—and she hadn't realized exactly how much until now.

The wind picked up, and snow flurries fell from the

sky and landed on Santa's striped stocking cap. He didn't shiver or show any signs of being cold, and still Jac couldn't stand the thought of him being stuck out in the elements.

"Listen," she said, "I realize that you probably have reservations at a hotel, but hotel rooms can be so cold and unfriendly—especially around the holidays. So why don't you stay with me? I don't have an extra bed now, but I'm sure I can get one delivered before the end of the day."

He studied her for a moment with intense blue eyes before shaking his head. "Thank you, but I couldn't do that. Especially with newlyweds."

Jac flashed him a surprised look. "How did you know?"

His gaze lowered to the wedding band. "You didn't have that on last time I saw you." He smiled. "Holiday weddings are always nice."

Nice wasn't exactly the word. *Brief* and *disappointing* would have been better descriptors. Not only for her wedding, but for her sex life.

"Nice enough," she said as she got to her feet. "Now come on." She took his arm and helped him up. "I won't take no for an answer."

"Well, that's awfully nice of you." He patted her hand, which curled around her arm. For a little old man, he had a surprisingly big bicep. "But I really couldn't—so much to do and so little time before Christmas. Although there is something you could do for me." He hesitated for only a moment before waving a hand at the family Jac had noticed earlier. Upon seeing Santa wave, the woman said something to the man fixing the car, and he stopped and wiped his hands on a rag before collecting the kids and ushering them over to the crosswalk. Within minutes they were standing in front of Jac.

"This is the Trujillo family." Santa made the introductions. "Mr. and Mrs. Trujillo, this is Mrs. McPherson. She has a place for you to stay."

Jac's eyes widened. "Excuse me?"

Santa's bushy eyebrows lifted. "You did offer."

"Well, yes, but..." She looked at the Trujillos. "Umm, I'm sorry, but I'm afraid that this man misunderstood. My condo is barely big enough for my husband, all our animals, and me. So I'm afraid that you'll have to find another place to—"

Suddenly, for no apparent reason at all, Gomer jumped to his feet and took off. He moved so quickly that he jerked the leash from Jac's hand. With no other choice, Jac raced after him. Tugging Gilmore behind her, she hurried down the sidewalk and around the corner of the building, using every command she could think of. "Stay! Sit! Halt!"

Gomer listened to none of them. Fortunately, he headed back to the condo. Or not to Patrick's condo as much as the one next door. The garage door was open, which seemed strange given that it hadn't been open when Jac left for the walk. Maybe someone had rented it. Although she didn't see any moving vans or vehicles parked in front. But that had to be the case because the door that led inside was cracked open, and Gomer had no problem nosing his way inside.

"Gomer!" she yelled just as Mr. Trujillo ran past her.

"Don't worry, miss," he said. "I get the *perro*."

The kids raced after their father, leaving Jac and the mother to bring up the rear.

Again Jac tried to explain. "I'm sorry I can't let you stay here."

"No worries," the woman said. "God will work things out. He always does." She smiled shyly as she adjusted the baby on her shoulder and followed Jac up the stairs of the condo.

At the top Jac found Gomer and the rest of the Trujillo family. Gomer had finished his race for freedom and was licking the kids' faces and making them giggle while their father looked on with a smile.

"Thank you," Jac said as he handed her the leash. "Patrick would've killed me if I lost his dog."

"Kill you?" Mr. Trujillo looked worried.

"Umm, no, not kill exactly," she said. "He'd just be very angry." She watched as the children stopped playing with the dog and looked around the empty condo with wide eyes.

"Is this our house, Mama?" the little boy asked in an awed voice.

His mother shook her head. "No, *mijo*. This is Mrs. McPherson's house."

"Actually, I live—" Jac started, but the little boy cut her off.

"But this is the house I asked Santa for." His eyes looked confused. "And he said he would get it. He promised."

The father's expression turned sad as he picked up his daughter and ushered his son toward the door. "Not this one. I'm sure Santa has a better one in mind for us."

As the family trudged down the stairs, a suppressed memory swelled up from the deep recesses of Jac's brain. She'd been five and Bailey ten when they had been evicted from their apartment and forced to live in their mother's beat-up Pontiac until she had gotten another bartending job. Jac could remember how scared she'd felt every night when she and Bailey had huddled together in the backseat while their mother slept in the front. Four walls and a roof, even in a roach-infested apartment, had been better than a car parked in a deserted parking lot.

Making a decision, Jac tugged Gomer and Gilmore down the stairs after the family. Patrick might not kill her for buying new furniture, but he was going to kill her for moving an entire homeless family in next door.

Chapter Twenty-One

So I was right."

Patrick glanced up from the computer screen to find his sister, Cassie, stepping in the door of the on-site trailer. She wore her usual work boots and jeans, along with a knit hat and ski jacket dusted with snowflakes.

"Right about what?" He closed the webpage he'd been looking at as she pulled off her hat and gave it a shake.

"Mom told me that you got married. Then she made me promise that I wouldn't bug you this week because you'd be spending time with Jacqueline." She flopped down in the chair in front of his desk. "But I bet Matthew money that you'd be back to work within a couple days."

"I'm glad I could add to the Sutton dynasty," he said dryly.

Cassie leaned up, her green eyes filled with concern. "I don't blame you, Paddy. We all know that you were forced into it and your marriage is nothing but a farce."

Patrick didn't know why his sister's words annoyed

him. His marriage was a farce. At least it had been. Now he didn't know what it was. He couldn't figure out the game Jacqueline was playing. For the last couple of nights, she'd been extremely accommodating. And he had to admit that he liked it. Liked it a little too much. Of course, what man wouldn't like coming home from work to a sexy wife with a beer in her hand? Not to mention the home-cooked dinners that had forced Patrick to add a few extra miles to his morning run.

And the sex...it had been amazing. His face heated with embarrassment. At least for him. He still couldn't believe that he'd fallen asleep. He had never left a woman unsatisfied in his life. Last night he'd planned on making it up to her, but then his foreman had called with an emergency, and by the time he'd gotten off the phone, Jacqueline had been sound asleep. Tonight he would turn off his phone. In fact maybe he wouldn't wait for tonight. Maybe he'd leave work early.

He smiled. "Actually, marriage isn't that bad."

Cassie's eyes widened. "What? Are you saying that you're happy being married to Jacqueline?"

He took a moment to consider the question and was surprised with the answer that came back. Regardless of the havoc Jacqueline had brought to his orderly life, he felt happy. Or maybe because of the havoc, he felt happy. No longer were his thoughts consumed with work and the stress that came with it. Now thoughts of Jacqueline slipped in when he least expected it. Her leaning over to pull a fresh-baked item out of the oven wearing nothing but his flannel shirt. Or her sitting at the breakfast bar enjoying dessert. Or her sleeping curled in the curve of his body. And instead of distracting him, these thoughts made his days more enjoyable—and far less monotonous. Which had Patrick wondering if maybe his Aunt Wheezie had been right all along. Maybe he had needed a wife to balance his life.

Not change it, but just balance it.

"Yes." He cocked an eyebrow at his sister. "And you shouldn't look so surprised. I thought you wanted me happily married. Which is why you kept trying to fix me up with one of Amy's friends."

"That was different. I was just giving you an option. I wouldn't have forced you into marriage."

"Well, Jacqueline didn't force me. It was a conscious decision that I made."

"Because of the baby?" When he didn't say anything, Cassie rushed on. "I get it, Patrick. You want your child to have two loving parents like we did, but that only works if the mother and father love each other."

At one time he would've agreed. But after a couple of days of marriage, he'd started to see things differently.

"Maybe my marriage didn't start like yours and James's, but that doesn't make it any less of a marriage."

Once the words were out, he realized their truth. And for the first time since making the decision to marry Jacqueline, he didn't feel scared, or angry, or confused. He just felt content.

Cassie studied him for a moment. "You're sure?"

"I'm sure." To prove it he leaned up and clicked open the baby furniture website. "Since you're here, you can help me pick out some baby furniture. I talked to Matthew today, and he and Ellie are getting the baby's room ready, which made me realize that I probably need to get started on a room for Lulu."

"Lulu?" Cassie looked at him as if he'd lost his mind. "You've already named the baby? And Matthew's baby is only a couple months away, Paddy. You have a good seven months to go."

"I know, but I like to be prepared."

"You should try buying a couch first," she said as she got to her feet and walked around the desk to stand behind him. "I'm surprised that Jacqueline didn't run screaming from your house when she first walked into that man cave."

Patrick sent her an annoyed look. "It's not that bad. Jacqueline doesn't seem to mind it."

"Which really worries me. What kind of a woman doesn't want a couch? Or to help pick out baby furniture?"

"I don't think Jacqueline is into shopping as much as cooking." He clicked on a plain walnut crib. "What do you think about this one?"

Cassie reached over his shoulder and took control of the mouse. "You'll need a bassinet first. I have this one, and it's great. It has these soothing water sounds that all my babies loved. I was so sad when Noel grew out of it."

Patrick glanced up. "Please don't start crying, Cass. Last time my crew thought it was an air raid siren and ducked for cover. Besides, Noel isn't even one year old yet. You've still got plenty of time to baby him. And if he's grown out of his bassinet, why don't you just give it to me?"

She put the bassinet in the online shopping cart before she answered. "Because I might need it."

Patrick's eyes widened. "Cassie, please don't tell me that you're pregnant again."

"Okay"—she stepped back and threw up her hands—

"so I'm pregnant again. It's not like it's the end of the world. Things like this just happen, and if anyone should understand that, you should."

Patrick couldn't help it. He tipped back his head and laughed. "Four kids, Cassie. At the rate you're going, you're going to beat out Mom."

A smile lit her face. "Not beat her, but maybe join her. After all, five is a perfect number."

It was funny, but Patrick discovered that he agreed.

After Cassie finished helping him pick out baby furniture, he took her to lunch at a local pub. Over brats and chips, she helped him make a list of things he would need to ask the obstetrician at Jacqueline's first appointment. Once lunch was over, he dropped Cassie off at her SUV and intended to head to another jobsite. Instead he headed home. Not because of Jacqueline, but because it was Friday. And everyone took off early on Friday.

He had just reached downtown when his cell phone rang. He didn't recognize the number, but this time he had no trouble recognizing the voice.

"Hey, Paddy!" Jonesy greeted him with the same enthusiasm that had gotten him voted captain of their college rugby team. "Since I haven't heard from you, I thought I'd check in and sweeten the deal. How about all the fried cheese sticks and hot wings you can eat?"

Patrick laughed. "How could a man refuse that perk?" His smile faded. He'd been putting off calling Jonesy. Now it looked as if he could put it off no longer. "I'm sorry I haven't gotten back with you, Jonesy. I've had a few things come up."

"I hope the family's okay."

"Yes. Everyone is fine. I just...got married."

There was a long pause before Jonesy's bellow of laughter came through the receiver. "You had me going for a second, Paddy. Married? Yeah, right."

"I'm not kidding, Jonesy. I got married three days ago."

This time it took a little longer for Jonesy to answer. "I don't know whether to be more pissed off that you didn't invite me to the wedding or that you didn't mention it when I talked with you."

There was no way to explain things to Jonesy without going into detail, and Patrick wasn't about to do that. So he kept it brief. "It wasn't a big wedding. And you know I've never been good at sharing personal information."

Jonesy snorted. "That's the truth. I would've never tried to steal a kiss from your sister if you'd mentioned her mean right hook." He laughed. "Okay, so things aren't going to be as raunchily fun as they were in college. I still want you to build my sports bars. I'm sure that a wife isn't going to change your work ethic."

Before he'd married, Patrick would've agreed. But now he realized that he wanted his wife to change his work ethic. He didn't want his life to be just about work. And that's exactly what would happen if he started his own company.

"Listen, Jonesy, I can't tell you how much I appreciate the offer," he said. "But I'm afraid I'm going to have to pass. Not only because I can't leave M&M, but because I want to spend time with my new wife." Once the words were out, it was like a huge burden had been lifted off Patrick's shoulders.

"Are you sure?" Jonesy asked.

"No," Patrick answered truthfully. "I'm not sure. There

will be days when my father is breathing down my neck and my brothers are annoying the hell out of me that I'll regret my decision, but deep down I know it's the right one."

"Okay, man," Jonesy said. "I'm disappointed, but I can't say as I'd want to change my life if I was in your shoes. You always were one lucky bastard. I'll call you next time I'm in town and maybe we can go to dinner. I'd like to meet the woman that finally hooked Patrick McPherson."

Jacqueline hadn't hooked Patrick. But she'd certainly taken over a part of his brain. As soon as he pulled into his garage, a fantasy took shape, one that included lifting his wife up on the breakfast bar, wrapping those pretty little painted toes around his waist, and sinking deep into her warm, welcoming flesh. Except that when he got to the top of the stairs, he didn't find Jacqueline cooking in the kitchen. His disappointment lasted for only a second. On his big pillow-top mattress, he could take his time making love to her and give her what he should've given her the first time.

But halfway to the stairs, he stopped and slowly turned around. For a second he thought he'd walked into the wrong condo. Not one thing, from the area rug to the red couch, was his. Gone were his desk, beer logos, and pool table; in their place were end tables, framed artwork, and lamps that matched the vase on the huge dining room table. A dining room table that looked like it belonged in Hearst Castle.

All sexual fantasies vanished behind a wall of anger. But before he started yelling, Patrick remembered what Cassie had said. Obviously his sister had been right.

Women liked couches. And now that he thought about it, he wouldn't mind cuddling with her on a couch. If they pushed the couch against the wall, it would still fit with his pool table. He glanced around. Where the hell had she put his pool table? Intending to find out, he climbed the stairs. But before he reached the bedroom, her voice drifted out into the hall.

"I'm not kidding you, Gerald. The man has become putty in my hands. And all it took was a couple of my grandma's old recipes and some sweet little old Southern charm. Yes, I actually talk like this. Sort of a mix between Scarlett O'Hara and Paula Deen, but more breathy like my mama when some new loser came to town." She paused. "Okay, so Patrick isn't a loser. He's just a workaholic who only comes home to eat and sleep. The vampire who gave me multiple orgasms has been replaced with a guy who falls asleep when things are just getting good." She giggled. "But there's something to be said for spending his money. I spent the morning shopping at the cutest little shops just blocks away, and I found throw pillows for the new couch and coats for the Trujillos, and I couldn't resist buying myself a pair of Jimmy Choos."

Angry was too gentle a word to describe how Patrick felt. *Furious* came closer. He strode into the room and found Jacqueline reclining on the bed with the dogs and cats. Two of the cats slept on the pillow next to her, while the other curled up on her lap. The dogs slept at the foot of the bed, completely unconcerned that their master was home. Although Gomer did lift his head briefly before going back to sleep. Patrick got a little more reaction from Jacqueline.

When she saw him, her blue eyes widened. "Gotta go,

Geri." She hung up and set the phone on the nightstand—a nightstand he'd never seen before—then moved the cat and got to her feet. She wore another one of his flannel shirts and bright-blue high heels that made her eye level with him. A hesitant smile lifted the corners of her mouth.

"I didn't expect you home so soon, dear." She walked toward him, her hips swaying provocatively. "I guess I better get dinner started." When he didn't move out of the doorway, she cocked her head. "Is something wrong, sugar?"

"Wrong? What could be wrong?" He glanced down at her heels. "New shoes?"

She followed his gaze and tipped her foot to the side. "Aren't they cute? I realize that I really don't have a place to wear them, but I just couldn't resist."

He stared into those innocent-looking baby blues and tried to keep from wrapping his fingers around her neck. "Where is my pool table?"

"So that's why you look so upset." She reached out and patted his chest. "Well, there's no need to worry. I didn't sell it. I just put it in the garage."

"The garage? I didn't see it in the garage."

She hesitated. "Not our garage. The one in the…empty condo."

"Matthew's? How did you get in?"

"Umm…well, I sorta had the alarm company come out and reset the code." She shrugged. "I didn't think you'd mind."

Anger welled up in Patrick, and pregnant wife or no pregnant wife, there was no pushing it down. "You didn't think I'd mind?" He leaned closer as his voice boomed. "And I guess you didn't think I'd mind when you completely redecorated my house. Or when you manipulate me with food and sex and then call me a loser for falling for your little game." He jabbed himself in the chest. "I'm not a loser. I'm just an idiot who made a big mistake in marrying you! Now give me the code."

Jacqueline stared back at him. Much to his aggravation, there was not one ounce of fear in her eyes. "My, but aren't we a grumpy bumpkin today."

He gritted his teeth. "The code."

"One. Two. Three. Four."

Patrick's mouth opened, then clamped shut. Afraid that steam would come pouring out, he refrained from opening it again. Instead he turned and stomped down the stairs. And the crazy woman followed him.

"Umm...there's something else that you probably should know," she said as she followed him through the living room. The sight of the big red couch in the spot where his pool table used to sit had him turning to her and holding up a finger.

"Not one more word. Do you hear me? If you say one more word, I won't be responsible for what happens."

"But..."

"Shht."

"I just think..."

"Holy hell." He headed down the stairs, hoping he could outdistance her in the heels. He should've known better. She caught up with him at Matthew's garage, seemingly unconcerned that she wore only his flannel shirt in twenty-degree weather.

"Are you crazy?" he said. "Get your ass back inside."

"I just need to tell you something before..." Her voice trailed off as the garage door opened. And since he hadn't punched in the code yet, he was more than a little baffled. His confusion deepened when two kids came racing out.

"*Hola*, Miss McPherson," the boy said. "Papa says to thank you for the new coats." He puffed out his chest as if to display the blue ski jacket he wore. "I zipped it all by myself."

The little girl stopped and struggled with the zipper tab on her pink fur-trimmed jacket. "I can't get mine," she said in frustration. Since Patrick was in shock, all he could do was stand there while Jacqueline leaned down to zip the little girl's coat.

"My sister always had to zip mine," she said. "But you'll learn. You just have to make sure that this metal piece is all the way down in the zipper." She demonstrated, not even aware of the wind that lifted the tail of her flannel shirt.

Patrick's eyes widened at the glimpse of bare butt, and before the kids noticed, he reached out and held it down. She glanced back at him and lifted an eyebrow like he was accosting her. Which made him even madder.

"So do you want to explain?" he said.

She arched a brow. "Now you want to listen?"

"Jacqueline."

"Fine." She finished zipping the jacket and took over the job of holding down the shirt. "These children are the Trujillos. I met their father and mother the other day, and since they didn't have a place to live, and since this place was vacant, I thought you wouldn't mind if I let them stay here for a few days. At least until we can find them another place to live." She waited for the kids to start playing with Gomer and Gilmore, who had followed them out, before she continued. "But I guess I was wrong.

I'll talk with Mr. Trujillo and pay for them to move to a hotel."

"You're going to pay? Sort of like you paid for the couch and those kids' coats and your new shoes?"

She swallowed and, for the first time, looked nervous. Or maybe she was just cold. "I know Bailey told you that I didn't have any money, but I'm going to get some. Then I'll pay you back for all my purchases—including the Trujillos' hotel bill. I give you my word."

"Your word?" He snorted as he pulled off his coat and hooked it around her shoulders. "After all your lies, your word means nothing to me."

Then he turned on his bootheel and would've headed back to his condo if he hadn't stepped in a pile of dog poop. It was par for the course. His life had suddenly turned to shit.

Chapter Twenty-Two

Jacqueline woke from her nap feeling like something wasn't right. The sound of a slamming door instantly reminded her of what that something was. Patrick had overheard her conversation with Gerald, and the jig was up. Surprisingly, she wasn't that upset about the truth coming out. It had been exhausting keeping up the sweet-Southern-girl charade. And regardless of his temper, she wasn't afraid of Patrick. Still, it wasn't a good idea to prod an angry bear. And after he'd stepped in the dog poop, she'd decided to give him a little alone time and had come back to the condo to take a nap.

But she couldn't very well hide out in the bedroom for the rest of her life. Especially when she was starving. Getting up from the bed, she quietly—or as quietly as you can with three cats and two dogs following you—made her way down the stairs. She wasn't surprised to see the pool table back in the living room. No doubt Patrick had called his herd of brothers to help him. Although his brothers weren't there now. And neither was Patrick.

A husky laugh came from the direction of the garage. Jac didn't hesitate to climb down the stairs and open the door. It was chilly outside, but she forgot about the cold when her gaze settled on her husband, who was standing in the open doorway of the garage way too close to a beautiful dark-haired woman. The same woman Jac had seen coming and going from the condo on the other side of the Trujillos.

"So are you sure you don't want to come over for dinner?" She batted her eyelashes at Patrick. "I make a killer pasta."

"Sorry, Dorothy—" Patrick started, but the woman cut him off.

"Deirdre. My name is Deirdre." She placed her hand on his chest. "But if you want to call me Dorothy, you can."

Jac waited for Patrick to remove her hand. He didn't, nor did he look guilty when he finally glanced over and noticed Jac standing in the doorway. Instead his gaze slid over her body and down to her shoes.

"Get those damned shoes off before you fall and break your fool neck."

The woman's hand on Patrick's chest and his arrogant command were the straws that finally broke the camel's back. Or the straws that finally unleashed Jac's Irish temper.

"And you can go straight to hell, you asshole!" she said before slamming the door and stomping up the stairs, stumbling in her heels and almost breaking her fool neck. But she didn't care. She had married a Neanderthal. An inconsiderate, self-absorbed, womanizing Neanderthal. She grabbed a billiard ball off the table as Patrick came in from the garage.

"What was that all about—?"

The pool ball missed his head by mere inches, leaving a dent in the wall before rolling across the floor with Hairball One chasing after it. He pulled his gaze from the ball and stared at her with a look of disbelief. She jerked up another ball and took aim, but he got to her before she could follow through.

"Have you lost your mind?" His hand tightened on her wrist as his eyes grew more intent. "Or is this the true Jacqueline? The one beneath the sweet, accommodating woman." He released her and stepped away as if he couldn't stand to touch her. "How stupid could I get thinking that a spoiled, selfish socialite would know how to cook?" His words stung, especially after all the hours she'd spent in the kitchen, cooking and scrubbing pots and pans.

"Spoiled and selfish?" She rubbed her wrist. "Let's talk about spoiled and selfish, shall we? You leave me in a two-bedroom frat house with nothing but a pack of animals and your blow-up sex doll to keep me company while you work fourteen hours a day. Then you stagger home too tired to do much more than suck down the dinner I spent hours cooking, get your jollies, and fall fast asleep."

"And that gave you the right to pull some Martha Stewart shit on me and charge up my credit card without once asking me if it was okay?"

"What other choice did I have?" She stepped closer as her temper gained momentum. After a week of Southern sweetness, it felt liberating to be able to speak her mind. "It was either that or live in a man cave with no furniture. I'd rather be tarred and feathered. So I gave you what you wanted in return for what I wanted. It was a fair deal."

"Fair to whom, the manipulator or the one being manipulated?"

"Aww." She pouted her lips. "Is the big, bad McPherson upset over getting played for a fool?"

"I'm not a fool!" He stepped closer with his fists clenched. "And you better shut up or I'll—"

"What?" She stood her ground. "You'll hit me. Well, go ahead. It's not like it hasn't happened before. And it will just prove my point that you are nothing but a loser." She poked him in the chest with her finger. "And no loser is going to bring down Jacqueline Danielle Maguire." She whirled and took the stairs two at a time, Gomer following on her heels. Once in the bedroom, she grabbed a suitcase out of the closet and flung it on the bed. She had just finished clearing out her underwear drawer when Patrick spoke.

"Who hit you?" She turned to see him standing in the doorway. He still looked angry. But the anger didn't seem to be directed at her. "Who hit you, Jacqueline? Was it the guy you mentioned on Halloween night—Mr. Darby?"

She was surprised that he had remembered the name. "It doesn't matter. All that matters is that you're right. This marriage isn't working."

He came into the room and ran a hand through his hair, releasing his breath in a long sigh. "So I guess you've called your big, bad sister to come rescue you?"

The thought had crossed her mind. But her days of

having her sister bail her out were over. Jac was a big girl. She needed to start acting like one.

"No. I'm going to a hotel." She walked to the armoire and jerked open the second drawer. She didn't know how she was going to pay for a hotel, but she would think of something. Before she could turn back to the suitcase with the armful of sweaters, Patrick blocked her way.

"Our marriage isn't working because all you've done since I've known you is lie."

"Fine," she said as she walked around him and dumped the sweaters into the suitcase. "I'll concede the point that I should've told you about using your credit card and the Trujillos if you concede the point that you haven't exactly been a model husband."

"And just what is your idea of a model husband?"

She turned and looked at him. "How about someone who doesn't work so much? Someone who doesn't come home so tired he can't string three words to-gether?" She hesitated. "Someone who doesn't suck in bed." She tried to move around him, but he took her arm and stopped her.

"Excuse me?" His eyes were filled with almost as much disbelief as when she'd thrown the pool ball at him. "You think I suck in bed?" While he stood there stunned, she pulled from his grasp and continued to pack. She had completely packed one suitcase by the time he found his voice. "You're right."

Jac stopped with her hand on the suitcase zipper and turned to him. "I'm right, you suck in bed?"

His eyes darkened. "I was referring to not being a good husband. I haven't spent very much time with you."

"Very much. Try none."

"All right. None. I guess this entire husband/father thing has me freaked out. And I did what I always do when I'm troubled by something." He shrugged. "I work."

"You think I'm not freaked out?" She swallowed hard. "I'm just as scared as you are, Patrick."

"How would I know that, Jacqueline, if you don't tell me?"

"How can I tell you if you're never home?"

Patrick stared at her for a moment before he nodded. "Point taken." He reached up and brushed a strand of hair off her forehead, his warm fingers leaving behind a trail of heat. "So where do we go from here?"

"Divorce court, I guess."

He studied her. "Is that what you want?"

"Isn't it what you want?"

After only a moment, he shook his head. "No. I don't want to get a divorce." He released his breath. "To be honest, this has been the best week of my life. I looked forward to coming home to dinner and having someone to talk to besides my dogs and cats." He smiled. "And Miss Featherbee." He glanced around. "Where is she, anyway?"

Jac blushed. "Umm, I sorta popped her."

Patrick's eyebrow lifted. "I assume it was a complete accident."

"Of course."

He laughed before his eyes grew intent. "I'd like another chance, Jacqueline. But maybe instead of trying to figure out how to be husband and wife, we can just try to be friends."

"Friends? Are we talking without sex?"

His gaze traveled over her body. "I don't think that will

work. Not when just the sight of you in one of my shirts makes me go crazy."

Her breath caught. "This old thing?"

He stepped closer, his voice low and husky. "So what do you say?" With his gaze locked on hers, he lifted a hand and undid the top button of the shirt. "Do you want to be friends, Jac?" He undid another button. "Friends with benefits?" She barely nodded when he jerked open the shirt, sending the rest of the buttons flying.

"I thought you liked this shirt," she said.

"I'll like it better without the buttons." With a flick he opened her front bra clasp, and she was encased in strong, warm fingers. There was something so erotic about being caressed by a man who spent his days doing hard manual labor. He handled her like a craftsman with years of experience. Although his touch was gentle, there was a tantalizing strength and confidence beneath each stroke. He caressed her for what seemed like hours before he lowered his head and took her nipple into his mouth.

The tug and pull of his lips made heat pool between her legs. Her eyes closed, and her head lolled back. There was no rush this time. He sipped on first one breast and then the other as if he had a hundred years to complete the task. He used his tongue and the edges of his teeth over and over again until Jac's knees gave out, and she sat down hard on top of her packed suitcase.

He pulled her up in his arms long enough to knock her luggage to the floor, then he followed her down to the bed and continued his slow torture. She knew he was trying to rid her of the idea that he sucked in bed. But rather than disprove it, he confirmed it.

The man sucked in bed.

Lord, how he could suck.

He sucked the crests of her breasts until she panted. Sucked the tender flesh behind her ear until she moaned. And sucked the moist spot between her legs until she pleaded. But he paid no heed to her pleas. Each time she got close to climax, he pulled back and kissed and nibbled on the inside of her thigh until her breathing calmed and her hips settled back on the bed. Then he would start the torture all over again.

Finally she could bear it no longer.

"Patrick!" she yelled as she grabbed fistfuls of his hair and tugged. "Please!"

"Please what?" he whispered against the top of her thigh. "I'm only trying to be a good husband and spend some time with my wife."

"Please." She tugged his hair.

"Whatever you want, Jac." He lowered his mouth.

It took no more than a few seconds of divine tongue swirling to send her over the edge. She pushed up against his hot mouth and yelled out as wave after wave of intense pleasure rolled over her. The strokes of his tongue followed the flow of her climax, strong at the peak and lighter as she eased down to earth. By the time she had melted into the mattress, only his soft breath touched her quivering flesh.

He gave her a quick kiss there before climbing off the bed and stripping out of his clothes. If she hadn't been so relaxed, she would've watched the show. But her eyelids refused to open. Not even when he rejoined her on the bed.

"Are you okay?" He ran a hand over her stomach.

All she could do was grunt. Even with her eyes closed, she could tell it made him smile. The man was arrogant.

Completely and totally full of himself. A smile broke over her face.

"What's so funny?" He continued to caress her stomach. It was endearing how gentle and caring he was, almost like he was trying to soothe their child.

"You and your ego," she said.

"After that crushing blow, what did you expect?" He kissed her belly button.

"Maybe I expected exactly what I got."

"Which was?"

Jac opened her eyes. No wonder the man was arrogant. Dressed the man was hot. Unclothed he was every woman's fantasy. From the top of his thick gold hair to the toes of his broad feet, every inch of the man reeked of virile male. The late-evening sun spilled in through the balcony doors and over the smooth, muscular lines of his broad shoulders and chest. Over the thick-corded neck, the square chin, the strong, whiskered jawbone. There was an amused smile on his lips and a curious look in his eyes.

"Well," he said. "What did you get?"

My dream man.

The thought popped into Jac's head without warning, leaving her stunned. Her dream man? Had she lost her mind? Patrick wasn't anything like her dream man. Her dream man didn't wear a tool belt or have a pool table in his living room. He didn't ride a motorcycle or drink Scottish ale. He didn't live in a small condo or drive a big, mud-splattered truck. No, her dream man wore designer suits and drove expensive Maseratis. Drank Ketel One and hundred-year-old bottles of wine. And her dream man expected nothing from her but money.

Looking into Patrick's deep green eyes, she realized that he expected more—much more—than she was willing to give.

"Don't tell me the question has left you speechless." He brushed his lips across hers. "What did you get, Jac?"

"Food. I need to get food." It wasn't a lie. She was starving, but she could've waited to eat if her wild imagination hadn't gotten the best of her. Patrick wasn't her dream man. It was just the aftershock of a great orgasm that had made her even think it. But before another wayward thought could pop into her head, she rolled out from beneath him and got to her feet.

"Where are you going?" he asked.

"To make something to eat."

"You've got to be kiddin'." He leaned on his elbows and watched in disbelief as she slipped into a pair of leggings and a sweater. "In case you haven't noticed, Jac, I wasn't exactly finished."

Oh, she had noticed. And she was having an extremely hard time keeping her eyes off his flexed man muscle. "I think my Granny Lou would call that 'tit for tat.'"

He groaned and fell back on the bed. "You're a cold-hearted woman, Jacqueline McPherson."

Jac didn't know what made her smile. Her married name or his pure frustration. Either way she discovered that Patrick might not be her dream man, but she liked him. Liked him enough that she couldn't let him go completely unsatisfied.

"Come on." She tossed his underwear at him. "I'll make you an omelet."

Chapter Twenty-Three

Patrick liked to watch Jacqueline cook. She moved around the kitchen with an efficiency and competency that he wished more of his crew had. It seemed that she had made the kitchen her own and knew where things were better than he did. Not that he had done much cooking—or shopping, for that matter. As she pulled items from the cupboards and refrigerator, he was amazed by how well stocked the kitchen was. Stocked with his favorite ale and all kinds of condiments and ingredients for making home-cooked meals. For the first time he realized the effort she'd put into cooking for him. She hadn't just thrown dinner together every night. It had taken planning, grocery shopping, and preparing. And she was right. He'd just shoveled in the food without one thank-you. Or one orgasm.

Which was exactly why he hadn't complained too much when she'd left him hard and wanting more. He deserved to go without an orgasm. He watched as Jacqueline leaned over to get a pan out of the oven drawer and took in the sweet curve of her shapely butt in the tight material of her leggings. At least he was willing to go without an orgasm until after dinner.

She glanced over her shoulder and caught him looking. "See something you like?"

"As a matter of fact, I do." He smiled, then said something he should've said days ago. "Thank you. I haven't eaten so well since I left my parents' house."

He expected her to gloat a little. Instead she looked surprised and a little embarrassed. "You're welcome."

"So how did you learn to cook?"

"From trial and error." She set the skillet on the stove and drizzled some olive oil in, then grabbed a bell pepper from the bowl on the counter and placed it on a cutting board. "It was either that or eat Bailey's cooking. And believe me, Bailey does a lot of things well, but cooking isn't one of them."

"So I take it that your wealthy aunt didn't have a chef?"

Jacqueline pulled a knife from the drawer and proceeded to chop the pepper with a dexterity and skill that surprised him. "No, Aunt Frances had a chef. But I learned how to cook before I got to my aunt's. Although once there, Chef Pete took me under his wing and furthered my culinary education. He tried to teach me gourmet cooking, but it didn't stick. Soufflés and rich sauces couldn't beat out pigs in a blanket."

He laughed. "I'm glad. I'm not much of a soufflé man."

She glanced over and smiled. "Why doesn't that surprise me?"

"Okay, I admit it. I'm a comfort-food kind of guy. But what I can't figure out is how a snooty rich girl became a comfort-food cook."

She put the pepper in the pan and started slicing the onion. "My Granny Lou knew how much I loved to cook and got me a subscription to *Taste of Home* magazine for my seventh birthday."

"Seven? You started cooking when you were seven? Where were your mother and father?"

She stopped cutting and hesitated for a moment before answering. "My father left before I was born, and my mama was gone most of the time. So I cooked for Bailey and me." She went back to slicing, leaving Patrick floundering.

Her words painted a much different picture from the one Matthew's research had painted, and Patrick had to wonder what picture was the most accurate. "So I take it that your mother wasn't as wealthy as your aunt," he said.

Jacqueline laughed. "You could say that."

He waited for her to put the onions in the pan before he asked, "What happened? Why did you have to go live with your aunt?"

"My mother died." She said the words as a matter of fact—like she was discussing the weather. "She went out for a motorcycle ride and never came back." She shrugged as she stirred the vegetables in the skillet as if it were no big deal, which stunned Patrick.

He'd never been a mama's boy like Matthew, but he didn't know what he'd do without her. Probably cry like a baby. But Jacqueline didn't shed a tear, not even from the onions. He should be glad. Tears made him feel awkward and uncomfortable. But for some reason, the lack of emotion made him feel just as awkward and uncomfortable. He had the urge to hug her. To pull her into his arms and tell her that everything would be okay. Instead he got up and moved around the counter.

"So what can I do to help?"

She shot him a surprised look. "You cook?"

"No, I eat. But I figure I can be your sous chef if you tell me what to do."

A devious expression entered her eyes. "You mean I get to order around the boss?" When he only lifted an eyebrow, she laughed and handed him a box of mushrooms. "Clean these."

"With soap?"

She took them back. "On second thought, why don't you just watch?"

He leaned back on the counter and crossed his arms. "I'm going to assume that soap is out as far as mushrooms are concerned."

The smirk on her face turned into a giggle. "As far as any food is concerned."

"Fine, then I'll do the dishes."

She brightened. "Now that's a job I'll gladly give you."

An hour later Patrick was finishing up drying the pots and pans while Jacqueline sat on the barstool and watched.

"What do you want to do tonight?" she asked. "I could pop some popcorn, and we could watch a movie. Although without a couch, we'll have to sit at the dining room table."

Patrick didn't want to watch a movie on a couch or at the table. He wanted to sink deep inside his wife's hot body. But he couldn't say that without sounding like the

Neanderthal she thought he was. And with the orgasm score so unbalanced, sex was now in her ballpark. He just had to figure out how to start the game.

He hooked the towel on the handle of the oven. "We could watch television in the bedroom."

She glanced at the clock. "It's too early to go to bed." She slid off the barstool. "How about a game?" While he tried to figure out a game that would get them into bed, she walked into the living room and chose a pool cue from the rack. Not just any cue. But Patrick's cue. One that had been perfectly balanced for his hands.

Hurrying over, he took another pool cue from the rack. "Here." He held it out to her. "Why don't you use this one?"

Her hands tightened on his stick as she sent him a placid smile. "This one is fine."

Since he couldn't very well jerk it away from her, he kept the one he had and rested it against the table while he racked up the balls. "So we'll start with something easy." He briefly ran through the basics of the game of eight ball. She listened intently before walking to the end of the table and picking up the white cue ball.

"So I just hit this ball into that triangle of colored balls?" Before he could even nod, she placed the ball on the center spot and took aim. If her perfect form hadn't been a dead giveaway, her expert pool stroke would have been. In one fluid motion, she drew back the cue stick and thrust it forward, sending the cue ball racing toward the racked balls. It hit with a crack and careening colors. Three balls found a pocket. Two solids and a stripe.

With a wide-eyed look, she chalked the tip of her stick. "Something like that?"

Patrick should've been pissed that she'd lied about

playing pool. Instead he had to bite back a smile. Jacqueline might have some major personality flaws, but if she played pool as well as she cooked and made love, he figured he could overlook them.

Without waiting for a reply, she moved to the other side of the table and took aim at the solid purple ball. It rocketed into the side pocket with a sturdy thump. When she looked up, she was smiling. Not a practiced smile, but a real one that made her blue eyes twinkle and a cheek dimple. "Beginner's luck."

"You don't say." It was hard to keep the smile off his face. "Well, then I guess we shouldn't make any bets. I wouldn't want to take advantage of a beginner."

She straightened and re-chalked. "Oh, but I love bets. It always makes things more interesting."

He shrugged. "Well, if you're sure. What should we bet?"

She thought for a moment before answering. "How about a pool table? If I win, it goes. And if you win, it stays." When he hesitated she quirked an eyebrow. "Scared you'll lose?"

"Not hardly." He nodded at the table. "I believe it's still your turn." He leaned on his cue stick and watched as she came around the table and stood in front of him.

"Excuse me," she said. He stepped back, and she bent over to take aim. He wasn't sure how it happened. One second he was admiring the curves of her ass in the leggings, and the next he was sliding his hand over one sweet cheek. He felt real bad that it happened right as she was taking the shot. She miscued, and the cue ball hit one of his striped balls into the corner pocket.

"Thanks, babe." Patrick moved around the table, chalking his stick.

"You did that on purpose," she fumed.

"What?" He tried to duplicate one of her wide-eyed looks. "I was just removing a little piece of lint, su-u-gar." He drew out the endearment like she did. "Besides, all's fair in love and pool." She released a frustrated huff as he bent over and slammed a striped ball into a pocket.

It took his second shot slamming home before Jacqueline gave up her anger and decided to play his game. Before he could bend over for his next shot, she was sitting on the edge of the table and pulling off her leggings.

"Is it hot in here?" She slipped her heels back on and plucked at her sweater, lifting it high enough for him to see her lacy panties.

"Not hot enough," he replied as his gaze ran up her bare legs. "At least not yet." He gave her a sly smile before leaning over and slamming another ball home. Before he could set up his next shot, she had moved around the table, her finger sliding along the smooth wooden edge.

"Do you feel warm?" she said in a husky voice. "Because I wouldn't want something like…heat distracting you from your game."

"I'm sure you wouldn't." He bent over, but just as he pulled the cue back, her hand curved around his butt cheek, sending a shaft of heat streaking to his crotch. He completely missed the cue ball. When he glanced over his shoulder, she shrugged.

"Lint."

Before he could straighten, she had grabbed her pool cue and was lining up for a shot. The solid ball hit the other balls in the pocket with a crack. But Patrick swore that would be her last good shot. Not only because he wasn't about to get rid of his pool table, but also because just the stroke of her hand had him as hard as the pool balls and he wanted to move on to another game.

"Good shot, Jac." He stepped directly behind her, pinning her between his hips and the table. "But I think your stroke was a little unsteady. Here," he settled his hands on her hips, "let me give you a few tips." He brushed his hard-on against her ass as he leaned over and whispered in her ear. "The key is a smooth, steady stroke." His fingers curled around the front of her bare thighs as he rubbed against her. "Not too hard and not too soft. That way, the ball won't skirt the pocket, but go inside. Deep. Deep inside." He slid a finger beneath the edge of her lace panties, briefly enjoying her wet heat before he released her and stepped back.

"Go ahead, honey. What are you waiting for?"

She took the shot, and a solid ball rolled into the pocket. Fortunately, so did the cue ball.

"That's tough luck." Patrick quickly retrieved both balls and took aim. Another striped ball disappeared into the pocket just as her hand settled over the bulge in his jeans.

"Nice one." She traced a finger over the fly. "But I think you have an advantage."

"And what would that be?" His voice was thick with desire.

"Your stick. I think it's straighter then mine." She unbuttoned his jeans and slid down the zipper. "Shall we see?" He couldn't help but moan when she released his cock to her hand. "See, I was right. It is straighter." She stroked down the length from tip to base. It took enormous willpower to keep from succumbing to Jacqueline's cool fist. But Patrick had always been competitive. Competitive enough to remove her hands and go in for the win. With single-minded determination and his manhood prominently displayed, he made short work of the last couple of striped balls on the table before calling the pocket for the eight ball and driving it home.

It hadn't even hit the bottom before he tossed the cue stick on the table and advanced toward her. He picked her up and set her on the table, spreading her legs and stepping in between. "I win."

Her gaze met his, and he was relieved to see as much heat in her eyes as he felt swirling inside of him. "You cheated."

"I have been known to do that when I want to win something badly."

She leaned back on her hands, displaying the pretty pink panties that looked more than a little damp. "The pool table?"

"Fuck the pool table." He moved her panties to the side and slipped deep inside her with one hard thrust, the tight, warm walls of her body enveloping him. "Jesus, Jac." He moaned out the words. "You're so hot, baby. So... wet." He slowly pulled out before thrusting back in.

He kept the pace slow and steady while he gained control of his desire. Wanting to make sure it felt as good to her as it did to him, he pulled her closer to the edge of the table, curving his fingers over her thighs with one thumb over her clitoris. Her head lolled back, and her eyes closed as she wrapped her legs around him, pulling him deep. He moaned and moved faster—harder—all the while strumming her with his thumb. He didn't know how much more he could take when her hips lifted off the table and she moaned out her orgasm. With a grunt and an awkward jerk, he followed, thrusting deep inside her as he found release.

She fell back on the table. He slumped over her, resting most of his weight on his forearms and his cheek against the soft curves of her breasts. She ran her fingers through his hair, and he suddenly felt extremely content. After a moment she spoke.

"Patrick?"

He liked the way his name sounded coming from her lips. "Hmm?"

"Could you let the Trujillos stay in the condo? Not forever, but just until they find a place to live?"

He lifted his head. "Did you really think I would kick them out? Although I wish you had asked me before you made the decision. I would've furnished the place so they wouldn't have been forced to sleep on the floor."

Her face lit up like the Fourth of July. "You plan on buying them beds?"

"Not me. Since you're so good at buying furniture, I figured I'd give that job to you."

A devilish look entered her eyes. "I know of a pool table they could have for free."

"Oh no. I won fair and square."

"More like low-down and dirty." Her hands were still in his hair, and her fingers brushed the tops of his ears. The simple caress shouldn't have made him hard, but it did. She must have felt it because her eyes widened. But instead of pushing him away, she tightened her legs and pulled him closer. "How about double or nothing?"

Patrick groaned as he sank deeper. "Okay, Jac, but you need to know that I play to win."

Chapter Twenty-Four

For the love of Pete"—Gerald's voice came from the thick branches of the Douglas fir—"this tree wouldn't even fit in your Aunt Frances's grand ballroom. It's sure as heck not going to fit in Patrick's condo."

Jac stood back and examined the tree Gerald held up. "You're probably right. Put it back, and we'll keep looking."

With a grunt Gerald flopped the tree back with the other ones leaning on the fence before brushing pine needles off his knee-length coat. "I don't even know why you're looking at trees. Since you decided to let Patrick keep the pool table, where are you going to put it?"

"I thought I'd put it in one corner of the bedroom."

"Now that makes perfect sense. Especially considering that it's where you spend all your time."

It was true. She and Patrick had spent the majority of the past week in bed. And not just having sex—although there had been plenty of that. But they'd also watched movies, played cards, and just talked. It had been wonderful. And just the thought of it brought a happy leap to her heart and a satisfied smile to her face. A satisfied smile that didn't go unnoticed.

"I can't believe it"—Gerald crossed his hands over his heart—"my little Jac has finally found true lust." His gaze sharpened as he looked over her shoulder. "And I can't say as I blame you. The man is delectable."

Jac glanced behind her and saw Patrick standing just inside the gates of the Christmas tree lot. He wore his usual flannel shirt, faded jeans, and work boots, but in deference to the cold temperatures, he'd added a green down vest that accentuated the muscles of his arms. All he needed was an ax resting on his shoulder to complete the picture of virile lumberjack. His searching gaze finally landed on her, and she couldn't seem to help the heat that filled her entire body. A slow, sexy smile eased over his face, and the feeling only intensified. She watched in a kind of airless happy bubble as he strode toward her, their gazes never wandering from each other, even when he dipped his head and brushed a kiss over her lips.

"Sorry I'm late. I stayed to help Juan Trujillo with some insurance forms." He kept an arm tucked around her, which was a good thing since her knees felt weak. "So did you find a tree you liked?"

With Patrick so close and so utterly handsome, she couldn't seem to form any words. All she could do was smile back at him. It took Gerald's startling exclamation to snap her out of her daze.

"Oh my God."

Jac glanced over to find Gerald looking back and forth

between them with a stunned look on his face. "What?" she said. "What's wrong?"

Gerald shook his head and adjusted the scarf around his neck. "Nothing. Nothing at all."

Jac studied him for a second more before making her own assumptions. "I think Gerald is referring to my choice in Christmas trees. I seem to be drawn to ones that would work better in Rockefeller Center than in our condo."

Patrick laughed. "Then I guess you're lucky that your husband owns an electric saw." He pulled her closer. "So where are these monster trees?"

Unlike Gerald, Patrick had no problem lifting each tree Jac picked out and holding it while she examined the branches for gaps. Nor did he complain when it took her a while to make her decision. Although he did seem as relieved as Gerald when she finally settled on a seven-foot Scotch pine. After handing it off to one of the teenage boys who worked the lot, he quickly chose another one.

"I'm not sure we'll have room for two," Jac said. "Especially with the pool table."

"This one's for my Aunt Wheezie. She wanted me to pick one up for her Christmas party this weekend." Patrick sent her a rather secretive smile. "But if you want two trees, I think we'll have room."

Confused, she shook her head. "One's plenty."

Still grinning, he hefted the tree and followed the young man to his truck, which was parked just outside the chain link fence. After he tied both trees down and paid the kid, he turned to Gerald, who was huddled in his coat and still looking between the two of them.

"I'm glad you came into town early, Gerald. I think

my aunt has bitten off more than she can chew with this Christmas party. And I was wondering, since you run an event business, if you could give her a hand. I'm more than willing to pay you."

"There's no need to pay him," Jac cut in. "Gerald would be more then happy to help." She sent him a bright smile. "Wouldn't you, Geri?"

He nodded weakly. "Of course, why wouldn't I want to start doing parties for free?"

Patrick laughed. "Maybe you can help, Jacqueline." He winked at her. "I'd love some pigs in a blanket. So is your sister going to make the party?"

"No, I'm afraid not. I talked to her today, and she said that she can't get away from work. So she won't get in until late on Christmas Eve."

"Flying?"

Jac nodded. "But she's not happy about it." A gust of wind sliced through her, and she shivered. Which resulted in Patrick pulling her into his arms and rubbing her back.

"You need to get out of this cold. And where is your hat?"

"Sorry, Dad," she teased. "I left it at school."

"Smart butt." He playfully smacked her bottom before adjusting her scarf up around her ears. "Since I need to drop off the tree at Wheezie's, how about if I pick up dinner and meet you and Gerald back at the condo?"

"I could make dinner."

He touched her bottom lip with his finger, and his eyes turned hot. "You've made dinner every night. Let me treat you for a change. Chinese?" She nodded, and he gave her a brief kiss before waving at Gerald. "Take good care of my girl, Geri." His words made Jacqueline feel even giddier, and she watched as he got in the truck and backed up. When he glanced over and saw that she was still standing there, he rolled down the window. "Get in the car, Jacqueline."

Blinking, she turned to discover that Gerald was already in the rental car with the engine started. She hadn't realized how cold she was until she climbed in and the blissful warmth from the heater enveloped her.

She shivered and held her gloved hands out to the heating vents. "I can't believe it's so cold this far south. It's every bit as cold as New York." When Gerald didn't say anything, she glanced over. He was watching her, his eyes intent and almost concerned. "Okay, what's going on?" she asked. "Are you mad that I made you lift all those trees? Or is this about me ignoring your calls this last week? Well, I'm sorry. But when you were dating Ramon, you ignored me. In fact I didn't hear from you for weeks at a time."

"Because I loved Ramon."

She reached over and took his hand, gently squeezing it. "I know. And I can't tell you how sorry I am that it didn't work out."

Gerald sighed. "So it's not lust. It's love."

"Of course I knew it wasn't lust." She released his hand and reached for her seat belt. "You wouldn't have ignored me for simple lust." She pulled the strap across her, but before she could lock it, Gerald placed a hand on her arm and stopped her.

"I'm not talking about Ramon, Jac. I'm talking about Patrick." He hesitated for only a brief second. "You aren't in lust with him. You're in love with him."

The seat belt slipped from her hand and zinged back to hit the door with a clatter. "What?" She tried to snort with derision, but it came out sounding more like choked hysteria. "Obviously you've spent too much time alone. You're starting to lose it. I don't love Patrick. I could never love Patrick."

"So you're telling me that you still think he's a loser?"

A loser? No, Patrick wasn't a loser. In fact in the last couple of weeks, she'd discovered that he was the complete opposite of the boyfriends her mother had brought home. He was a man who loved his job and his family. A man who didn't mind getting his hands dirty and taking on whatever task needed to be done. A man who believed in fairness and doing what was right. Whether it was marrying the woman he'd impregnated or giving a job to a man down on his luck.

She'd found out about Patrick hiring Mr. Trujillo the morning after they'd had pool table sex. She'd been making pancakes and Patrick had been taking a shower when the intercom buzzer had gone off. She answered it, but no one was there. When she went outside to check, she found a small bag of biscochito cookies with a homemade note from the Trujillo children—not only thanking her for the place to stay and the food and coats, but thanking Patrick for the job. Jacqueline walked back in with the cookies to find Patrick just coming down the stairs. She didn't even wait for him to reach the bottom before she flung herself into his arms.

The pancakes had to wait.

"You were right, Gerald. Patrick isn't a loser," she said.

"Of course he's not. Which explains why you've fallen in love with him." She started to deny it, but Gerald held up his hand. "Believe me, Jac. That look you just gave him wasn't an I-think-you're-a-nice-guy look. Nor was it an I-want-to-jump-your-bones look. It was a you-are-the-center-of-my-universe look. And I should know because it was the same look I used to give Ramon."

"No." She shook her head, suddenly feeling more than a little hysterical. "You're wrong, Gerald. I-I don't...I can't love Patrick. These sappy feelings that I have are just because of the great sex. Because I've never had such amazing orgasms with another man. That's all."

Gerald gave her a sympathetic look. "I understand your fear of love, Jac. I don't know much about your mother, but I know how cold your aunt was—just as cold and unloving as my parents. And like my parents, she taught you that love wasn't nearly as important as money. But money can't buy happiness, Jac. Your aunt and my parents are perfect examples of this. Which probably explains the weird stipulation in your aunt's will. She wanted you to be as miserable in your loveless marriage as she was in hers." He leaned closer. "But love does buy happiness, Jac. You and Bailey have taught me that. Without you as my friends, I never would've survived after my family cut me off for being a homosexual. Your love is what makes me happy. So don't be afraid of loving Patrick."

As if all the strength had suddenly drained out of her body, Jac slumped back in the seat. Love? Was it possible? Could she be in love with Patrick after only a few weeks?

As with the jigsaw puzzles she and Gerald used to put together on rainy days, her mind pieced through the memories and tried to organize a cohesive picture of her relationship with Patrick. It wasn't easy. Their relationship hadn't started out like most. It had started by accident and continued because of the tiny person that was growing inside her. But these past few weeks hadn't been an accident. Or about the baby. They had been about two people getting to know one another. Getting to know one another and becoming friends.

Jac couldn't deny that she liked Patrick. She liked the way his green eyes crinkled up at the corners when he laughed and the way he looked all content and satisfied after he finished eating one of her meals. And she liked the way his hand rode on her back when they went anywhere together and how intent he looked when she read to him from one of the baby books she'd purchased. But most of all, she liked going to bed snuggled against him at night and waking up snuggled against him in the morning. If she was truthful with herself, she didn't like these things as much as love them.

She was so consumed with her thoughts that she was surprised when Gerald pulled up to the condo's garage. He kept the engine running and waited for her to speak. When she finally did, she didn't deny her love. She couldn't. Instead she faced her greatest fear.

"What if he doesn't love me?"

"Aww, honey." Gerald released his seat belt and pulled her into a hug. "Then that's his loss. But somehow I don't think that's the case. Not if the dopey look on his face was any indication." He pulled back. "But you need to tell him, Jac. You need to tell him everything. Not just about being in love with him, but about your aunt's will and the reason you married him."

"But he'll hate me for lying and manipulating him."

"Probably at first. But if he really loves you, he'll forgive you."

She sent him a skeptical look. "I'm not so sure. You've seen his temper."

Instead of reassuring her, Gerald thought for a moment before nodding. "Maybe it would be better if you waited to tell him about the will when you're in a crowded place—and when his power tools aren't within reach."

"Thanks a lot, Gerald. That makes me feel so much better." She opened the door. "Come on. We need to unbox the decorations we bought and put hooks on them before Patrick gets back."

He reached into the backseat and grabbed the bag of decorations. "I think I'm going to let you two lovebirds decorate your tree without me."

"But Patrick's bringing you dinner."

He handed her the bag. "Since you're eating for two, you can eat my portion."

She got out. But before closing the door, she leaned back in. "I love you, Geri."

He smiled. "Ditto. Now get going before I run out of gas."

With the temperature being so low, Jac didn't waste any time punching in the code and getting inside. Once in the door, she was almost bowled over by an enthusiastic Gomer. She corrected him for jumping, but she couldn't help giving him a good scratch on the ears. The cats and Gilmore waited at the top of the stairs. She was crouched down giving them each some love when she glanced over at the living room.

Her heart stopped.

The pool table was gone and the couch, chairs, and end tables were arranged around the fireplace, a lit fireplace with three red furry stockings hanging from the mantel. Each one had been embroidered with a name.

Patrick.

Jacqueline.

And Baby Lulu.

Chapter Twenty-Five

Throwing a party wasn't as easy as it had been when Wheezie was twenty years younger. With only minutes left before people started showing up, she was up to her sagging chin in preparations. It didn't help that her hip was bothering her more than normal. Or that Barkley had disappeared for two days and wasn't answering his cell phone. Hopefully, he was still getting someone to pose as Gabby's father. Of course with Barkley, it was hard to tell. The man had a mind of his own—and another life Wheezie knew nothing about.

The only bright spot of the day was Patrick's early arrival with Jacqueline and Gerald. Not only because Wheezie could use the help, but also because she was finally able to witness for herself how the newlyweds were doing. From the looks of things, pretty damn well.

"I told you to stay out of that oven, Patrick McPherson." Jacqueline swatted at Patrick with a dish towel. "If you keep opening the door, the pigs in a blanket are never going to get done."

"But I'm hungry," Patrick pleaded. "I haven't eaten anything since your skillet egg dish at breakfast."

She took a carrot stick from the vegetable-and-dip tray on the counter. "Here, eat this."

He took the carrot from her hand, but didn't bite into it. Instead he pulled Jacqueline into his arms and nibbled on her neck. "How about if I eat this?"

Wheezie's heart warmed. She couldn't remember the last time she'd seen Patrick so playful and happy. It looked like he'd finally discovered the joys of marriage. Which meant that Wheezie's days of soul mating were coming to an end. She didn't know why she suddenly felt so depressed. Wasn't that what she'd been asking for? A little rest and relaxation? Of course now wasn't the time for rest and relaxation.

Having found the napkins she'd been looking for on the kitchen table, Wheezie took them back into the dining room. Gerald was putting the finishing touches on the huge floral arrangement that sat in the center of the table while Gabby feasted on the pigs in a blanket Jacqueline had sneaked by Patrick and placed on the table earlier.

"These are great, Geri." Gabby spoke with a full mouth. "With the way you arrange flowers and Jacqueline's cooking skills, I don't understand why your event planning business hasn't taken off."

Gerald carefully placed another white rose in the midst of the bright-red poinsettias. "Probably because we pretty much suck at the business side of things. I'm good at planning parties and creative with flowers and design, and

Jac can cook, but neither one of us are good at managing time or money."

Wheezie arranged the cloth napkins in a neat column. "It sounds to me like you just need an office manager... and maybe some new clientele in a new city."

Gerald shot her an inquisitive look that quickly turned to a knowing one. "Are you talking about moving the business to Denver, Miss Wheezie?"

She loved a quick mind. It saved so much time. "Why not? It's as plain as the purple velvet of your sports coat that Jacqueline will miss you something terrible when you return to New York City. And since we can't have a mother-to-be upset, I'm thinking that Denver is a perfect place for you to restart your business. Why, with Mary Katherine's friends alone, you'll have more business than you can handle."

"She's right," Gabby said. "My grandma's friends love to throw parties. And if you move here, you could hire me to be your office manager. My dad says I have a real business head on my shoulders."

Gerald sent her a genuine smile. "I'm sure you do. But while I like Denver, I can't leave Bailey. Especially now that Jacqueline isn't going back."

Wheezie stopped arranging the napkins. "Now that she's not going back? Was she going back before?"

Gerald's face turned as red as the poinsettias. "Did I say *now*? What I meant was since—since Jacqueline is married and won't be living in New York, I don't want to leave Bailey."

"Gabby," Wheezie said, "why don't you go see if Jacqueline needs any help in the kitchen?"

That was the good thing about the teenager: She knew

how to take a hint without a lot of questions. She glanced between Wheezie and Gerald before she grabbed another pastry-wrapped cocktail frank and left the room. When she was gone, Wheezie sat down in the chair.

"So let's not beat around the bush, Gerald. Was Jacqueline planning on leaving Patrick?"

He swallowed hard and glanced at the kitchen. "Yes. But she's not planning on leaving him anymore."

"And I suppose that her leaving had to do with Frances's will?" She wasn't surprised when he nodded. She knew the will had played into their marriage somehow, but had been unable to find out exactly how. "What was the stipulation?"

Releasing his breath, Gerald sank down in the chair across from Wheezie. "In order to inherit her aunt's money, she needed to marry a man in her aunt's social circle and stay married to him for a year."

Wheezie hesitated for only a second before stating her mind. "Why that crazy bitch."

Gerald laughed. "She was crazy and a very unhappy woman. Which was why she hated Jac so much. Jac has always looked on the bright side of things. And Mrs. Rosenblum never forgave Jac for writing the letter and pretty much forcing her to acknowledge her orphaned nieces—and her poor upbringing. I really think Mrs. Rosenblum put the stipulation in her will hoping to make Jac as miserable as she was. She must be rolling in her grave knowing Jac has finally found happiness."

Wheezie studied him. "Has she?"

He met her gaze. "I truly believe that Jac loves Patrick, Miss Wheezie. And once she loves someone, she'll be loyal to them until the day she dies."

"So I guess Patrick doesn't know about the will."

"Not yet. But Jac's going to tell him soon."

Wheezie got to her feet and pointed a finger at him. "Absolutely not. Sometimes it's best to let sleeping dogs lie or hot-tempered Scots stay in the dark. If Jacqueline loves him, telling him about the stipulation will make no difference now."

"But I thought the best marriages were built on truth."

"That's poppycock. The best marriages are built on love. And sometimes you need to love someone enough to save them from the truth." The phone rang, and she waved a hand at the kitchen. "Now get in there and make sure Jacqueline keeps her lips zipped."

Once Gerald was gone, Wheezie shuffled over to the buffet and answered the phone. She was surprised when Mary Katherine's voice came through the receiver.

"How's the party going, Louise?"

"So far, so good," Wheezie said. "Although the majority of the family hasn't gotten here yet. And Cassie just called and said that she and James had to cancel their trip to see his parents because Jace came down with an ear infection and couldn't fly. Where are you? I thought you'd be somewhere over the Atlantic by now."

"Oh, Louise"—her usually calm voice broke—"I've really messed things up this time."

"Take a deep breath, Mary Katherine, and tell me what happened."

"We're stuck in Kansas City in a blizzard. No flights are coming in or going out." She sniffed. "Now I'm not going to spend Christmas with my family or on a cruise ship with my husband."

Wheezie might've felt sorry for her niece if Mary hadn't

made her own bed. "Which is exactly what you deserve for not telling Albert the truth in the first place."

"And you don't think that I don't know that, Louise?" She sniffed. "I should've told him long before tonight."

"So how did he take it?"

"The ornery man laughed. And not just a chuckle, but an out-and-out belly laugh. Then he picked me up off my feet in a bear hug before he walked off without a word. I wouldn't be surprised if he's left me for good."

Wheezie snorted. "That's doubtful. We McPhersons don't give up on people that easily. I'm sure he's gone to see if he can't find a way home."

"You think?"

"Either that, or a shot of whiskey." Something Wheezie could certainly use. The doorbell rang, and with everyone in the kitchen, it was up to her to answer it. "Listen, Mary Katherine, I've got to go. But I want you to stop feeling sorry for yourself and find that nephew of mine and do some serious kissing up."

Within fifteen minutes of her hanging up with Mary Katherine, Wheezie's house was filled to the rafters with celebrating Scots. Christmas music came from Gabby's phone, which she'd plugged into a small speaker, and laughter rang out as the relatives fueled up on spiked eggnog and Jacqueline's hors d'oeuvres. Wheezie would've liked to try one herself, but she was too busy answering the door as more and more people arrived.

"Merry Christmas, Wheezie," Sidney, Ellie's best friend, said as she stepped inside.

"Merry Christmas yourself." Wheezie nodded at the bag of packages she carried. "It looks like you've done some shopping."

"They're Matthew and Ellie's gifts for you." She held the bag in one hand while Wheezie helped her off with her coat. "They dropped them by before they left on Friday morning."

"Have you heard from her and Matthew?"

"I talked with her this morning. And I couldn't help but get the feeling that she and Matthew would've been happier staying here in their new home."

"Well, I guess that makes sense," Wheezie said. "With the baby coming, Ellie's in the nesting stage."

"Thankfully, that's something I know nothing about." Sidney held up the bag. "Where do you want these?"

Wheezie led her over to the Christmas tree in front of the window and helped her take the presents from the bag and stack them beneath the tree.

"Before I forget," Sidney said, "Rory called and wanted me to change the tickets for the Polar Express from tonight to earlier this afternoon. I guess they missed Gabby and wanted to cut their trip short. They should be here any moment." Gabby came into the room, and Sidney leaned in to whisper. "But don't say anything. I think they want to surprise her."

Oh, it would be a surprise all right. Especially if Wheezie couldn't get ahold of Barkley and stop him from walking in with Gabby's fake bio dad. Unfortunately, as if on cue, the doorbell rang, and before Wheezie could shuffle over there, Gabby beat her to it. If the hesitant, uncertain look on Gabby's face was any indication, it was too late to call Barkley.

"Hi," Gabby said in a soft voice. "Won't you come in?" She held open the door, and a bald, studious-looking man with glasses stepped in who had to be five inches shorter than Gabby. Wheezie rolled her eyes. This was supposed to be a truck-driving redneck who'd played quarterback in high school? It was the last time she would trust Barkley.

"Hello," the man said as he fidgeted with the lapels of his overcoat. "I hope I'm not intruding, but the need was too great to put things off any longer."

Oh, brother. Talk about overacting. Wheezie was really going to bawl out Barkley for hiring this yahoo.

Gabby's brow knotted. "But if you felt that way, why didn't you come sooner?"

"I tried to make contact before, but things didn't work out. Running a charity takes a lot of time and energy—especially during the holidays."

Wheezie decided it was time to jump in. "That being the case, I'm sure you can't stay long." She glanced out the window, hoping Amy and Rory got stuck in traffic. "In fact, why don't you and Gabby exchange numbers and you can call each other and gab at a more convenient time. Like when you get back from your missionary work in Africa."

"Africa?" Gabby's eyes widened. "You're going to Africa?"

The not-too-swift actor shook his head. "No. There must be some mistake. My charity work isn't in Africa. I run a nonprofit organization here in the States."

Wheezie rolled her eyes. Great, they had an ad-libber on their hands. The doorbell rang and, fearful it was Amy and Rory, Wheezie grabbed both Gabby's and the actor's arms and pulled them toward her sun-room. "Why don't you two sit and chat in here for a moment while I run and get some snacks." She pushed them inside the room and closed the pocket doors before shuffling back to answer the front door. She opened it to find Barkley standing there with a tall man in a cowboy hat, Western suit, and boots. They had barely stepped inside when Barkley growled at the man under his breath.

"Remember your manners."

Looking fearful, the man doffed his hat and smiled weakly. "Hello, ma'am. Merry Christmas to you."

Wheezie looked at Barkley in confusion. "Please tell me that this is your date for the evening."

"His date?" Gerald suddenly appeared holding a tray. His eyes traveled Barkley's length before he smiled like a cat with a canary. "I knew I loved you, Aunt Wheezie." He held out the tray to Barkley and batted his eyelashes. "Pig in a blanket?"

Barkley ignored the obvious come-on. "No, thanks." He glanced around. "Where's Gabby?"

It finally dawned on Wheezie who the man with Barkley was. She studied the man in the suit. At least this one looked like a redneck quarterback. But if he was the actor, then who was with Gabby?

Just then the door to the sun-room opened, and Gabby stepped out. Her gaze wandered around the room until it stopped on Wheezie's. The disbelief in her eyes pretty much said that the jig was up. But before Wheezie could figure a way out of the mess she'd made, Rory came in the door carrying Douglas.

"Surprise!" he yelled as Amy followed behind him with a bright smile on her face. Neither one of them hesitated before walking over to Gabby and enfolding her in a group hug.

"We couldn't leave our Gabriella on Christmas," Rory said. "I don't care how old and mature she thinks she is."

"So that's my kid?"

Everyone turned to the cowboy in the suit, who was staring at Gabby. "She sure don't look a thing like me," he said. "She looks just like her mama." He glanced at Amy. "Hey, Amy. How's it goin'?"

Amy's eyes widened. "Luke?"

"In the flesh." He tipped the hat he'd put back on.

"But what are you doing here?"

"Some old woman called and invited me. Of course, with my work and all, I had to turn her down." His gaze moved over to Barkley. "But then this guy showed up at my trailer and told me he would break my fingers if I didn't get on a plane with him." He shrugged. "So here I am."

"An old woman?" Rory's eyes turned to Wheezie, and everyone else followed suit.

Since there was no way out of it, Wheezie said the only thing she could. "Does anyone else need a shot of scotch?"

Chapter Twenty-Six

Patrick had never been much on Christmas Eve parties. Crowds, even crowds of family, had always made him feel closed in. So he was more than content to stay in the kitchen with Jacqueline as she hustled around pulling hors d'oeuvres from the oven and filling trays. When cooking at home, she liked to wear one of his old flannel shirts, no makeup, and her hair clipped up in a mass of curls. But tonight she had dressed for the occasion and wore off-white pants and a fuzzy blue sweater that turned her eyes an even deeper shade of blue. She'd artfully applied makeup and fixed her hair to fall around her shoulders in soft auburn waves. With the diamond studs in her ears and the designer heels on her feet, she would've fit into any high-society gathering. And yet here she was in his great-aunt's kitchen working harder than one of those television chefs in a cooking competition. Patrick couldn't have been prouder, or happier, that she belonged to him.

It was a male chauvinistic thought. One his sister Cassie would've socked him for if she'd been there and could've read his mind. But he couldn't help it. Since the pool table sex, he'd taken possession of his new bride. As far as he was concerned, Jacqueline did belong to him. And he had started to wonder if he didn't also belong to her. For the last week, he certainly hadn't been himself.

Work was no longer the center of his life. He had no urge to get a beer with his buddies after work. Or invite his brothers over for a game of pool. In fact he was thinking about selling the pool table he'd stored in the Trujillos' garage. What use did he have for the pool table now? An image of Jacqueline stretched out naked on the green felt had him reevaluating. Okay, so maybe he wouldn't sell it. Maybe what he needed was a bigger house. One that had a basement for his pool table and a couple of spare rooms for kids.

Kids. Yes, he wanted more than one. Maybe not as many as his parents or Cassie, but three seemed like a good number. A couple of boys and one cute little Irish/Scottish lass with red ringlets exactly like her mother's.

He slipped off the barstool and took the cookie sheet away from Jacqueline and set it on the stove. "You've done enough work for the night. In fact I think we should go home and have a nice, quiet Christmas Eve by the fire." He pulled her into his arms. "Naked."

She encircled his neck and beamed up at him. "That sounds wonderful. But I think you're forgetting a few things. Like picking up Bailey from the airport and midnight mass. Your aunt would be terribly disappointed if we didn't attend with her."

"She would live. And I thought Gerald was picking up Bailey."

Jacqueline smiled. "He's changed his mind. It seems he's found the love of his life. Although I'm not so sure Barkley reciprocates the feelings."

"Barkley? My aunt's chauffeur? I don't think he's—"

"Excuse me."

Patrick turned to see a short, bald-headed man standing in the kitchen doorway. Since his aunt Wheezie had a thing for bald guys, Patrick figured he was her newest boyfriend. He was about to introduce himself when Jacqueline stiffened in his arms.

"Mr. Darby?" she breathed.

The name had Patrick's gaze narrowing as the man spoke.

"Forgive me for intruding on your holiday, Ms. Maguire," Mr. Darby said in a hesitant voice. "But I'm afraid I couldn't put it off any longer."

"Mrs. McPherson," Patrick said as he released Jacqueline and stepped in front of her. "I'm her husband, Mr. McPherson. And what exactly can't you put off?"

Before Mr. Darby could do more than swallow, Gerald rushed into the room with a half-empty tray of pigs in a blanket and a wild look in his eyes. "I'm not sure, but I think there's going to be a fight out there. Your family members are getting pretty wound up."

Since Patrick couldn't remember one Christmas Eve that hadn't ended in a fight—or at least a heated argument—he wasn't all that surprised. You couldn't get that many stubborn Scots in the same house without someone losing their temper. He was more concerned with what was going on in the kitchen.

"Where were you on Halloween night, Mr. Darby?" He took a step closer to the little man. "Because if you've ever done anything to harm my wife, I'm going to squash you like a bug."

"Of course I haven't." The little man looked appalled. "I would never harm your wife—or anyone. I'm only here to see if she would continue her aunt's tradition and be willing to donate money to my charitable organization. The sum her aunt gave every year went a long way to helping those in need." He fidgeted. "And I'm afraid without it, many children and families will go without."

"That's how you knew my aunt?" Jacqueline stepped around Patrick. "So you weren't trying to kill me?"

Mr. Darby's eyes widened. "Why would I want to kill you, Ms. Ma—McPherson?"

Jacqueline giggled. A giggle that quickly turned into an out-and-out laugh that had Patrick smiling. His smile faded when his brother's voice boomed from the other room.

"You did what, Aunt Wheezie?"

Patrick looked at Gerald. "Rory's here?"

He nodded. "I guess they cut their trip short to be with Gabby for Christmas. Except Gabby doesn't look real happy about her parents being back. Of course I think she's upset about having three dads." He looked at Mr. Darby. "Although if you're Jacqueline's Mr. Darby than you can't be one of Gabby's dads."

Completely confused, Patrick headed for the living room. When he arrived he discovered his entire clan of relatives circled around like a bunch of kids at a playground fistfight. He pushed through the crowd until he reached the people in the middle. Rory, Amy, Gabby, Wheezie, and a stranger in cowboy boots.

"What's going on?" he asked.

Everyone started talking at once. The only one not talking was Wheezie, which told Patrick everything he needed to know. Since he wasn't about to deal with the entire group, he took Wheezie by the arm and escorted her to the sun-room. As he'd predicted, the ones who were the most upset at his aunt followed. Rory, who looked more hurt than mad. And his wife Amy, who just looked pissed.

"How could you contact Gabby's father without asking me, Wheezie?" she said. "You had no business doing something like that."

Instead of answering, Wheezie walked over to a cabinet and pulled down a bottle of scotch. Without even looking for a glass, she unscrewed the cap and took a big swig. She released a sigh before turning to Amy.

"You're right. It wasn't any of my business. And I apologize. I just thought it would be nice if Gabby got to meet—"

"It's not her fault." Gabby came charging into the room. "I was the one who wanted to meet my biological dad." She thumped her chest. "I was the one who talked Wheezie into calling him and inviting him here while you were in Durango."

Amy stared at her daughter. "You? But why didn't you just tell us that you wanted to meet your father, Gabby? Why did you have to go behind our backs?"

Gabby's face fell. "Because I didn't want to hurt Dad's feelings." She glanced over at Rory, and tears filled her eyes. "I didn't want you thinking that I didn't appreciate all that you've done for me, all the love you've given me over the years. I especially didn't want you thinking that

I don't thank God every day that he gave me such a great dad like you."

Some of the hurt left Rory's face, to be replaced with overwhelming love. "Oh, Gabs." He walked over and pulled his daughter into his arms. "I know you love me. And I thank God every day that he gave me such a great kid for a daughter." He pulled back. "Yes, it's hard to share. But I realize that you have a biological father, and it's only natural that you want to meet him. I just wish you had told me how you felt."

"Me too." Gabby looked at Wheezie. "And I'm sorry for putting you in the middle, Wheeze." Her eyes crinkled in confusion. "But what I still can't figure out is who that man is that you were trying to pass off as my biological dad."

Wheezie shrugged. "I guess I had a little bout of dementia. But we shouldn't let that ruin a good Christmas Eve party." She waved everyone out the door. They all complied, except for Patrick, who just wasn't buying it.

"Dementia?"

Wheezie smiled. "It happens." Carrying the bottle of scotch, she shuffled out the door.

By the time Patrick got back to the kitchen, Mr. Darby was gone and Jacqueline was refilling a cookie tray and humming "Have a Holly Jolly Christmas." He felt a little jolly himself as he slipped his hands around her waist and kissed her neck.

"So do you want to explain what made you think that Mr. Darby was trying to kill you?" he asked between kisses.

"There's something you need to know about me." She turned in his arms and looped her hands around his neck.

"I watched a lot of television growing up, and it gave me a vivid imagination that sometimes gets the best of me. Something that happened with Mr. Darby."

"Well, if we're sharing secrets, I guess you should know that I was the serious, logical kid who couldn't come up with a fictional story to save his soul." He gave her a quick kiss on the tip of her nose. "So I think we're pretty well matched. You can be the one who dreams up the dragons, and I'll be the one to slay them."

Her eyes turned dreamy. "I think that might work out quite well." She gave him a kiss that had him mentally searching for a place in his aunt's house where he could get her alone. Unfortunately, before he could pull her into the pantry, Wheezie came in.

"Enough of the smooching." She pulled Jacqueline away from him. "I want to introduce my new niece-in-law to the family."

There was nothing for Patrick to do but follow them back to the party. A party that got wilder as the night went on. Aunt Hester and Aunt Mae got into it over who had brought the best fruitcake, and the argument ended with a taste test that got Aunt Hester's husband, Ray, in big trouble for choosing Aunt Mae's fruitcake over his wife's. Cousin Jen had too much spiked eggnog and announced that she'd had an affair with an encyclopedia salesman fifty years earlier. Since she'd been a widow for five years, no one seemed too upset by the news. Gabby's biological father turned out to be as big of a jerk as everyone had thought he was. After eating most of the cheesy tater tots, he made a pass at Amy, which resulted in Barkley physically removing him from the party and driving him back to his hotel.

By eleven o'clock Patrick was more than ready to leave for the airport. Unfortunately, he couldn't seem to locate his wife. He finally found her asleep in a spare bedroom amid a pile of coats. She clutched a down jacket to her chest like a teddy bear and a soft smile curved her lips. Since he couldn't bring himself to wake her, he covered her with a blanket. He figured he could make it to the airport and have Bailey back before Jacqueline woke up.

"I guess being pregnant makes you tired."

He glanced up to see Gabby standing in the doorway. He figured that she had to be upset about the scene her biological father had made, but he didn't know what to say to make it better. So he kept the conversation light as he tucked the blanket around Jacqueline. "I guess so. Being a man, I don't have a clue."

"Men are pretty clueless." She moved into the room. "So do you love her?"

Leave it to a kid to cut to the chase. He started to deny it, but then he looked at Jacqueline sleeping so peacefully, and the truth just came out. "Yeah. I love her."

"I'm glad," Gabby said. "It will make things a lot easier for your kid."

The sadness in her voice made Patrick realize that there was no way around a conversation about her father. Moving away from the bed, he chose his words carefully.

"I'm sorry about your dad, Gabs, but I've done some pretty stupid things when I've had too much to drink."

"No. It wasn't Aunt Wheezie's eggnog. He's just a jerk." She shrugged. "Something I figured out after five minutes of conversation. He wasn't interested in me at all. All he wanted to talk about was what a great football player he'd been in high school and how many girlfriends he had—as if I wanted to hear about that. And it doesn't really matter. When your dad doesn't contact you for sixteen years, you kinda figure that you're not going to be best buddies."

"I don't think dads are supposed to be best buddies," Patrick said. "Big Al and I aren't that close."

Gabby looked surprised by the words. "Just because you don't always agree with Grandpa Al doesn't mean that you're not close, Uncle Paddy. In fact my dad says that Grandpa likes locking horns with you as much as you like locking horns with him."

Damn, the kid was smart. He smiled and walked over to ruffle her hair. "So are you going to be okay about Luke?"

She picked up a picture from the dresser. A picture of the entire McPherson family—Gabby included. "Yeah. I don't know what I expected. Maybe I just needed to meet him. To have him meet me. No-regrets kind of thing." She glanced over. "You know what I mean?"

Patrick pulled her into his arms. Resting his head on top of hers, he released his breath. "Yeah. I know exactly what you mean. I also know that you're a cool kid. And I hope my kid is half as cool."

Gabby tipped her head and grinned. "Hey, with me as a cousin, how could they not be?"

Patrick made it to the airport just in time for Bailey's arrival. After checking the flight status on the monitors, he moved to the security gate to wait. He was surprised at how many people were flying on Christmas Eve. Hordes of travelers squeezed through the gate, hurrying off to baggage claim or stopping to greet the friends and relatives who waited for them.

"Hey, Patrick!"

He turned to see Jonesy coming toward him. His hair was longer than the last time Patrick had seen him, and as usual he looked like he had just rolled out of bed.

"What are you doing here, man?" Jonesy threw an arm around him and pulled Patrick in for a quick hug. "I thought you spent Christmas Eve with your family."

"I do," Patrick said, "but I have to pick up my wife's sister. What are you doing here? I thought you left last week."

"I planned to, but then I met this girl at a Starbucks and…" He flashed a grin. "It's nice being the boss. And speaking of being the boss, I talked it over with Mike and we still want you to build the sports bars." When Patrick started to speak, he held up a hand. "Even if that means I have to go with M&M and whoever you and your crazy family hires for my on-site project managers. I want you on my team, man."

Patrick grinned. "That's great, Jonesy."

He pointed his finger. "But I still expect you to supervise—even after you're rolling in your wife's money." When Patrick sent him a confused look, Jonesy socked him on the arm. "You sly dog you. No wonder you decided to get leg-shackled so quickly. I would get married too if all I had to do was stay married for a year to get billions. Mike couldn't believe it when I told him who you married. I guess he knows the last dude Jacqueline left at the altar, and Gerhardt told Mike all about the stipulation in the aunt's will."

While Patrick tried to piece things together, Jonesy went on. "According to Mike, Gerhardt was only going to get a small percentage. Please tell me that you worked out a better deal with Jacqueline before you signed the prenup." He glanced at his watch. "Shit, I'm going to miss my flight." He thumped Patrick on the back. "I'll call you after the first, and we'll get everything in writing." He turned and hustled off.

For a moment Patrick couldn't seem to catch his breath. He felt like he had been plunged under water without any warning and was now floundering to find the surface.

Needing air, he headed for the exit. Once outside he pulled in greedy gulps. The sharp coldness expanded his chest and brought with it the stark truth.

Jacqueline had played him for a fool. She was exactly who he'd first thought she was. A manipulative, spoiled socialite who loved one thing—money. She hadn't married him because of their mutual attraction. Or because of their baby. She'd married him to get her hands on her aunt's inheritance. And that had probably been her plan all along, and the reason she'd come to Denver in the first place. Her standoffish behavior had been a ruse to throw him off—to make him think that marriage was all his idea.

Betrayed was too mild a word to describe how Patrick felt. He felt blindsided. As if sleepwalking, he headed to the parking garage. He didn't pay any attention to the travelers who bumped him as they hurried home to their families, or care about leaving Bailey stranded. He only cared about one thing.

Ending the hoax of his marriage.

Chapter Twenty-Seven

W hat do you mean Patrick isn't there?" Jac didn't wait for Bailey to answer her before she pulled the phone away from her mouth and addressed Gerald, who sat in the front seat of Aunt Wheezie's car with Barkley. "Geri, didn't Patrick say that he was going to the airport to pick up Bailey, and if he didn't get back in time, he would meet us at the church?"

Gerald sent her an annoyed glance for interrupting his conversation with Barkley about spring fashion. "That's what he told me." He turned back around. "So where was I, Barkley? Oh yes, I was telling you about the new teal tennis shorts I found at Neiman Marcus…"

Now more than a little worried, Jac returned to her conversation with Bailey. "Do you think something happened to Patrick? Maybe he got in an accident. Or some mugger accosted him in the parking garage. Or he got hit by one of those rental car buses. Those guys always drive so reckless—"

"Calm down, Jac," Bailey said. "I'm sure Patrick didn't get in an accident. He's probably just parking. It's a madhouse here. I'll text him and meet him at the pickup area outside. Now, what's this I hear about church?"

Jac cringed. She had purposely kept the entire midnight mass thing to herself. Bailey didn't believe in God and had spent her adult life avoiding church. Which was more than likely due to their mother's religious craziness. Every six months she would drag them to church, where she would sob and carry on in a dramatic display of repenting her sins. Then, less than twenty-four hours later, she'd be sinning again. Jac didn't hold that against the church as much as against their mother.

"The McPhersons always go to midnight mass on Christmas Eve," she said. "And I thought that maybe you'd like to—"

"No." Bailey cut her off. "I don't mind suffering through the entire McPherson Christmas, but I refuse to spend Christmas Eve in church. I'll have Patrick drop me off at the hotel, and I'll see you in the morning."

Jac wasn't happy about having to wait to see her sister, but there was no arguing with Bailey when she made up her mind. "Fine. I'm making you your favorite French toast for breakfast, but without the cream cheese because Patrick doesn't like cream cheese. And with a side of bacon because Patrick loves bacon. And we'll have to wait to eat until after Patrick and I go on our morning run."

"Patrick has you exercising?"

"It's not really exercising, and I don't really run. I walk while Patrick laps me, then we walk to the bakery a couple blocks over and he buys me a chocolate croissant.

Although, with it being Christmas, the bakery will probably be closed tomorrow."

There was a pause before Bailey spoke in an awed voice. "Gerald was right."

"Right about what? Did he tell you about Mr. Darby?"

Bailey groaned. "Please, Jac, I refuse to listen to one more crazy story about Mr. Darby trying to kill you. I was talking about you being in love with Patrick."

Try as she might, Jac could no longer deny it. Somehow, some way, she had ended up in her own romantic comedy. A romantic comedy where the heroine falls head over heels in love with her hero. Uncaring that Wheezie sat in the seat next to her listening, Jac finally allowed the truth to spill out. And with it came a giddy sense of rightness. "I do love him, Bay. And I don't know how it happened. One second he was this arrogant, macho man, and the next second he became everything I've ever dreamed of." Jac couldn't keep the smile from her face. "I thought we were so different that we could never get along, but our differences are what make us so compatible. He likes to eat comfort food and I like to make it, he likes to listen and I like to talk, he likes to make money and I like to spend it. So it turned out that we are perfectly matched. He's like my..." She struggled to find the right word and was surprised when Wheezie helped her out.

"Soul mate."

Jac glanced over to find the old woman's eyes sparkling. Jac nodded. "Soul mate. Patrick is my soul mate."

"Well, I think I just spotted your soul mate," Bailey said. "So I'll talk to you tomorrow."

Even after she'd replaced her phone in her purse, the bubble of happiness continued to swell in her heart. Although the happiness was mixed with awkwardness when Wheezie spoke.

"So you thought my nephew was an arrogant, macho man?"

Jac cleared her throat. "Maybe a little."

Wheezie tipped back her head and laughed, which caused Jac to start giggling. They were both still laughing when Barkley pulled up in front of the large Catholic church.

"I'm going to drop you off at the steps so you ladies don't have so far to walk," he said.

"You aren't coming in?" Gerald shot him a disappointed look.

"Barkley never comes in," Wheezie said as she pulled on her gloves. "Which leads me to believe that he's a vampire and worried about turning to dust."

Gerald glanced over at Barkley and sent him a seductive smile. "Jac and I have always had a thing for vampires."

Barkley didn't reply, and Jac had to wonder if he was as interested in Gerald as Gerald was in him. He didn't appear to be very happy when Gerald decided to skip midnight mass and keep him company. Wheezie, on the other hand, found the entire situation funny. As Jac helped her up the flight of stone steps that led to the entrance of the church, the old woman chuckled.

"It serves him right for not telling me about Gabby's father."

The church was a beautiful building with vaulted, ornate ceilings, huge stained-glass windows, and a reverent silence that freaked Jac out.

Unlike Bailey, Jac believed in God. Not as the burning

bush in *The Ten Commandments*, but as a bigger, sterner version of George Burns in *Oh, God!* As she followed Wheezie down the long aisle, she waited for him to hover over her with his cigar and get after her for all the lies she'd told over the years. Which probably explained why she jumped when Al McPherson popped out of nowhere.

Big Al was just as scary as God.

"There you are, Wheeze." His booming voice echoed off the high ceiling, causing more than a few people to turn and stare. Their annoyed expressions didn't seem to bother Big Al, or Wheezie, who laughed as she gave her nephew a hug.

"I figured you two would work things out and get back here in time to spend Christmas with your family."

He smiled, a smile that looked just like Patrick's. Which made Jac a little less scared of him. "We would've been here a lot sooner if Mary Katherine wasn't so stubborn."

Mary swatted at her husband. "Lower your voice, Albert. We're in church."

He looked around, and his smile got even bigger. "We are, aren't we?" He gave his wife a resounding kiss on the cheek before turning to Jac. "Where's that ornery son of mine?"

Since it took a moment for Jac to find her voice, Wheezie answered for her. "He went to the airport to pick up Jacqueline's sister, but he should be here anytime now."

Big Al gave Jac a thorough once-over. "You're Catholic, I take it."

She swallowed hard. "No, sir."

His eyes crinkled as he studied her. "Well, I'm sure

Mary Katherine can change that. And not sir. Just Al...or Dad." He pulled her into his arms and gave her a bone-crushing hug. "Merry Christmas, Jac, and welcome to the family." Before she could get over her surprise, he released her and ushered his wife into a pew. A pew already filled with McPhersons. Since they had been at the Christmas Eve party, Jac had expected to see Rory, Amy, Gabby, and Douglas. She hadn't expected to see Jake, Melanie, and their children. And neither had Wheezie.

"What happened to your ski weekend?" Wheezie asked.

"The kids got bored with skiing. And since Rory and Amy came home early, we figured we would too," Jake said.

Melanie leaned around him. "It wasn't because of Rory and Amy's decision as much as Jake's bad mood the moment we left the city limits. My husband does not like changing tradition."

A scowl settled over his features. "Okay, so I like tradition. What's wrong with that?" He glanced down the pew at the aisle. "And it looks like I'm not the only one."

Matthew and Ellie entered the pew. "We caught a late flight," Matthew said as he helped Ellie off with her coat. "After Ellie's parents renewed their vows, they pretty much pushed us out the door. I think they plan to spend their Christmas in bed." He dodged Ellie's playful swat. "Well, it's the truth. And I can't say as I blame them. I'm looking forward to sleeping in my own bed." He winked at his wife. "Or not sleeping."

"Shush, Matthew." His mother got after him. "Sit down and behave yourself."

"Things never seem to change. Do they, Mattie?"

At the words, everyone looked at the aisle to see Cassie filing into the pew, followed by James. It appeared that the McPhersons didn't like to be away from one another at the holidays. And Jac understood exactly how they felt. She wished Gerald and Bailey were there. But mostly she wished that Patrick were there, hooking his arm around her and pulling her close like James did with Cassie.

Cassie smiled up at her husband before she addressed her family. "When James's dad and stepmom heard about Jace's ear infection, they decided to come here for the holidays. Since they were tired from the trip, they volunteered to stay with the kids while we came to church. I didn't realize the entire family would be here."

"Not the entire," Wheezie said. "But Patrick will be here soon. Now everyone sit down so I don't have to crane my neck."

The family followed her orders. Once seated, the McPhersons stretched the entire length of the pew. They were an imposing group. And a loving one. Jac watched as Amy snuggled Douglas to her shoulder, and Rory pulled Gabby closer and kissed the side of her head. Jake collected the cell phones from his two daughters and turned them off before handing them to Melanie, who had just finished taking earphones and a video game from their son. Matthew whispered something to Ellie that made her blush, and Cassie whispered something to James that made him laugh. And Big Al presided over it all with a content smile on his face.

This was what Jac imagined when she dreamed of a family—all the loyalty, laughter, and love. Suddenly everything became as crystal-clear as the cross that hung above the altar. Gerald was right. Money didn't buy happiness. The McPherson family proved it. They weren't happy because they had money. They were happy because they had love. Because they woke up every day knowing they were cherished. Jac had been no happier living with Aunt Frances than she had been living with her mother. In fact, the happiest moments of her life had been spent with Gerald and Bailey when she had very little money...and with Patrick in a small condo with a herd of stray animals and a large pool table.

It turned out that Jacqueline didn't want money.

She wanted love.

She looked up at the stained-glass window closest to her—at the savior with the soft blue eyes and loving smile—and she prayed. She prayed a prayer of thanks to God for having known what she needed when she hadn't.

It seemed fitting that Patrick would appear at that moment, his hair mussed and cheeks red from the cold. His gaze found her, and she discovered that his cheeks weren't the only things that looked cold. Her joy fizzled, and fear took its place. Especially when Patrick made no effort to move down the pew toward her.

"Sit down, Patrick," his mother whispered under her breath. But he ignored her and motioned to Jac.

Terrified that something had happened to Bailey, Jac got up and scooted past the legs of every McPherson as she made her way to the aisle. Once she was there, Patrick took her arm and quickly propelled her toward the front doors. When they got outside the church, he released her.

"What is it?" she asked. "Is it Bailey? Did something happen to Bailey?"

He turned from her and walked over to the stairs, his hand running through his hair. "Why did you marry me?"

Her shoulders sagged in relief. "You brought me out here to ask me that? Geez, Patrick, you scared me to death."

He turned back around, his features hard and unyielding. "Just answer the question, Jac. No lies. No manipulation. Just the damn truth." His anger and desperation finally got through to her, and she felt almost as scared as she'd been before.

He knew. He knew about the will.

"Bailey?" she whispered. "Bailey told you?"

"No. I didn't wait for Bailey at the airport. Which is a good thing since I probably would've strangled her. She knew. Gerald knew. My friend from college knew. The only person who didn't know was the fool you suckered into marrying you. You care nothing about the baby—or me. You just care about your own selfish needs."

She released her breath, and it turned to fog in the cold air. "You're right. I did want my aunt's money to begin with. To me, it was security. Something I never had in my life. But you're wrong if you think I don't love our baby, Patrick. I love our baby as much as I love you."

He froze, his finger in midair. Then, just as quickly, it dropped limply to his side as he shook his head. "I'm not falling for your act, Jacqueline. Not again. You don't love me. You don't know what love is. When the year is up, you're planning on being long gone. And you're going to take my child with you. Admit it. That's the plan, isn't it?"

That had been the plan. But somewhere along the line, it had changed. Instead of one year, she wanted a lifetime. A lifetime of loving Patrick. But the look of hate in his eyes caused that dream to evaporate like her steamy breath in the cold air. Once it was gone, so was the desire to defend herself.

"Yes," she said. "That was the plan."

He stared at her a moment, her pain reflected in the clear green of his eyes. Behind her the door of the church opened.

"What's going on?" Wheezie asked. "Why did you leave church, and why are you two standing out here in the freezing cold?" When neither one said anything, she drew her own conclusions. "So I'm going to guess that you're having your first married squabble. Well, the holidays are notorious for putting undue stress on a relationship. It never failed that Neill and I got into it at least once between Thanksgiving and New Year's."

"This isn't just a squabble, Aunt Wheezie," Patrick said without taking his eyes off Jac. "It seems that Jacqueline married me because of a stipulation in her aunt's will."

Wheezie shuffled up next to Jac almost as if she were choosing sides in a game of kickball. "I know."

"You what?" Patrick finally looked at his aunt. "You knew and you never told me? Why?"

"Because it wasn't important." She shrugged her bony shoulders. "People marry for a lot of reasons, Patrick. Babies and money are just some of them. But what matters is why they stay married." She flapped a hand. "Now apologize to each other and let's get back to the service."

"No," Patrick growled. "I'm not going back to the service. I'm not apologizing. And I'm sure as hell not staying married to a woman who loves money more than she loves me." He turned and started down the stone steps.

Jac wanted to stop him. To yell out everything that was in her heart. But somehow she knew that it wouldn't be enough.

But Wheezie wasn't letting her nephew get away so easily. "Now wait one darn minute, Patrick!" She went to follow him down the steps, but her leg gave out and she fell forward.

"Wheezie!" Jac grabbed onto the sleeve of her coat and pulled her back. Unfortunately, when Wheezie came back she stumbled into Jac. And in her heels, Jac lost her balance and fell down. She might've been all right if she hadn't tried to break her fall. Her weight and Wheezie's were too much for her wrist to take. There was a crack of bone, followed by searing pain.

"Wheezie! Jac!" Patrick's voice sounded distant, like he was yelling their names from miles away instead of feet.

Wheezie was lifted off her, and only a few seconds later Patrick knelt next to her. "Tell me what hurts, Jac." He tentatively touched the arm she cradled. "Is it your wrist? Is it broken?"

There was little doubt that her wrist was broken. But looking into Patrick's green eyes, it was her broken heart that hurt the most.

Chapter Twenty-Eight

"You're lucky I ran into Wheezie before I ran into you."

Patrick glanced over at Bailey, who sat on the edge of the bed in Jac and Patrick's bedroom next to her sleeping sister. Instead of a no-nonsense business suit, she wore faded jeans and a wrinkled sweatshirt. But her expression was all ball-buster. She had arrived at the emergency room right after they had x-rayed Jacqueline's broken wrist, but before they had done an ultrasound to make sure everything was okay with the baby.

Patrick glanced back at the images he held in his hands. Images of the tiny little being that grew in Jacqueline's uterus. He was surprised at how the image already looked like a baby—and even more surprised at the lump of emotion that swelled in his throat.

"I don't know what Wheezie told you," he said. "But I am responsible."

"Because you got ticked about the will." Bailey got up from the bed and walked over to the French doors that led to the balcony. The early-morning sun was hidden behind a heavy layer of clouds, giving the sky a twilight feel. "I'm responsible for that. I thought it would be best if you didn't know the details."

"Best for who? You and Jacqueline?"

She turned back around. "Whatever you might think, I never wanted my sister to marry for my aunt's money. I wanted her to marry for love. I thought she had the best chance of that with someone closer to her own age— someone she was attracted to. Someone who was attracted to her as well." She released her breath. "But you're right, I shouldn't have kept the information from you. I guess I thought that it would be a deal-breaker."

"It would've been." He paused. "Still is."

Bailey's gaze flickered back to the bed. "You want a divorce?"

He rested his head on the back of the chair. With no sleep the night before, he was running on fumes. Or maybe just emotion. "Cut the shit, Bailey. You know as well as I do that Jacqueline plans to leave me as soon as she has the money. Why would I wait?"

"That might've been true to begin with, but it's not true now."

"And what makes you think that? Let me guess, your sister told you that she loved me and you believed her." When she didn't deny it, Patrick continued. "Of course you did. She's your sister. But look at things from my perspective, Bailey. How can I possibly believe a woman who's lied to me from the moment I met her? She wasn't coming from a party on Halloween. She was running away from a wedding. Which makes me wonder why she didn't run away from ours. Of course she couldn't, could she? The deadline was almost up, and if she didn't marry me, she'd be out billions of dollars." He snorted in disgust. "What kind of crazy woman puts that stipulation in her will?"

"One who hated anyone who had anything to do with her past."

His eyes narrowed. "Your aunt hated you? Then why did she agree to take you in?"

Bailey walked back over to the bed and sat down. She looked as exhausted as he felt. "I'm sure she was worried about what people would think if word got out that Frances Rosenblum had ignored a couple of poor orphans. So she took us in and then promptly shipped us off to boarding school. I think we reminded her of a past she wanted to forget. I figured it out and stayed away from her. But Jac"—she smiled sadly—"Jac always looks on the bright side of things. She thought if she just worked harder at fitting into our new life, Aunt Frances would accept and love us. But the truth is that Aunt Frances was more like our mama than we thought. She was a manipulative bitch who cared nothing for us—who wanted control long after she was dead."

It was hard not to feel hatred for a woman who couldn't open her heart for her two orphaned relatives, but Frances Rosenblum's behavior didn't justify Jacqueline's. "But she didn't control you. You chose not to follow your aunt's stipulation."

"Money doesn't mean that much to me."

"Just to Jac."

Her shoulders stiffened. "That's easy for you to say, Patrick. You grew up with loving parents and plenty of money. The most you had to worry about was making your bed and getting your homework done. You didn't grow up with a bartender mother who loved men more than her children and thought it was a real funny joke to name her two daughters after brands of liquor."

It took a second for Patrick to figure it out. "Jack Daniel's and Bailey's Irish Cream?"

She released an exasperated huff. "If Mama hadn't had a hysterectomy, I'm sure there would've been a Seagram, José, and Bacardi. She was a real jokester, our mama. Unfortunately, she wasn't as funny to her two kids as she was to the horde of losers she brought home. Losers who used and abused her—or maybe she used and abused them. I never could figure out which. About every six months, she'd get in a major fight with one of them and move us to another town, where she'd start the cycle all over again. It would've continued if one loser hadn't killed her by crashing his Harley into the back of a semi."

Patrick face must've shown his shock and sympathy because Bailey quickly continued.

"You don't need to feel sorry for us. Everything turned out for the best. Or I should say that, thanks to Jac, everything turned out for the best. If not for her, we would've spent the rest of our childhoods living with our Uncle Bud." Something crossed her features that could only be described as fear. And since Bailey had never shown an ounce of fear, Patrick figured Uncle Bud had been a real bastard.

"It was Jac who remembered our Aunt Frances," Bailey continued, "and got it in her head that we were destined to be the next Little Orphan Annies. And once she fixates on something, there's no changing her mind. She bombarded Aunt Frances with phone calls and letters until the woman gave in."

Too exhausted to comment, Patrick just sat there in a fog until the doorbell went off.

"That's probably Gerald." Bailey started for the doorway.

Patrick got up. "I'll get it. You need to stay here with Jacqueline in case she wakes up."

On his way down the stairs, he tried to process what he'd just learned. Step by step, things began to fall into place. Jacqueline knowing how to cook and play pool. Her love of pretty things and her strong desire to make his house a home. It all made sense. By the time he reached the bottom of the stairs, the two different pictures he held of his wife had become one. One heartbreaking picture of a survivor.

When he finally got to the garage and opened the door, Gerald was standing on the other side with a cardboard tray of coffee cups and a pharmacy bag. While Patrick and Bailey looked like they'd been pulled out of a trash compactor, Gerald looked neat and crisp in his red sweater and skinny jeans.

"I had to drive all over to find a pharmacy that was open on Christmas morning, but thankfully coffee shops aren't as religious." He handed Patrick the tray. "I figured we could use a little pick-me-up after the night at the emergency room." He rubbed his temple. "Not to mention my hangover." He followed Patrick inside. "Who would've thought that eggnog could knock you on your ass? What did Wheezie put in it?"

"I would say an entire bottle of scotch." Patrick set the tray on the breakfast bar and motioned at the coffee. "Which one?"

Gerald put the bag down and pulled out a cup. "I didn't know what you took, but I figured black and strong. Somehow I don't see you as the caramel-latte-with-extra-whipped-cream kind of guy."

"Good guess." Patrick accepted the cup and took a deep drink. "Thanks."

"You're welcome." Gerald opened the bag and took out a bottle of aspirin. He tapped three out and popped them into his mouth before washing them down with his caramel latte. "I got Advil for Jac like the doctor recommended. How's she doing?"

"She's asleep right now. But I'm sure Bailey would appreciate the coffee." Patrick took his coffee and walked over to the recliner that had arrived only a day earlier. Since Bailey had evicted the dogs from the bedroom so they wouldn't accidently injure Jacqueline's arm, Gomer and Gilmore were sleeping on the couch. His mother hadn't allowed animals on the furniture, but Jacqueline didn't have the same rule. She seemed to enjoy cuddling up on the couch with all the dogs and cats. Unless that was a lie too.

"Bailey can't drink coffee." Rather than head upstairs, Gerald took the only space left on the couch, cautiously eyeing Gomer as he sipped his coffee. "She's wired enough without caffeine. The one time she drank a cup, she stayed up for three nights straight. And believe me, you don't want to deal with Bailey when she hasn't slept for three days. Picture Godzilla mixed with Richard Simmons."

If he hadn't felt so shitty, Patrick might've laughed. Instead he rested his head back. The chair was damned comfortable. "I guess she and Jacqueline were pretty much on their own when they were kids."

"I think that's an understatement. Their tough child-hood probably explains why Jacqueline is so protective."

Patrick lifted his head and looked at Gerald. "You mean Bailey?"

"I mean your wife," Gerald said. "Her protection isn't as physical as yours. Or as verbal as Bailey's. Jac's protection of the ones she loves is much more subtle." He set down his cup and turned toward Patrick. "I know you're not going to believe this, but Jac didn't want the money for herself—she wanted it for Bailey and for me. She wanted to make sure that we'd never go without, like she and Bailey had to. And the baby only made her more determined to get her hands on her aunt's billions. It was the only way she could figure out how to protect all of us."

"That doesn't make her lying right."

"No. But hopefully it makes it understandable." Gerald paused, no doubt waiting for Patrick to say that he was no longer mad at Jacqueline. Patrick wasn't mad at her. The fear of her being injured and of losing the baby had wiped all his anger right out of him. Now he just felt numb. No, more like hurt. Hurt that Jac hadn't trusted him enough to share with him everything that Bailey and Gerald had.

"It's probably not my place to tell you this," Gerald continued, "but I think you should know. Jac plans to sign over most of the money she inherits to a charitable orga-nization run by none other than Mysterious Mr. Darby. It seems that Aunt Frances wasn't as evil as we all thought. She had been funding the organization for years and knew that Jac would continue to do so if she didn't marry a deadbeat who lost it all." Gerald got to his feet. "I guess

I'll take the Advil upstairs in case Jac wakes up and needs them."

Patrick only nodded. His mind was too exhausted to make any sense of the jumble of information it had received that morning, so he leaned his head back and closed his eyes. It felt like he'd only closed them for a moment, but when he opened them, the lighting was different in the room. Someone had plugged in the lights of the Christmas tree and turned on the gas of the fireplace. The three stockings seemed to jeer at him.

Blinking the sleep from his eyes, he sat up and glanced at the window. It was still light—perhaps midmorning or early afternoon. It was hard to tell without the sun. The gray clouds had finally produced snow. It fell past the multi-paned glass in a swirl of winter white.

"I'm glad the storm didn't hit last night."

The words were spoken so close that Patrick's muscles tightened. He turned to find the Santa Claus bum sitting on the couch between Gomer and Gilbert, his holey stocking feet resting on the coffee table. He smiled, and his eyes twinkled merrily.

"A bad winter storm always makes flying much more difficult."

Patrick's eyes narrowed on the bum. "How did you get in here? And don't tell me that you came down the chimney, because I don't have one."

The bum chuckled. "No. I came up the stairs."

"Not likely. I closed the garage door when I let Gerald in."

"Then Gerald must've been the one who left it open."

Patrick's brow knotted. "Gerald's gone?"

Santa bent his leg and examined the hole in his stocking.

"Gerald. Bailey. Jacqueline. They're all heading home." He shook his head. "I'll have to get Mama to fix this."

"Home? You mean my parents' house?"

The bum glanced at him. "I mean New York City."

"Bullshit!" Patrick jumped up. "They wouldn't leave without saying good-bye." He took the stairs two at a time, arriving in the bedroom completely out of breath. Not from running up the stairs, but from fear. The fear intensified when he found no shoes scattered across the floor. No flannel shirts draped over the nightstand. No bras hanging out of the drawers. Or cosmetics cluttering the top of the girly vanity. In fact the room looked much like it had before he married Jac. And that didn't just scare him. It terrified him.

A flash of plaid caught his attention, and he walked over to the kilt folded on the top of the dresser. The same kilt that Jacqueline had stolen Halloween night. A small folded piece of paper rested on top. His hand shook as he picked it up and opened it. The handwriting was as loopy and sprawling as Jacqueline. And damned if it didn't make his heart tighten before he even read the words.

Patrick,

You deserve pages upon pages of apology. Unfortunately, I've never been good at putting words to paper. So I'll keep it simple. I'm sorry. I'm sorry I lied. Sorry I rearranged your life. Sorry I married you under false pretenses. But I'll never be sorry that I stumbled into your cabin. That I carry your child. That I got to know the man beneath the scowl.

You made me realize that good men do exist. I just wish I'd realized it sooner.

Jacqueline

P.S. You don't have to worry that I'll keep your daughter from you. She couldn't have a better father, and I want her to get a chance to find that out like I did.

"It does make things easier, doesn't it?"

Patrick glanced over his shoulder to see the bum standing in the doorway.

"This way there are no messy good-byes." The old guy moved farther into the room. "Your life can go back to the way it was."

Patrick looked around the bedroom and, for the first time, realized what his life had been without Jacqueline—a cold room filled with only the bare necessities. No redhead in a flannel shirt. No laughter. No love. Just a sad construction worker who didn't know how to forgive. He glanced down at the letter, but he was having trouble seeing through the haze of pain that enveloped him.

"She just signed, 'Jacqueline.'" His words came out in barely a whisper. "If she loves me, why didn't she write, 'Love?'"

"Perhaps she didn't think that you wanted to hear it."

Patrick shook his head. "It shouldn't matter whether I want to hear it or not. If you love someone, you should say it."

There was a long pause before the bum's hand settled

on Patrick's shoulder. It was amazing how warm the little guy was. The heat of his hand seemed to penetrate through Patrick's shirt and into his very skin.

"Then say it, Patrick," he said in his kind voice. "Tell her what's in your heart."

It was strange how such simple words could finally open a man's eyes and make him see what a fool he'd been. After all the years of allowing his brain to rule his life, Patrick finally allowed his heart to lead the way. It pointed him in one direction.

Jacqueline.

"When?" He turned to the bum and took his arms. "Do you know when she's leaving?"

The old guy glanced at his watch. A damned nice watch for a bum. "I'd say you've got just enough time to get to their hotel before they leave for the airport."

Not even questioning how he knew that, Patrick headed for the door. But before he got there, the bum stopped him. "Not so fast, Patrick. I think you're forgetting something." Patrick turned to find the white-bearded man holding out the kilt and grinning. "When you give someone a present, it's always best to have it wrapped."

Chapter Twenty-Nine

"What you need, Jac, is a good cry." Gerald stopped packing long enough to toss Jac a box of tissues.

Due to the cast on her arm and her heavy heart, Jac made no move to catch it. Luckily, Bailey snagged it before it hit Jac right between the eyes. "Shut up, Gerald," Bailey said.

"Why? It's true." He went back to meticulously folding his fur-lined hoodie. "Both you and Jac could stand a good cry. It might help get rid of all that pain and anger you've carried around with you since childhood."

"I don't have pain and anger," Bailey snapped.

"And I'm not gay." Gerald shot her a sugary smile. "I just like to sleep with men and decorate my apartment in subtle shades of pink and purple."

Jac would've laughed if she hadn't felt so miserable. Gerald was right. She did need a good cry. It was too bad that all her tears seemed to be locked inside the hard knot lodged in her throat.

"Speaking of gay"—Bailey went back to packing her own suitcase—or more like haphazardly tossing her clothes in—"who was the mean-looking guy you were fawning all over at the emergency room?"

Gerald released a deep sigh. "Only the second love of my life. Unfortunately, the information I got turned out to be false. Barkley is as straight as Jennifer Aniston's hair. I would've known that if my gaydar hadn't short-circuited after the third mug of Aunt Wheezie's eggnog." He shrugged. "Oh well, you never know until you try. So when does our flight leave?"

"In a few hours." Bailey zipped her suitcase with a zing.

A few hours? The knot inside of Jac tightened. In just a few hours, she'd be on her way back to New York. Back to Gerald's small apartment. Back to Saturday movie nights and Sunday-morning coffee and pastry. Back to her old life. Except she didn't want to go back to her old life. She wanted to stay right here in her new life. Unfortunately, that was no longer an option. Patrick no longer wanted her to stay here—with or without the baby. She could keep her tears in, but she couldn't seem to keep her bottom lip from quivering. It didn't go unnoticed by Bailey. With a look of concern, she sat down on the edge of the bed and took Jac's hand.

"We don't have to go, you know. We could stay right here until you and Patrick work things out."

"No." Jac shook her head. "there's no working it out. You heard him, Bay. He thinks I manipulated him. And he's right. I did manipulate him. So I understand perfectly why he wants a divorce."

"So you weren't sleeping," Bailey said. "I should've

known. And since you were eavesdropping, you should know that Patrick didn't say *divorce*. I did."

"But he didn't deny it. Nor did he say that he loved me."

Gerald finished packing his skinny jeans and sat down on the opposite bed. "Patrick has never struck me as the type of man who's in touch with his emotions. Maybe he loves you, and he just doesn't know how to admit it."

It was strange how the well-meaning words could strike such a chord in Jac. Probably because her mother had used the exact words every time one of her loser boyfriends had dumped her. *He loves me. He just doesn't know how to show it.* But the sad truth was that not one of her mother's boyfriends had ever loved her. If they had, they would've stayed with her, regardless of her Irish temper and two bastard daughters.

True love conquers all.

Jac still believed that—would always believe that. If Patrick had loved her, he would never have let her go.

"No," she said, "he doesn't love me. And I'll have to live with that." Getting up from the bed, she started to pack. With one arm in a sling, it wasn't easy. But then again, neither was life. The knot in her throat was still there. In fact she didn't know if it would ever go away. Or if she would ever stop loving Patrick. But for now she had a baby to grow. A child to raise. And she intended to do a much better job than her mother had.

Bailey exchanged looks with Gerald before getting up from the bed. "So you want me to start the divorce papers?"

"Yes," she said. "And while you're at it, you can inform Aunt Frances's lawyers. I already planned on giving Mr. Darby most of the money anyway. He turned out to be a very nice man with a very kind heart, and I'm thinking about volunteering for one of his low-income housing projects when we get back." She expected some kind of reaction to the news. Instead there was a long stretch of silence that had her turning around. Bailey wore a half smile while Gerald's was much bigger.

"Well," he said, "I guess we need to come up with another business plan. What do you think about a food service that delivers? We could call it the Gay Gourmet."

Bailey rolled her eyes. "That's ridiculous."

"It's not that bad, Bay," Jac said. "After my hors d'oeuvres went over so well at Wheezie's Christmas Eve party, I think we have a chance with catering. We just need to stay away from weddings and do more casual cuisine. 'Country Catering.' I think it could work."

"And if it doesn't, I'm sure you two will think up something else," Bailey said as she pulled them into a bear hug. "Now let's get to packing so we can check out."

Fifteen minutes later they were on the elevator with their luggage and a very talkative bellboy.

"So you're leaving on Christmas day? That's a bummer. What? Did you get in a fight with your family? My dad got in a fight with my uncle one year when we went back to see my grandparents in Tennessee, and we left first thing Christmas morning. Pissed off my mom like you would not believe."

Regardless of how upset she was, Jac couldn't let the boy's stab at conversation fall flat. "It's too bad that you had to work on Christmas."

The teenager shrugged. "I don't mind. My family celebrates on Christmas Eve, and I get time and a half for working today. Besides, you get to see some strange shi—stuff on holidays."

"Do tell," Gerald said. "I love strange shit."

The young man leaned closer. "Well, last Fourth of July, we had this country band staying here. And the groupies that follow them rented out a room on the fifth floor. They called because they'd run out of beer in the minibar, and when I brought more up, this one girl answered the door in nothin' but cowboy boots and a smile."

"And what about the cowboys?" Gerald said. "Were they naked?"

The teenager looked confused. "Umm...I didn't notice. But the guy who showed up today was close to naked."

"A cowboy?"

The kid shook his head. "No. I think he's Irish or something. Anyway, you'll get to see him when you leave. He's right out front and hasn't moved for the last half hour. Although how he's not freezing his ass—butt off, I don't know."

Before Gerald could ask any more questions, the elevator stopped, and the doors pinged open. A huge Christmas tree with brightly wrapped packages beneath graced the sitting area in the lobby, and artificial boughs of greenery and ornaments hung along the front desk and above the revolving front door. They followed the bellboy to the set of doors to the right of the revolving door, and Gerald held one open so the bellboy could push the brass luggage cart through.

"So where is this naked guy?" Gerald asked once they were outside.

The bellboy nodded to the left. "I'd say he's in the middle of that crowd of people." Jac followed his gaze to the people huddled around a horse and carriage, snapping pictures with their phone cameras.

"Come on, Jac." Gerald took her arm. "Let's go take a look."

Jac pulled back and shook her head. "You go on, Geri. I'll wait for the valet to bring around the car."

"Come on." He pulled her along. "Bailey can wait for the car. Being asexual, she won't be interested in a naked man anyway." Having gotten their pictures, two young women ducked out of the crowd, giving Gerald an opening. Jac followed behind him, stepping on his heels when he stopped suddenly.

"What is it?" she asked as she tried to see around him. "And please don't tell me it's the third love of your life."

"Umm...no," Gerald said. "He's not the love of my life." He turned with a very knowing and happy smile on his face. "I think you're about to get your fairy tale, Jac." While she looked at him with confusion, he stepped to the side.

It took a moment for Jac to comprehend what she was seeing. Not the horse and carriage—she had seen the vehicles around downtown Denver—but the man who stood next to it. He wore nothing but scuffed work boots and a Scottish kilt that hugged his waist. His golden hair fluttered in the stiff wind, and snowflakes landed on his thick muscled arms before quickly melting into the heat of his skin. He paid little attention to the cold or the crowd that clicked its pictures. His gaze was focused on the revolving door of the hotel, his brow knotted, and his eyes intent.

"Did you bring your bagpipes?" a man asked. "Are you going to play Christmas music on your bagpipes?"

"Yeah, sweetie," the woman next to him said, "show us your bagpipe."

"Yes, do play your bagpipe," another woman yelled from the back.

The comments might've gotten even raunchier if Gerald hadn't shouted, "Hey Patrick! She's over here."

Green eyes swept over to Jac, and suddenly she forgot how to breathe. The feeling grew worse as he moved toward her. He stopped only inches away. So close that she could feel the heat radiating from his body and take note of his red face. Since Jac had never seen him embarrassed before, it took her a moment to figure out the reason behind the color.

"Obviously, the bum has a few screws loose," he said. "And I have a few loose for listening to him." He seemed to have trouble meeting her eyes. "I guess I was willing to try anything to keep you from leaving."

At one time that's all it would've taken to have Jac flinging herself into his arms. But now she needed more.

"Why do you want me to stay, Patrick?"

He swallowed. "Because I like what we have, Jacqueline. I like coming home and finding you there. I like playing pool with you, and watching movies, and going for runs. I like the way you cook, and care for my pets, and drool when you sleep."

"I do not drool."

"You drool." He smiled, and it was like the sun had come out from behind the clouds. Heat warmed her entire being from the top of her head to the tips of her toes as he took her hand and cradled it between his. "Come home with me, Jacqueline."

It would've been so easy to agree. Her body was already leaning toward him. But despite all the beautiful things he'd said to her, there was one he'd left out. One that she needed to hear before she could ever completely give her heart and soul to a man. But she wasn't going to spell it out for him. If his love wasn't given freely, she didn't want it.

She leaned in and brushed a kiss over his lips. "Good-bye, Patrick." She turned and walked through the crowd of people, who now watched her as much as they had Patrick. Bailey was tipping the valet when she looked up and saw Jac. Always able to read her sister, Bailey immediately grew concerned.

"What happened—"

"Jacqueline!" Patrick bellowed as loudly as his father as he pushed through the crowd. "You are not leaving," he ordered, and then lowered his voice when she looked at him. "You can't leave me, Jac. Not when I love you— when I've loved you ever since you dropped into my life that Halloween night."

The words had the lump in Jac's throat melting like the snowflakes on the concrete. Tears that she had held in submission for so long leaked from the corners of her eyes and rolled down her cheeks. And she had no strength or desire to stop them.

"I love you too," she sobbed. "And I have ever since you took a bite of me."

In two strides Patrick had her in his arms. "Don't cry, baby. Please don't cry." He cradled her chin and brushed the tears from her cheeks with his thumbs before he lowered his head and kissed her. At the first touch of his lips, the world ceased to exist. It was just her and Patrick floating in a bubble of happiness.

"Excuse me, sir?"

They pulled apart to find a man dressed in livery standing there.

"I'm sorry, but the hotel says I need to move." The man opened the door of the carriage. "So if you're ready?"

Patrick looked at Jac in question and held out a hand. She didn't hesitate to take it. He helped her up into the carriage. On the seat were a fuzzy blanket and a pastry box. She glanced back at him, and he shrugged.

"I figured a chocolate croissant couldn't hurt." He moved the box and picked up the blanket, waiting for her to take a seat before sitting next to her and tucking the blanket around them both. When she was cuddled in his arms, Gerald and Bailey stepped up to the carriage.

"I guess the Gay Gourmet will have to wait," Gerald said.

Since the thought of her best friend leaving made her sad, she didn't reply. Fortunately, Patrick answered for her. "Not if you move to Denver. I think Jacqueline could use something to keep her out of the shopping malls."

Gerald smiled. "You're right. And I hear that Denver's a great place to fall in love."

"The best," Jac said as she grinned up at her husband. He rewarded her with a kiss that made her sigh. Then he turned to Gerald and Bailey.

"I expect to see both of you back at my parents' house. Since Mom didn't get to throw her Christmas Eve party, she's gone all out on a Christmas wedding reception."

Jac looked at him with surprise. "You and your family were pretty sure of the outcome. What if I hadn't agreed to stay?"

He flashed a smile that warmed her heart. "Then I would've chucked the romantic crap and kidnapped you. It's not like McPhersons haven't done it before."

"Kidnapped?" Jac smiled and snuggled against Patrick's warm, broad chest. "Now that's romantic."

Chapter Thirty

It was surprising how much a family of McPhersons could get done in a short time. Albert and Mary Katherine's house was completely decked out for Christmas, from the large Douglas fir that filled one corner of the family room to the Santa and reindeer on the front lawn. The house even smelled like the holidays. Cinnamon candles burned on the mantel. Vanilla-laced sugar cookies cooled on the counter. And a rosemary-infused prime rib roast baked in the oven.

"It was lucky that Melanie had planned on making the roast for New Year's," Mary Katherine said as she finished the rum cake batter. "Otherwise we'd be eating peanut butter and jelly sandwiches."

"All things work out if you let them." Wheezie's gaze scanned the great room. The McPhersons were living proof of things working out.

What had started out as a disjointed Christmas with the entire family headed in separate directions had ended up bringing everyone even closer together. Jake and Melanie and their three children helped Rory and Amy and their two kids finish decorating the tree. Gabby held Douglas up so he could reach the higher branches, then once the ornament was hung, tickled him until he squirmed and giggled. Her biological father had sobered up, but then left town without a word to anyone. No matter how much Gabby said she didn't care, Wheezie figured it had to hurt. She also figured that Gabby had enough love in her life to heal that hurt.

In the opposite corner of the room, Cassie and James tried to corral their energetic son, who had recovered from his ear infection and was diving from the back of the couch with his new play sword. His little sister was calmly sitting between James's parents, listening to her grandfather read a story. And one-year-old Noel was being spoiled by Matthew and Ellie. With the content smiles on their faces, there was little doubt in Wheezie's mind that they were thinking about the time when they would hold their own child.

Patrick and Jacqueline didn't seem to be thinking of parenthood. They stood at the window looking out at the snow that fell from the sky like a lacy doily. Patrick's arms were wrapped tightly around Jacqueline as he whispered something in her ear that made a blush tint her cheeks.

"They look happy, don't they?"

Wheezie turned to see Mary watching the newlyweds with tears brimming in her eyes. "My last baby is married now and starting a family of his own," she said. "Where did the time go, Louise? It seems like only yesterday that I was cuddling Patrick in my arms."

Wheezie didn't know where time went. Her time on earth had slipped through her fingers like sand through a sieve. But there were still a few grains left. And she sure as hell wasn't going to waste them by getting caught up in the past. Waiting until Mary turned to check on the roast in the oven, Wheezie picked up the bottle of rum and added more to the cake batter. Once she emptied the bottle, she slipped off the barstool and reached for the walker that she'd parked next to the stool. It wasn't the plain aluminum one the doctor had given her. This one was bright purple with big off-road wheels and a nifty basket for her purse and cell phone.

Wheezie was still trying to figure out which one of her ornery nieces and nephews had sneaked into her house and left it under her Christmas tree. They all had denied it, and the card tied on with the candy-cane-striped bow had read only two words: *Love, Santa.* Of course it didn't matter who had given it to her. All that mattered was that it had been given with love.

Clicking off the brakes, she wheeled the walker into the family room, where Big Al, Gerald, and Bailey had just finished handing out flutes of champagne to most of the adults and sparkling apple juice to the children and pregnant women. Albert waited for Mary to finish in the kitchen before he handed her a flute of champagne and Wheezie a glass of what looked like good scotch whiskey.

With a broad smile on his face, he lifted a glass and made a toast.

"Merry Christmas and a happy and prosperous New Year. May your brogue remain thick and your life long."

Wheezie smiled. She couldn't have said it better herself.

A titan in the boardroom and the bedroom, billionaire Deacon Beaumont vows to save a failing lingerie company. But in this glamorous world of corsets and supermodels, a sexy, savvy businesswoman is the one in real need of rescue...

Please see the next page
for a preview of

*A Billionaire
Between the Sheets.*

Deacon was playing a game he had no business playing. Especially when the money he was playing it with wasn't his own. It was his brothers' as well. And both Nash and Grayson wanted him to sign the contract and make them millionaires as quickly as possible. They had no desire to be owners of their uncle's lingerie company. And Deacon didn't want that either. Which didn't explain why he'd refused to send the contract back with his uncle's lawyers. Or why he had shaved his beard, cut his hair, and traveled all the way to California to deliver it in person.

Obviously something had gone a little haywire in his brain. Something that had gotten even worse when he'd seen Olivia's opulent office, stood looking at the spectacular view, and finally turned to find a spoiled executive in a suit that probably cost more than his entire wardrobe. And now, whether he had a right or not, he wasn't through making Olivia sweat.

Although she didn't appear to be sweating too much.

"So I guess you want me to beg," she said. When he didn't reply, she shrugged. "Okay. You want me on my knees or will a couple of *pretty pleases* do?"

He stopped twirling the pen through his fingers and called her bluff. "Knees would be nice." He expected her to tell him to go to hell. Instead she walked around the desk and, without the slightest hesitation, lifted her sexy-as-hell skirt just enough to flash him a peek of pretty pink garter belt fasteners and thigh-high stockings before kneeling in front of him.

Her piercing green eyes pinned him as she spoke in a voice that was anything but humble. "Please, Deacon. Please sign the contract."

It was his fantasy all over again. Technically, the desk and office were his. And while Olivia wasn't exactly in rags, she was on her knees. Which didn't explain why all the fun had drained right out of the game. Probably because he knew what it felt like to be forced to beg. Knew exactly the feeling of humiliation that came with needing something someone else had.

"Get up," he said.

"Why?" She gave him a wide-eyed look. "Did I do it wrong, Deacon? Sorry, but I'm not as good at begging as the Beaumonts."

The pen slipped from his fingers, and the leather chair creaked as he sat up, bringing his face inches from hers. "Shut up."

"Or what? You won't sign the contract?" She laughed, her breath coming out in a puff of heat. "We both know that you won't walk away from fifty million."

Her condescending attitude took Deacon from angry to flat-out pissed. So pissed that he couldn't even put together a reply that would wipe the smartassed smirk off her face. That being the case, he chose a nonverbal way to do it.

He kissed her.

Not a soft kiss, but a hard, forceful one that ended with him sucking her plump bottom lip between his teeth and giving it a nip. When he pulled back, Olivia was staring at him with shocked eyes. He expected her anger and didn't even tense when she lifted her hand. But instead of delivering a stinging, much-deserved slap she slid her hand over the stubble on his jaw before pulling him back for another kiss.

She kissed much better than she begged. He actually believed that she was enjoying it. He sure as hell was. Her lips were hungry and aggressive, her mouth hot and wet, and her tongue slick and teasing.

Deacon opened his legs, and she moved right into the space like a moored ship. Her hands curled around his neck while his curved over her ass, lifting her knees off the plush carpeting. As he squeezed the firm cheeks, his mind ran through the list of things he would need to accomplish before he could be surrounded by the heat of her body. Lift skirt. Remove panties. Unzip jeans. Pull out cock. Get condom—damn.

He pulled away from those scorching lips. Then, just to make sure he didn't succumb to a pair of desire-drugged eyes, he shoved the caster chair back a good three feet. But even with the added space, it took a while for him to get ahold of his raging hormones.

Olivia didn't take quite as long.

After only a few blinks, she got to her feet, took two wobbly steps toward him, then hauled off and gave him the stinging slap he'd expected earlier. By the time his ears stopped ringing, she had the pen and contract in hand.

"I did what you asked," she said through gritted teeth. "Now you sign."

It was difficult to keep up the smiling-asshole part with a hard-on that could easily have been used as a battering ram, but he did his best. "I didn't force you to beg. I merely asked. And you deserved it when you weren't exactly honest about how many shares Uncle Michael left us."

"The number of shares was in the contract."

"True. But you didn't explain that we owned the company."

"You don't own it. You own controlling interest."

"Which we both know is the same thing." He glanced around. "So this would be my office?"

Her eyes narrowed as she enunciated every word. "This. Is. My. Office."

Now that he was back in control, he asked the questions that had been circling his brain. "So what horrible thing did you do to get cut out of Uncle Michael's will completely? Forget to put your napkin on your lap? Burp at a dinner party? Get caught showing someone your panties?"

The look that entered her eyes was a combination of anger and hurt. "I didn't do anything. And I wasn't cut out completely. He left me all of his money and his house."

Deacon already knew this. After his father had gotten the lawyers high on the moonshine he always carried in his trunk, they had become loose-lipped. He knew exactly what his uncle had left Olivia. According to the lawyers, the value of the estate was the same amount she was willing to give Deacon and his brothers.

He studied her. "Sorry, but I just don't get it. If you were Uncle Michael's beloved stepdaughter, why wouldn't he just leave you the shares in the company? Didn't he know how much you love French Kiss?"

She turned away. "He knew." A buzzer went off, and Olivia reached out and pressed a button on the phone. "Yes?"

"Sorry to interrupt." Kelly's voice came through the speaker. "But your mother is on line one and says that it's an emergency."

Olivia's shoulders tightened. "Thank you, Kelly." She glanced back at Deacon. "Do you mind getting out of my chair?"

"Not at all." He got up and slid the chair over.

If looks could kill, he would be six feet under. Which made him smile even broader. He liked this feisty Olivia much better than he liked the poised businesswoman Olivia. Or maybe he just liked knowing that he could get under her skin.

He moved to the sitting area and sat down on the couch. It was as hard and uncomfortable as it looked. He picked up a French Kiss catalog from the coffee table and thumbed through it. It wasn't the first time. He was on their mailing list—under an alias, of course. An exasperated grunt had him looking up from the hot model in a lacy bra and panties to the ticked-off woman in a business suit. It didn't sit well that he found Olivia almost as hot.

"So I guess you're not leaving," she said.

He shrugged. "I don't have anywhere to go. This poor Beaumont only had enough money for the plane ticket." It was an out-and-out lie. He might not have had enough money to build his condos, but he had enough to cover a plane ticket and hotel. But damned if he wasn't enjoying toying with Olivia. However, the kiss had been a mistake. One that wouldn't be repeated.

She sent him a glare before pressing a button on the phone and talking into the receiver. "I'm sorry I kept you waiting, Mother, but I'm kind of busy right now. So what's the emergency? Did…" Her gaze met his before she swiveled the chair around and lowered her voice. "Did she throw another temper tantrum?" She only paused for a second before speaking in a voice at least three octaves higher. "Jail? She's in jail!"

Although he continued to thumb through the catalog, Deacon was all ears.

"What happened? Oh, good Lord." With the phone cradled to her ear, Olivia swiveled back around and placed her checkbook in the briefcase. "No, we can't leave her there, Mother." Another pause. "No, I don't have a clue how to bail someone out of jail, but I'm sure I'll figure it out." Hanging up the phone, she stood and grabbed her briefcase.

Deacon flipped down the catalog and got to his feet. "You'll probably need a bail bondsman."

She stopped on her way to the door and turned to him. "Excuse me?"

"That's what you'll need if you want to bail your friend out of jail."

"Oh." She nodded. "Thank you."

He flashed her a smile. "Anytime."

She studied him for a long moment before heading for the door. As soon as she had it open, she spoke to her assistant. But not as to an employee as much as to a friend she didn't want to offend. "Umm, Kelly, do you think you could reschedule my morning meetings? I need to drop... something off at my house and won't be back until the afternoon. And once Mr. Beaumont signs the paperwork on my desk, would you mind making him a reservation at a nice hotel and taking care of anything else he might need before he leaves town?" She glanced over her shoulder, her eyes almost daring him to contradict what she'd just told her assistant. "Good-bye, Deacon. Have a safe trip home."

Then, with the twitch of shapely hips and the click of purple high heels, she strode toward the elevators. Once she had disappeared around the corner, Kelly spoke.

"Is there a hotel you prefer?" She gave him a slow once-over, followed by the flirtatious bat of her overly long eyelashes. "Or if you like cozy, you could sleep on my couch, Mr...."

"Beaumont. And whatever hotel you choose is fine."

Kelly's eyes widened. "Beaumont? Are you related to Michael Beaumont?"

"He was my uncle."

"So you're his nephew? The one he willed the company to?"

Deacon nodded. "That would be me. But you don't have to worry. I don't have any plans to take over."

Her excitement dimmed. "That's too bad. What French Kiss needs is someone to take charge. Ms. Harrington is nice and all, but she's a bit of a pushover. Which might explain why we're going bankrupt."

"Bankrupt? French Kiss is going bankrupt?"

She glanced in both directions before she leaned in. "Since I've only worked here a few months, I don't have all the details. But rumor has it that, once you find out about the company's problems, you're going to sell it to the highest bidder. Which is going to suck for me since my roommate moved out with her rat bastard of a boyfriend and left me with the lease. And do you have a clue how expensive it is to live in San Francisco? Not that I'm hinting for a raise or anything. I would just like to keep my job."

Deacon was stunned. Last he'd heard, French Kiss was pulling in billions a year. Now it was going bankrupt? It didn't make sense. And why would Olivia spend all her money on a company that was going under?

As if reading his mind, Kelly continued. "Although I think Ms. Harrington has something up her sleeve to save the company. I overheard her talking to her mother about a secret weapon."

"A secret weapon?"

She nodded. "Some Paris designer. Unfortunately, now that person is in jail for sexual assault." Obviously Olivia's assistant didn't mind eavesdropping on phone calls.

"Do you know what jail Ms. Harrington went to?"

"No, but I do know that once she bails the designer out of jail, she's taking her back to her house." She turned to her computer. "And I have that address."

Fall in Love with Forever Romance

A BAD BOY
FOR CHRISTMAS
by Jessica Lemmon

Connor McClain knows what he wants, but getting Faith Garrett into his arms this holiday is going to require more than mistletoe...

SNOWBOUND
AT CHRISTMAS
by Debbie Mason

Grayson Alexander never thought being snowbound in Christmas, Colorado, for the holiday would get so hot. But between working with sexy, tough Cat O'Connor and keeping his real reason for being there under wraps, he's definitely feeling the heat. And if there's one thing they'll learn as they bring out the mistletoe, it's that in this town, true love is always in season...

Fall in Love with Forever Romance

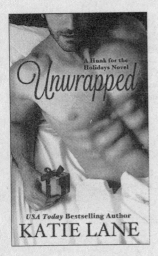

UNWRAPPED
by Katie Lane

Contractor Patrick McPherson is deeply committed to his bachelor lifestyle. But as the Christmas season approaches, he still can't quite forget his curvalicious one-night stand. Then Jacqueline shows up unexpectedly, and all holiday hell breaks loose. Because this year, Patrick is getting the biggest Christmas surprise of his life…

PLAYING DIRTY
by Tiffany Snow

In the second book in Tiffany Snow's Risky Business series, Sage Reece must choose between bad-boy detective Dean Ryker and sexy power-player Parker Anderson. Caught between a mobster out for revenge and two men who were once best friends, Sage must play to win—even if it means getting dirty…

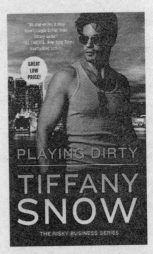

Fall in Love with Forever Romance

THE TAMING OF MALCOLM GRANT
by Paula Quinn

The beautiful and blind Emmaline Grey risks everything to nurse the mysterious Malcolm Grant back to health. But can she heal his broken heart too? Fans of Lynsay Sands, Karen Hawkins, and Monica McCarty will love the next book in Paula Quinn's sinfully sexy Scottish Highlander series.